KU-549-849

PRESERVE THE DEAD

Brian McGilloway

corsair

CORSAIR

First published in Great Britain in 2015 by Corsair
1 3 5 7 9 10 8 6 4 2

A CIP catalogue record for this book
is available from the British Library.

ISBN: 978-1-472113-16-0 (paperback)
ISBN: 978-1-472113-19-1 (ebook)

Typeset in Stone Serif by Saxon Graphics Ltd, Derby
Printed and bound in Great Britain by Clays Ltd, plc

Papers used by Corsair are from well-managed forests
and other responsible sources.

MIX
Paper from
responsible sources
FSC
www.fsc.org   FSC® C104740

Corsair
An imprint of
Little, Brown Book Group
Carmelite House
50 Victoria Embankment
London EC4Y 0DZ

An Hachette UK Company
www.hachette.co.uk

www.littlebrown.co.uk

For Tanya, with love

Also by Brian McGilloway

The Inspector Devlin Series

Borderlands
Gallows Lane
Bleed a River Deep
The Rising
The Nameless Dead

The DS Black Series

Little Girl Lost
Hurt

Tuesday, 17 July

Chapter One

The bruising extended from his temple, around the curve of the eye socket and down almost to where the fold of his laughter line curled round to meet his lip.

Lucy gently touched the purpled skin with the tips of her fingers, afraid that too much pressure might cause him to wake. She moved back slightly and traced down along his neck to where she saw a second shadow on the skin, this time the injury aged and yellowed around the edges, just visible above the collar of his vest. Wisps of grey hair curled over the material, rising and falling lightly with each breath.

She drew back the blanket from him, seeing for the first time the leather strap that encircled the safety bar at the side of his bed, its other end fastened around her father's wrist.

'Dad?' she whispered, tapping him lightly on the arm in an attempt to rouse him. 'Dad, what happened?'

For a moment, his eyelids fluttered, his face inclining towards hers. Then he settled back on the bed again, his head barely denting the pillow. His brow shone with perspiration, despite the presence of a portable fan in the room.

She pushed back from the bed, opened the door and went out into the corridor. Seeing no staff, she moved up towards the main workstation on the ward. Just as she approached, an orderly came around the corner.

'DS Black? Just the person.'

'What happened to my father?' Lucy demanded. 'His face? What happened?'

The man raised his hands in placation. 'I'm sorry, Miss Black. I thought you'd been ... He became aggressive with some of the other patients and took a fall,' he said.

'He's chained to the bed,' Lucy said.

'He's not chain—' he said, seemingly swallowing back his protest at her comment. 'We had to restrain him to stop it happening again; he was uncontrollable.'

'He has a bruise on his chest, too.'

'I don't know – it ... it may have been when he was being subdued. Look, I understand you're annoyed. And I know you're off duty, but ... well, we think there's a body in the river.'

Gransha Hospital, in whose secure unit her father had been placed, sat on the outskirts of Derry city, alongside the River Foyle, nestled in the shadow of the Foyle Bridge. The bridge, a kilometre-long structure, had been designed with an arch high enough over the river to allow access for ships to pass under in order to reach the city docks. However, soon after completion, the docks were then moved north of the bridge, and the majestic arch's function became purely aesthetic.

The height of the bridge made it a frequent spot for suicide attempts in the city. In the previous decades, over five hundred people had already lost their lives to the river, more than ninety from the Foyle Bridge alone. If there was a body in the water so close to the bridge, Lucy felt fairly certain that it was as a result of a suicide jump.

She went with the orderly, down from the block in which her father was being held, cutting across the grounds, onto the field running down to the train tracks along the river's edge. She pulled out her mobile and called the sighting in to the Strand Road station as she ran. Doing so would not only alert the Police Service of Northern Ireland, but, more importantly, also Foyle Search and Rescue, a charity group in the city, made up of volunteers who patrolled the river and assisted in recovery operations. That the city needed such an organization was a reflection of the frequency with which people went in the river.

As they approached the river's edge, she could see a group had already gathered, most dressed in either blue or white scrubs, suggesting that they were staff from the hospital. The air was heavy with the stench from the water, the odour of the exposed sediment banks along the river's edge having built all day, ballooning in the intense heat. Even now, despite the fact it was past nine, the evening was still humid enough that the effort of jogging down through the field had caused Lucy to sweat.

The orderly led her through, pushing those gathered aside, announcing that she was 'the police'.

Lucy scanned the water, the glare of the evening light shattering on its surface forcing her to shield her eyes with her hand.

'There,' the orderly said, pointing up to her left.

She followed the line of his arm and finally saw the arm and head of a man breaching the river.

'Hello. Can you hear me?' she called, but there was no response save the rhythmic rise and fall of the man's arm on the water, as if the river itself were drawing breath.

Chapter Two

The man seemed to have snagged on a tree branch then become lodged in the sediment as the water retreated, only becoming exposed when the tide lowered. Lucy could tell that the rescue boat wouldn't be able to reach him without running aground itself in the mudbank. He would have to be recovered from the shoreline.

'Listen,' she called, waiting for the assembled group to quieten. 'He could still be alive. We need to go out and bring him in quickly. I need some volunteers. We need to make a chain. I'll go to the front, but I'll need someone holding on to me so I can reach out and try to pull him in.'

She waited a beat to see if anyone would offer to take her place. She was, she reckoned, at least ten years and two stone lighter than anyone else there.

The orderly with whom she had come down stepped forward. 'I'll hold you,' he offered.

'Thanks ...' Lucy said. It wasn't quite what she'd hoped, but at least it was something.

'Ian,' he said, assuming her hesitation was because she couldn't remember his name.

A few of the others mumbled offers of assistance and began to step down onto the shoreline from the grass verge where they stood. Lucy turned and tried to trace a path across the mudflats to where the man remained in the water. She was able to spot the sharp edges of rocks that protruded through the surface of the shore. With a bit of luck, and some careful balancing, she reckoned she could make it to within a few feet of the man.

'Follow me,' she said.

She picked her way across the rocks, quickly at first for the ground was solid. As she got closer to the water, though, her progress slowed, for the rocks were slippery here, their edges hidden beneath blades of seaweed. She turned, expecting Ian to be close. Instead, he was some fifteen feet behind her, lumbering from rock to rock, swinging his arms as if to build momentum before lurching from one step to the next.

She only needed to step across to one more rock in order to reach the man, whom she could now see clearly. His face was turned towards her, his mouth and eyes shut. His hair, plastered to his scalp, might have been grey, though the silt of the river made it difficult to tell.

'We're on our way,' she called, though again without response. His eyes appeared to be closed, but his features carried none of the injuries she might have expected had he been in the river long.

She waited until Ian had caught up with her, then nimbly moved onto the final rock. She could feel its jagged edge through the soles of her trainers, and had to move to get a better foothold. In so doing, she shifted too quickly to the left and lost her balance. She flailed her arms, desperately trying to centre herself when she felt the thickness of Ian's arms encircle her waist with such force it winded her. Her foot skidded off the rock and, for a brief moment, she was suspended in mid-air until Ian drew her back to the relative safety of the rock on which he stood, her body pressed tightly against his own.

'You all right?' he asked, breathless from the exertion.

Lucy nodded. 'Thanks,' she said, patting the breadth of his arm, which still held her.

'I'll hold on to your belt,' he said. 'Then I'll follow you across. You grip mine,' he instructed, turning to the man behind him.

Lucy felt his fingers work their way between her belt and jeans. 'I've got you,' he said.

She stepped forward, taking her time, finding her balance. She felt the tension of his grip behind her, then felt it slacken as he stepped forward too, following her.

The man in the water lay five feet from her now, his arm outstretched, the sleeve of his jacket caught on a branch only two feet away. She decided to use the branch for some support, gripping it with her left hand as she reached for the man's hand with her right.

'You're good,' she heard Ian say, once he'd got his own footing. She leaned her body forward, realizing for the first time the level of trust she was placing, not just in the people behind her, but in the thin strip of her leather belt. For a second she panicked, regretting her decision, bending at the waist to try to reach, but it was no good. She had to lean her entire body forward.

9

As if sensing her reluctance, Ian called, 'I've got you, Sergeant.'

'Lucy!' she called. 'I'm Lucy.'

'I've got you, Lucy,' he repeated. 'Trust me.'

She took a deep breath, then leaned out fully now and felt, behind her fear, a momentary flood of exhilaration in the freedom of ceding all control, giving complete responsibility for her safety to someone else.

She stretched and felt the cuff of the dead man's jacket. Gripping it, she tugged, managing to move him a little closer to her.

'Grip his hand,' Ian shouted. 'We'll pull you back in.'

Lucy nodded, stretching further. Her face was slick now, her hair hanging in front of her eyes, her mouth filled with the bitterness of the smell of the mudflats. She felt the man's hand, was strangely surprised by its coldness in contrast with the heat of the hand that held her belt. She tightened her grip, as best she could against the slickness of the mud that coated the man's palm.

'I've got him,' she called. 'He's freezing. I think he's dead.'

She felt Ian's grip tighten, felt the tension in the cloth of her jeans stretched taut now across her buttocks. Then she felt herself begin to move, her body begin to straighten up. The heat, the stench, the angle at which she had been, all conspired against her and she felt dizzy, felt as if she would lose her balance again. Then she heard a low, long slurping sound as the dead man's remains pulled free of the sucking mud, and she moved more quickly, falling backwards against Ian. He wrapped his arms around her, holding her against him, stopping her from falling.

She leaned her head against him as she tried to catch her breath, could feel the thudding of his heart, the rapid rise and fall of his chest from the exertion. She felt a strange intimacy as she held, in her other hand, a dead man's grip.

'That was something else,' Ian managed. 'Are you OK?'

Lucy nodded, unable to articulate satisfactorily in words both the sudden thrill she felt at simply being alive and how alien a sensation it was.

Chapter Three

Lucy trudged back up through the reed bed, following the group now bearing the body she had pulled from the river up to the morgue in the hospital where the Medical Examiner would meet them. She took out her phone, wiping her hands clean on her trousers before calling Tom Fleming, her Inspector in the Public Protection Unit in which she was based.

'Lucy? Everything OK?'

'I'm down at Gransha,' she said. 'Visiting my dad. We've just fished a body from the river. He looks like an older man. Well dressed.'

'How well?'

'Suit and tie. Grey-haired. Is that ringing any bells? I can't think of anyone.'

DI Fleming was quiet for a moment. All Missing Person reports would go through the PPU first so, Lucy figured, if the victim was someone local who'd been reported missing, either she or Fleming would have come across the report. Most of the men she could think of on the list were younger than this one had appeared in the admittedly brief time that she had seen the corpse.

'How long has he been in?'

'Not long, I think. One of the doctors down here is on her way across so I can't say for certain, but there's little sign of bloating or discolouration.'

'I heard at my meeting this evening that one of our sponsors, a man called Terry Haynes, hasn't been seen in a while. He's Dublin born but has been living here for years. He's missing a few days now. He's a … he's a friend.'

Fleming was a recovered alcoholic who dried out after finding Jesus, but not before losing his driving licence and his family. As part of his outreach work with his church, and perhaps in penance for his own problems in the past, he worked with the local street drinkers, helping to man soup kitchens and delivering food to them which had been donated from local shops when it reached its sell-by date. Lucy assumed by a 'meeting' he meant his Alcoholics Anonymous group and that Haynes must be a recovered alcoholic who was now supporting new members.

'What's Haynes like?'

'Heavy, seventeen, eighteen stone maybe. He's grey-haired. He's not the suit type, mind you. He works with the street drinkers quite a bit.'

'I don't think it's him,' Lucy said. 'This guy doesn't look heavy, even allowing for bloating in the water. Has Haynes formally been reported missing?' she added, not recognizing the name.

'Not yet. I only just heard; a new group member was asking if he'd been seen around. She'd not heard from him in a few days. Called at his house and got no answer. He's her sponsor, which means that he's supposed to help her through the twelve steps. She'd been in contact with him every day. She had a slip and took a drink when she couldn't get in touch with him. That's not his fault, but it is out of character. Terry's helped a fair few of us; he knows the score.'

'Maybe he's had a slip himself?'

'Maybe,' Fleming agreed. 'I hope not.'

'I'll take a closer look at the body with the ME and let you know,' Lucy said, before ending the call.

Ian, the orderly, had drawn level with her now, his uniform splattered with mud. 'I'm sure you weren't expecting all this excitement when you came to see your dad,' he said, smiling.

Lucy returned the smile briefly. 'Listen, the man in the river? Have you any patients reported missing?'

'A couple. No one recent. There must be a fair few in this city, mind you.'

Lucy thought of all those who had been reported as Missing Persons. There were almost a hundred in the Foyle district alone, never mind those that might have been reported missing in the rest of the North, or indeed the Republic.

'More than a few,' she agreed.

Those carrying the body laid it on the examination table in the morgue, then filed out, as a doctor from the hospital pushed in through to examine the corpse and confirm death.

Lucy likewise squeezed her way in past the exiting group then closed the doors to the room. The doctor, an older woman, who introduced herself as Elma, pulled on a pair of gloves, then handed Lucy a pair. She pressed her hand against the man's cheek.

'He's freezing,' she said. 'He's not just after jumping in, then.'

14

'But there's very little damage,' Lucy observed. 'To his face and that. You'd think he'd look worse if he'd been in the water a while. I wasn't even sure he was dead until I felt his hand.'

Elma frowned. 'Yes. There's very little visible bloating, so you'd think he couldn't be dead *that* long. You know, he looks quite peaceful actually,' she added, stepping back a little and regarding the body.

The victim was an elderly man, his hair, though muddied and entangled with weeds from the water, was undoubtedly greying. His eyes remained closed, his mouth pursed. Lucy could see now that, rather than wearing a suit, as she had told DI Fleming, the victim wore grey trousers and a navy blazer, over a cream shirt and a blue tie.

'So what do you reckon?' Lucy asked. 'Suicide?'

'Presumably,' Elma said. Suddenly, she leaned down close to the body, her attention caught by something just visible in the man's nose. 'Wait a minute.'

She straightened and, moving across the room to one of the drawers, pulled out a pair of tweezers.

'What are you doing?' Lucy asked, edging in closer.

'He has something in his nose,' the woman said. She held the tweezers between finger and thumb and, using them, reached up into the nasal cavity, gripped the edge of the object protruding from it and pulled. As she did so, a roll of dirty material emerged.

'Jesus,' Lucy said, her stomach turning. 'What is that?'

'Cotton wool, I think,' Elma said, angling her head as she examined the material under the light before setting it down in a metal kidney dish on the bench

15

next to her. She moved across to the body again, leaned down and shone a small pen torch into the man's nostrils.

'Do you know what?' she said, straightening up. 'Not only is this man dead, but I think he's already been embalmed, too.'

Chapter Four

'Planning your own funeral is one thing, but going through with the thing *before* you throw yourself in the river? That's a remarkable feat,' the doctor commented a few minutes later.

The victim lay on his back on the table at the centre of the room, stripped to his underwear. Several incision marks were evident on his trunk in addition to roughly stitched wounds inside his thighs.

Elma pointed to them with a gloved finger as they examined the body. 'They must have used the femoral artery for the embalming drain,' she'd said. 'See?'

Lucy nodded, not quite wanting to look too closely. Instead, she stared at the side of the man's head, the slightly sunken cheeks creating the impression of a waxy hollow above his jawline. For a moment, she was reminded of examining her father's damaged face only an hour earlier.

'So, not only was your victim already dead before he went in the water,' Elma said, peeling off the gloves now and dropping them in the waste bin by the table. 'But he'd already been embalmed.'

'And judging by his clothes, possibly waked and boxed, too,' Lucy added.

It was traditional that, following death, the remains of the dead would be embalmed, then laid in an open coffin for a two-day wake, before the funeral on the third day, so that mourners could pay their final respects before burial. Generally, the deceased would be well dressed. If that was the case here, Lucy reasoned, then the man had been dead for a few days at the very least.

'So, if he was waked, how the hell did he end up in the water?'

'That's one question,' the doctor noted. 'The other is "Who is he?"'

Lucy nodded. 'I'll contact the local undertakers and see if anyone recognizes him. Any indications of how he actually died?'

Elma shook her head. 'Natural causes, by the looks of it.'

'No PM stitching?' Lucy guessed. Had his death been suspicious, he would have been subject to a post-mortem and his chest would have carried the telltale Y incision marks.

'And no signs of violence on the body,' the doctor added. 'The wounds we can see are consistent with those made during the embalming process.'

Lucy moved across to where the man's clothes lay piled on a chair next to the table. She lifted his jacket and, opening it, patted through the pockets. She folded back the jacket, examining the label protruding from the inside pocket.

'Looking for his name? Is it not just schoolkids who have their names on their clothes?'

Lucy nodded. 'He's old. My father is in here and they have his name written on all his labels so nothing gets lost or mixed up. I thought maybe it might've been the same with him, if he's been in a home or something.'

As she folded the jacket she noticed, for the first time, a small insignia on the breast pocket of a small golden castle, with, beneath it, two oak leaves. Under that was the word Captain.

'City of Derry Golf Club,' Elma said, pointing to the logo. 'He must have been a recent captain. They keep the blazer when they finish their year. The club changed their logo a few years back. The one on his jacket is the new version.'

'How did you know that?' she asked, bemused.

'I was a ladies' captain in Donegal,' she said. 'I recognized the City of Derry badge. They'll be able to tell you if any of their past captains have died recently. Being captain was clearly important to him, if he'd wanted to be buried in the club blazer.'

Chapter Five

Lucy considered driving up to the golf club on her way home; it lay just a few miles past Prehen Park on the road towards Strabane, but glancing at the clock on the dashboard display she realized it would probably already be closed for the evening. That, and the stench of the sediment mud still spattered on her clothes, drove her home for a shower instead. She reasoned that she would call in the morning, when she might have more luck in speaking to someone who would be able to help her. Then she would report it on to Mark Burns, the Chief Super of CID in the city. Let them deal with it then. Her curiosity needed only to know the dead man's name, having been involved, in a manner of speaking, in his recovery from the river.

The house smelt musty when she opened the door, a combination of the heat building inside all day and the aged furniture which had been bought by her father almost twenty years earlier, and which she had not replaced. She opened some of the windows downstairs to air the place out a little.

She stripped off and, after bundling her clothes into the washing machine, climbed into the shower. She was just drying herself when she heard someone knocking at her front door. Glancing at her watch, she saw that it was already past eleven.

Pulling on her dressing gown, she padded downstairs and peered through the peephole installed in the door. Standing outside was one of her neighbours, a man called Dermot who lived in a house opposite hers. She'd met him a few times; once he'd removed graffiti off her gable wall for her. Beyond that, and the occasional wave and smile as they passed in their cars, she didn't really know him. She didn't even know his wife's name, or those of his children, of whom there seemed to be quite a number.

She opened the door the few inches allowed by the security chain. Dermot smiled, in preparation of greeting, then seemed to notice that she was wearing her dressing gown and blushed. He wore a sweat-darkened grey T-shirt and running shorts.

'Lucy. I'm really sorry for bothering you,' he said.

'It's fine,' Lucy said. 'Is something wrong?'

Dermot glanced across furtively at his own house, then moved closer to her door again, the movement carrying with it the waft of sweat on the warm air.

'I ... ah ... look, I know it's late. It's the wife's sister. She's called with us. She's ... she's in pretty bad shape. We think her partner's hit her.'

'I'll call someone for you. They can come out straight away,' Lucy said.

'No,' Dermot said, stepping closer. 'No, please. She's not saying he did it, but ... well, her lip's bust and that. The missus wanted her to call the cops – to call you – you know what I mean, but she's refused. She doesn't want the police involved.'

'That's pretty common,' Lucy said.

21

Dermot stood, expectantly. Finally, Lucy said, 'Look, let me get changed and I'll call over.'

Dermot smiled briefly. 'Would you mind? That would be great. I didn't say I was coming across for you; I told them I was going out for a jog. I'm sure she didn't want me sitting there anyway.'

'I'll be over in a few minutes,' Lucy said, moving to close the door.

'One thing,' Dermot said, arresting its movement with his hand. 'Sorry,' he said, when he realized what he had done. 'Look, would you maybe say you're a friend of the family rather than her thinking you're there as a police officer. Maybe just have a chat with her.'

Ten minutes later, Lucy was crossing the street. She'd tied her hair back in a short ponytail, and wore jeans and a light-blue polo shirt. She knocked at the door and waited. A moment later, Dermot answered.

'Lucy. Come in,' he announced. To his rear, four small children peered down at her from the stairs, already dressed for bed, but obviously too excited by the drama below to sleep.

'Thanks very much for this,' Dermot muttered as he led her into the living room. On a wide sofa sat a woman Lucy recognized as his wife, her arm around the shoulder of a younger girl, in her late twenties perhaps, who bore little familial resemblance to her older sibling.

'Lucy's here,' Dermot announced again, pointing her towards one of the free armchairs.

The elder woman glanced at Dermot, then smiled towards Lucy. 'Hi, Lucy. Good to see you. This is my sister, Fiona.'

Fiona glanced up at Lucy. Her upper lip was split and swollen around a livid bruise.

'Hi,' Lucy said.

'Who's she?' Fiona asked, nodding towards Lucy but clearly addressing her sister.

'Lucy's one of our neighbours. She's a ... she's a friend.'

'Calling at eleven at night for a visit?'

'Sorry, I ...' Lucy struggled to explain the timing of her visit. She touched at her wet hair. 'I meant to call earlier, but I was swimming. I had to shower afterwards.'

It seemed to placate the girl enough for she made no comment.

Lucy smiled, encouragingly. 'It's good to meet you,' she said, clasping her hands between her knees. 'That's a nasty-looking cut.'

'It's fine,' the girl said. She shook her sister's arm from around her shoulder and straightened a little. 'I need to use the bathroom.'

'I'm going to grab a shower myself,' Dermot said quickly, sensing perhaps that left alone with his wife, she might have something to say about Lucy's presence. 'The downstairs loo will be free. Beside the kids will torture you upstairs.'

The two left Lucy and the elder sister sitting in the living room.

'How is she?' Lucy asked. 'Dermot explained what happened.'

'We don't *know* what happened,' the woman said. 'She'll not tell us anything.'

'What's her partner like? Is he abusive?'

The woman shrugged. 'I don't really know. They met two years ago. Whirlwind romance; he proposed a few months back, took her to Rome, swept her off her feet. I've barely seen them since they started dating, but they *seemed* happy. Cut themselves off from everyone, mind you. I was surprised she was able to remember where our house was this evening.'

Lucy nodded. 'Look, anything I can do to help, I will. There's no point pushing things too hard. If Fiona thinks you're forcing her into siding against her partner, she'll clam up and head home.'

The woman nodded. 'Don't let on you're police. You're a family friend.'

Lucy nodded agreement.

'And my name's Jenny, by the way.'

Fiona came back into the room a few moments later, a little more composed than previously. 'Sorry,' she said to the room in general.

Lucy smiled at her. 'So you're Jenny's sister?'

Fiona nodded. 'And you're a friend of the family? I've not seen you before.'

'You've not been here in two years,' Jenny retorted, then seemed to regret having done so.

'What do you do for a living?' Lucy asked.

'Nothing,' the younger girl commented.

'Lucky you!'

'I used to work in HMV,' Fiona said, quickly. 'I left it.'

'I was sorry to hear about that. When it closed. I used it a lot,' Lucy said.

24

'Yes. No, I left before that. My partner thought it wasn't really ... I was a bit old for it.'

'You're younger than me,' Lucy said. 'I'd love to work in a music shop. Just listen to stuff you want all day.'

'I don't really like music,' Fiona said.

'You *loved* music,' Jenny said quickly. 'She had a CD collection that took up a whole bookcase.'

'Yeah, I ... outgrew it,' the girl said, with little conviction. 'What do you do?'

Lucy hesitated. 'I'm ... I was a fitness instructor,' she said, finally. It wasn't a lie as such, she reasoned.

'Really?' Jenny asked, with genuine surprise. 'I didn't know that.'

Lucy nodded. 'I used to be really fit.'

'You're still pretty fit,' Fiona commented.

Lucy smiled. 'You're not so bad yourself,' she joked, causing Fiona to smile against her will. The girl winced at the gesture, then dabbed her thumb at the cut on her lip, which had reopened.

'Do you want me to take at look at that for you?' Lucy asked.

Fiona shook her head. 'It's fine,' she said. 'I banged into the cupboard door at home. I'm so clumsy sometimes,' she added.

'She might need a stitch,' Jenny said to Lucy. She turned to her sister. 'I told you, I thought—'

'It's fine,' Fiona said. 'I don't need a stitch.'

Lucy understood the girl's reluctance. Going to the hospital would necessitate repeating her explanation for the injury to another group of people. Clearly, unconvinced by it herself, she'd decided the less scrutiny it was subjected to, the better.

'Have you a chapstick?' Lucy asked. 'It'll sting a bit, but it'll seal it up.'

Fiona stared at her.

Lucy shrugged. 'I've taken my fair share of knocks and bumps,' she said. 'One of the tricks of the trade.'

'I might have one upstairs,' Jenny said, getting up to go and check.

Fiona smiled gratefully as her sister closed the living-room door. 'Thanks for that. She'd have been nagging at me all night, otherwise.'

'She's just worried,' Lucy said. 'She means well.'

Fiona nodded.

'So what actually happened?'

The girl looked at her, her eyes wide with panic. 'I told you, I banged it on the door. The cupboard. I'd left it open and …' The excuse faded into a mumble.

'It's OK,' Lucy said, just as the door opened again.

'Here we go,' Jenny said brightly, handing the stick to Lucy. 'Anna had one for when she comes out of the pool. Her lips are always dry,' she added unnecessarily.

'Can I?' Lucy asked, kneeling in front of Fiona, who nodded as she leant forward a little.

'How's she getting on?' she asked her sister to offset her embarrassment.

'The best,' Jenny said, watching Lucy work.

'I love swimming,' Lucy said. 'I've not been in ages.'

'I thought you were there tonight?' Fiona asked sharply.

Lucy stumbled on her answer. 'That's what I meant,' she managed. 'Until tonight.'

Jenny rushed to her aid. 'We used to go swimming every day,' she said to Lucy. 'Fiona and me. Then, you know ...' She glanced at her sister.

'Then you had kids,' Fiona said. 'It just became too difficult to arrange.'

'We should go for a swim someday,' Jenny said. 'I could be doing with getting back into it again. Just us girls. It'd be nice.'

Fiona smiled tentatively, as if testing the sealed cut, nodded a little uncertainly. 'That would be nice,' she echoed.

'Lucy?' Jenny said. 'How about it?'

Lucy stared from one sister to the other. She assumed Jenny had included her out of politeness and that to decline might seem rude. Besides, paradoxically, Fiona might be more inclined to spend time with her sister if a stranger was also present to prevent the conversation becoming too probing.

'Maybe,' she managed. 'I'll call you to arrange something at some stage.'

Wednesday, 18 July

Chapter Six

City of Derry Golf Club was situated on Victoria Road, just a few miles past Prehen Park, where Lucy lived. The course extended almost six kilometres, running from the main roadway alongside the river, up towards Gobnascale. Indeed, one of the holes of the course abutted the rear of Lucy's house in Summerhill. On the odd occasions that she actually managed to go out and cut the grass of the back lawn, she could hear the crack of the balls and the snippets of conversations as the players strolled past. A few times, she found the odd wayward ball hidden within the long grass of her garden.

The car park was almost empty when she arrived. Out on the fairways, the first four-balls of the day were starting their play. Inside, a handful of men were sitting at the Nineteenth Hole bar, drinking tea or eating fried breakfasts before beginning their game. Rather than going into the bar, Lucy knocked on the door of the shop.

A young man in a pink polo shirt was standing at the till, annotating the receipt roll as he worked through it with a blue biro.

'We're not open yet,' he said, when Lucy pushed open the door.

'I'm DS Black with the PSNI,' Lucy said. 'Can I have a moment?'

The man straightened, closing the till drawer. 'Of course. How can I help?'

Lucy came into the shop, taking out her phone and opening the pictures folder. She showed the young man the picture she had taken of the dead man's jacket. 'Is this from here?'

The man took the phone and, widening the image, examined it. 'Yeah, that's one of ours. A past captain's blazer. Why?'

'We recovered a body from the river last night,' Lucy said. 'He was wearing this. I was hoping you might be able to help us identify him. Maybe you have a list of all the past captains?'

'Oh my God! Is he dead?'

Lucy nodded. 'Would you have those names?'

The man nodded quickly. 'Come with me,' he said.

He led her out to the entrance to the bar where two large wooden boards had been erected on which was listed the names of all the club's captains and ladies' captains, tracing back to 1911.

'That's them all.'

'Have you a copy of the list you could give me?' Lucy asked. 'On something smaller. A sheet of paper, maybe. And the men only; I don't need the women's names.'

'Of course,' the man said. 'A lot of the older ones are dead. Do you want me to leave those off?'

Better to leave off those still alive, Lucy thought, but she said nothing. 'Perhaps just mark those you know to be deceased.'

'Of course,' the man repeated. 'I'll get the club secretary to do it when he gets in. He should have it all handy somewhere.'

Lucy glanced at her watch. It was nine thirty.

'That should be fine,' she said, handing him her card. 'He can fax it through to me at that number.'

'That's desperate news,' the man said, shaking his head. 'That's the second past captain who's died this week. You know what they say about these things happening in threes?' He rubbed his arm, as if suppressing the urge to shiver.

'Who was the other one who died?' Lucy asked.

Chapter Seven

'Cancer, apparently,' she said. 'His funeral was a few days ago, according to the Pro Shop keeper.'

Tom Fleming sat next to her, in the Strand Road office of Chief Superintendent Mark Burns. The heat had already begun to build and Burns had both a fan running in his room and the small window opened wide in the hope of a breeze. The air, though, was still and hot.

'Stuart Carlisle,' Burns said. He lifted the picture that Lucy had taken of the victim pulled from the river and compared it with one she had found on the golf club's website of a presentation taken a few years earlier. 'It could be him,' he agreed. 'As much as people can look like themselves when they're embalmed.'

'We thought it a CID investigation rather than PPU,' Fleming said. Then added, 'Sir.'

Burns shrugged. 'We've the whole team out at the moment at the city's waste plant at Maydown. The lorries were coming in to offload all the early morning collections and they found a man's body in one of the compactors.'

'Jesus,' Lucy said. 'Was he dead or alive when he went in the truck?'

'That we don't know,' Burns said. 'The team are working on it. So, look, if you have a name for this guy, check with the next of kin and find out what happened. Maybe it was a burial at sea kind of thing that went wrong.'

Fleming glanced across at Lucy, not bothering to hide his scepticism, but Burns was already standing up to indicate that the meeting was over.

Within the hour, Lucy had traced through the Registrar's office that Carlisle's death certificate had been issued to his nephew, Tony Henderson. Henderson lived on Balloughry Road, on the outskirts of town, not far from the border with the Republic of Ireland. She and Fleming went out together.

Henderson's house was a bungalow, sitting squat against the roadside. The driveway running along the side of the house had once been gravel, but time and use had worn deep gouges in the mud beneath, which sat in caked ridges now, as Lucy stepped over them towards the house.

A mongrel dog appeared from the rear of the property, small and white, with scraps of tan on its fur that suggested a Jack Russell had been involved somewhere in its parentage. It yapped several times at them, then lowered its head and hobbled forward, reaching Lucy and sniffing around her feet.

'Can I help you?'

Lucy looked up from the dog to where a thin, middle-aged man stood at the corner of the house, a paintbrush in one hand, a small can of paint in the other.

'Tony Henderson?' Tom Fleming asked.

'That's me. Is something wrong?' The man set the can on the ground and laid the paintbrush across the opening of the top. He straightened and pulled a rag from his back pocket on which to wipe his hands.

'We'd like to talk to you about your uncle, Stuart Carlisle?'

'Great-uncle,' Henderson said. 'What about him?'

'We believe we pulled his body from the river last night,' Lucy said.

The man laughed with relief, then realized it was not the appropriate reaction to the news of a recovery from the river. He raised a paint-stained wrist in front of his mouth. 'Sorry,' he said. 'You've got the wrong man. My uncle's already dead; he died last week.'

'We know,' Lucy said. 'Maybe we could go inside.'

Henderson's living room was narrow, one side dominated by an old china cabinet, the other by two armchairs. There was no sofa. Lucy sat on one seat, Henderson on the other while Fleming moved across to the window, as if to lean against the sill.

'I wouldn't do that,' Henderson said. 'I've just painted the woodwork.'

Instinctively, Fleming stepped away, wiping at the back of his legs lest some paint had transferred on to them.

Henderson stared from him to Lucy. 'If you know my uncle's already dead, why do you think he was the one you pulled from the Foyle?'

'Would you mind taking a look at this?' Lucy said, offering the man a photograph, a headshot of the body they had recovered. 'Is that your great-uncle?'

Henderson studied the image, angling it towards the light entering the room through the one narrow window to the front, across which hung a lace curtain. 'I've smudged it,' he said and pulled one tacky thumb from the picture before handing it back to Lucy. 'Sorry. That looks like him all right, but—'

'He was wearing a City of Derry Golf Club blazer?'

'Aye, that's right. I don't understand, though. We had his funeral.'

'When?'

'Monday. He was waked in the funeral parlour then they had the service for him at one. They took him off to be cremated in All Hallows in Belfast.'

'Cremated?' Fleming asked. Generally, Irish people tended not to cremate the dead, suitable land for burial plots not being an issue in the country. It was the exception rather than the rule. So much so, the only crematoriums in the North were in Belfast.

'Did you take the body up to All Hallows yourself?'

The man shook his head. 'I'd an appointment in the hospital in the afternoon,' he explained. 'The undertakers handled it all. I've to call for his ashes at some stage.'

'I see,' Lucy said.

Henderson clearly sensed something in her voice for he continued. 'I never knew him. He wasn't close to us. He was my granny's brother. He never bothered with our family. It was the home help contacted me to say he was dead. Going to the funeral service was as much as I figured he needed. What difference would it make seeing his coffin going into an oven, eh?' The man stared at Lucy, willing her to respond.

'That's understandable,' Fleming said, instead. 'Look, you're certain it was your great-uncle in the coffin at the service? Did you see him?'

'Aye. It was an open coffin at the wake. All his golfing buddies were there.'

'Did *anyone* accompany the body to All Hallows?'

'The undertakers, just,' Henderson said. 'All his golfing friends were the same age as him; they weren't going to start driving nearly two hours to see him being burned.'

'When did you last see him in the coffin?'

'At the start of the service. They closed the lid and sealed it, then we had the service, then they took the body out to take him to Belfast.'

'And that was the last you saw of it?'

Henderson nodded.

'Who was the undertaker?' Lucy asked.

'Duffy, on the Strand Road. Did they throw his body in the river, instead of taking him up to be burned?' he asked. 'They were paid out of his estate. They charged plenty for it. Bloody undertakers would drain you dry.'

'What about the rest of your great-uncle's estate?' Lucy asked, earning a scowl from Fleming for the nature of the question.

'It'll all come to me, I think,' Henderson said. 'All that effort and saving, just to have your money go to someone you hardly know when you're gone, eh?'

Chapter Eight

Duffy and Sons operated out of a converted mechanic's garage along the quay on the Strand Road. They were recently opened, and had managed to position themselves with a view of the river from their main service room on the first floor of the building. When they arrived, they were met by the owner, Gabriel Duffy, before being led up to the service room. Despite the volume of traffic along the main arterial route through the city just outside the window, the building was hushed, the air sweet and heavy with incense.

'We did handle Mr Carlisle's service,' Duffy said, his voice soft and sibilant.

'His "remains" were recovered from the river last night,' Lucy said. She produced the image she had shown Henderson and gave it to Duffy. He rubbed at the white-paint fingerprint on its surface.

'That does look like Mr Carlisle, but I can assure you, it can't be him. He was taken to All Hallows and cremated the day before yesterday. We have all the paperwork to show the transfer from us to the crematorium. Mr Carlisle's ashes are waiting for his great-nephew to collect. We have them here.'

He stood, and padded across the room and out through a different doorway from the one through which they had been brought in. Lucy assumed he was going to the preparation room beneath. A moment later he reappeared with a small box, slightly bigger than a milk carton. Attached to it was a sticker with Stuart Carlise's name and the date of his death.

'Is that it?' Lucy asked.

'You can pay for nicer ones,' Duffy said. 'Mr Carlisle's next of kin wanted a basic receptacle.'

Lucy took it from the man. It was heavier than she expected, perhaps the same as a bag of flour, she thought. 'Is this definitely Stuart Carlisle?'

Duffy nodded. 'My son drove the body up. He's downstairs finishing an embalming; he'll be up in a moment. The coffin was sealed at the service, taken out to the van and delivered to All Hallows. Ciaran waited in Belfast until the cremation was completed, a few hours later, then brought back the ashes.'

As if on cue, the rear door opened again and a young man came in, pushing the door closed with a click. He came across to where Lucy and Fleming sat.

'This is Ciaran,' Duffy said. 'The officers are asking about the Stuart Carlisle cremation.'

Ciaran nodded. 'Yes?'

'We believe we've found his body in the river,' Lucy said. 'Are you sure he was cremated?'

'Absolutely,' Ciaran said, quickly. 'I drove it up myself. We loaded him into the crematorium and I waited about until it was finished. I brought his ashes back.'

'Can we see the ashes?' Fleming asked.

Duffy looked at his son for a moment. 'It's a little irregular,' he said. 'It's really meant to go to the next of kin.'

'Do you think the next of kin cares?' Lucy asked. 'We just need to check that what's in that box is human remains.'

Duffy glanced at his son again. The boy nodded. 'I don't see why not,' the boy said. 'Show them.'

Duffy unsealed the box and opened the lid. Inside was a clear plastic bag containing what appeared to Lucy to be more like shingle than ash.

'Is that how they're meant to look?' Lucy asked.

Duffy nodded. 'The bones don't burn so they have to crush them instead,' he said. 'That gives it that texture.'

'So that's definitively a person in there.'

Duffy nodded. 'As best as I can tell by looking,' he said.

'You didn't remove the body from the coffin on your way up, did you?' Fleming asked Ciaran Duffy.

The boy blinked at him, then shook his head. 'No. Why would I do that?'

'Could someone else have removed the body?'

Ciaran shrugged. 'No. I left here and took it straight to All Hallows. They took it from me and I called back a few hours later.'

'You called back?'

'I went into Belfast a run,' Ciaran said, glancing at his father. 'It takes three hours sometimes to burn the deceased.'

'Did you stop along the way? Could someone else have swapped the body?'

Ciaran shook his head. 'No. I called into the shop at the bottom of the Glenshane for a can of Coke, but that was it. A couple of minutes at most. And the van was sitting in the shop forecourt the whole time.'

'If anyone did swap the body, it must have been in the crematorium. Check with them. Either that, or the man you pulled from the river isn't Stuart Carlisle,' Gabriel Duffy said, standing up and moving to beside his son.

Chapter Nine

Lucy was just pulling into Maydown station, where the PPU was based, when her mobile rang. It was Tara Gallagher, a DS in CID, who had started in Foyle District around the same time as Lucy.

'Burns wants you to come across,' she said. 'The body in the bin. We think he was a homeless man. Burns is hoping you might be able to identify him.'

Fleming nodded when Lucy passed on Tara's request. 'I'll call All Hallows on the way across; get them to check whether Stuart Carlisle's remains ever made it as far as Belfast. Can I use your phone? My own's out of charge.'

Lucy handed it across to him. 'Do you think Duffy is lying?'

'One of the Duffys is lying. I'm undecided which one.'

Lucy glanced across. 'There wouldn't be a chance that someone in All Hallows was involved?'

'And drove the body back down to Derry to get rid of it?' Fleming shook his head. 'I don't see it. We'll check and see, but I think that *whatever* happened to that body, it happened here.'

The waste disposal unit from which DS Gallagher had called was only a few minutes away, in the industrial estate in Campsie. Even as they approached, they could see the activity outside the building. Several CSIs, clad in white paper suits, were already coming out of the building.

Tara met them at the entrance and waited as they were signed through at the cordon set up at the doorway.

'I thought the city dump was in Culmore,' Fleming said.

'It was, apparently,' Tara explained. 'That closed a few years back and this crew have been handling all the waste disposal for the city since. The lorries bring it all back here and then it's sorted and taken on to landfill or recycled.'

'Look at you,' Lucy said, nudging Tara. 'An expert.'

'On rubbish, yeah,' Tara said, reddening. 'That's why I became a cop.'

'What's the story with the body?' Fleming asked. 'You think he's homeless?'

'He's dressed like it,' Tara said. 'They ran his prints through the system and got a hit. He was lifted for drunk and disorderly a few years back. He gave his address back then as a hostel in Derry.'

'If they have his prints on the system, they must also have his name. Why do you need us to identify him?'

Tara cracked a smile. 'I'll let the Chief Super explain that one,' she said.

The Chief Superintendent was standing in the main yard of the building, next to a bin lorry. The compactor unit at the back was raised above the vehicle as two CSIs squatted inside the rear section, sifting through the rubbish.

'Looking for clues?' Lucy asked.

'Looking for the remains,' Tara said. 'Of the remains. The rest is across there.'

At their approach, Burns turned and lowered his face mask. Lucy guessed its use was more due to the smell in the yard than for the preservation of the scene, particularly as the yard wasn't the scene of death anyway.

'Tom, Lucy,' Burns said, nodding. 'How did you get on with the family?'

Fleming nodded. 'Fine. Next of kin was at the man's funeral. The funeral home took him to Belfast to be cremated and have both the paperwork and the ashes to prove it.'

'Then how the hell did he get pulled out of the river?'

Fleming shrugged. 'That's the question. All Hallows in Belfast are to come back to me on it.'

'Run a PM and DNA tests on the corpse to confirm identity.'

Fleming nodded. 'Already on it,' he said, though Lucy knew that they weren't. Still, she guessed, Fleming wouldn't give Burns the satisfaction of knowing that. 'What's the story with the body in the bin? You think he's homeless.'

'I think it's safe to assume, considering he was sleeping in a bloody bin. Do these people not realize what could happen to them?'

'These *people* probably have no alternatives,' Fleming replied tersely.

'There are always alternatives,' Burns commented. 'Regardless, we need your expertise: we have ID on record for the victim,' he said. 'Just not the right one.'

45

'How do you know it's wrong?'

'He was lifted a few years back for being drunk and disorderly. He provided one of the hostels in Derry as his address. The only identification he had was a driving licence which listed an address in Poland.'

'Did that not have his name on it?' Fleming asked.

'It had *a* name on it. Prawo Jazdy.'

'So what's the problem?'

'When we tried running it through this morning we found out that Prawo Jazdy is not a name. It's the Polish for "driving licence".'

Lucy managed to stifle her laugh; Fleming on the other hand didn't even try, guffawing loudly at the comment. 'Morons,' he managed.

Burns smiled stiffly. 'It's a bit embarrassing for the District. And it doesn't help us at all.'

Fleming nodded. 'Of course,' he said. 'What hostel did he give as his address and when? We can check the names of any Poles who used it regularly.'

'There can't be that many,' Burns said, hopefully.

Chapter Ten

'There have been loads,' Niall Toner said, as he brought them into the Foyle Hostel. Situated off Bishop Street, the hostel was opened in the early seventies in response to the levels of chronic alcoholism affecting the men in the city.

'Really?' Lucy asked.

'Yeah. A lot of them were construction workers who came over for the building boom during the Celtic tiger. When the downturn hit, they couldn't find work, or, if they did, it was for fairly crap wages.'

'Unemployment and social deprivation,' Fleming commented.

'The breeding ground for alcoholism,' Toner said. 'It could have been the motto of this city for years. Not so much any more.'

'Why didn't they just go home?' Lucy asked. 'Not to get all BNP about it or anything. If there was no work for them any more.'

'Some of them fell into relationships here. Or had destroyed their relationships at home. There was the promise of all the work that would come too, with the A5 and A6 expansions. Of course, that hasn't quite worked out.'

Lucy nodded. She was well aware of the A5 debacle, it being the main road that ran from Derry along the river, past Prehen and all the way south to Aughnacloy some fifty-five miles away. The road was the main link between Derry and Dublin. At the height of the boom, the Irish government and the Northern Irish Assembly announced plans for a joint road-building programme, to open up the west with a dual carriageway replacing the dreadful single lane road currently in place. The project was to cost in excess of £300 million, partly funded by the Irish government despite the road not being in the Republic; the rationale was that it would increase trade to the Republic by improving infrastructure. When the crash came and the Irish government went bust, the promised money vanished. Then a group of landowners along the route took the project to the High Court in the North, which ruled against the expansion after finding that an environmental assessment of the impact on two salmon rivers had not been completed properly. Since then, the project had stalled, despite almost £60 million having already been spent, most of it on consultants' fees. The promised boost to the construction industry had not happened.

The A6 was the main road leading from Derry to Belfast which, likewise, had languished as a single carriageway for years, despite the fact that many major towns and cities in the east of the province had long since been dualled. That the two main routes out of the second city of the North were allowed to languish in the state they were in for so long was seen as testament to the lack of political will in the North to fund works in the west of the province. The first section, to Dungiven, was rumoured to start in

2015 at a cost of £100 million; no one really believed it would ever happen.

'Do you have a picture of him? I might remember him,' Toner asked, bringing them into his office. It was small room with three mismatched easy chairs in front of a desk on which an old PC hummed nosily.

'You'd not recognize him, Mr Toner,' Lucy said. 'Not the state he was left in.'

'I didn't quite catch you on the phone. Was he found in a bin?'

Lucy shook her head. 'We think he was in a bin. It was emptied last night into one of the lorries doing the night round. He was in the compactor for some time.'

Toner blanched. 'Jesus,' he said, blessing himself quickly. 'What a horrible way to go. Was he alive before he ... you know?'

'We don't know,' Lucy said. 'If he was sleeping in the bin, then it's likely that he was. On the other hand, maybe someone dumped his body in there just to get rid of him.'

Toner shook his head. 'I'm sure when he came across here from Poland he didn't think he'd end up sleeping in a bin.'

'Or dying in one,' Fleming commented.

Toner nodded. 'When was he here? We take notes of all admissions.'

'He was arrested on 16 October 2010,' Lucy said. 'He'd been in a fight and was drinking. He gave his address as here.'

'Why have you no name for him?'

'The officer who took his name recorded the wrong thing.'

49

'They thought the Polish for "driving licence" on his ID was actually his name. Prawo Jazdy.'

'And the man himself would hardly have corrected their mistake,' Toner commented.

'Not if he was so drunk they'd had to lift him.'

'The PSNI'd normally contact us the next day to tell us they had him. If they'd given us that name, we'd not have had him listed as a resident,' Toner said. 'October 2010,' he repeated to himself, standing and moving across to one of the filing cabinets behind his desk. He unlocked the third and pulled out the middle drawer, flicking through the various folders, then pulling out the one he wanted.

'These are all the admissions for October of that year, as well as those longer-term residents who were with us.'

'How many have you got in here?' Lucy asked.

'Twenty-five at a time,' Toner said. 'All single men. We don't take anyone with a history of violence or certain criminal offences. Beyond that, we'll try to help anyone we can.'

'How many are alcoholics?'

'Almost all,' Toner said, without looking up. 'We try to support them into drying out and turning things around. Here,' he added, pulling out a sheet. 'These are the twenty-five we had registered for that week. Most of them were here longer-term, so if he was here, he'll be one of these.'

He laid the sheet on the desk and they scanned down through it, looking for Polish names. Only one stood out: Kamil Krawiec.

'Give me a second,' Toner said, standing. 'I should have a copy of his ID somewhere.'

Within a few minutes, he produced a folder from the first cabinet this time. He opened it and handed the top sheet to Fleming. 'Is that him?'

Fleming studied the picture. 'I'm not sure. Can I take this?' He passed the sheet to Lucy. It was a blown up photocopy of the man's driving licence, with 'Prawo Jazdy' indeed printed at the top. The man in the image looked in his late twenties, sharp featured, his hair cropped tight against his scalp, staring unsmiling at the camera.

'I'll do you a copy,' Toner said. 'I remember him, I think. He was a construction worker, right enough.'

'When did you last see him?'

Toner flicked through the file. 'He left us in June 2011. I've not seen him since.'

'Any ideas where else he might have been living?'

'Your guess is as good as mine. Since the factory on the Foyle Road collapsed, the street drinkers have had to find new places.'

Lucy remembered the building. It had once been a shirt factory, next to the Craigavon Bridge, long since disused. Indeed, she had visited it once, with Tom Fleming, to find a woman who had once known her father in a previous case. A year or so after the case, the building had collapsed one night. Luckily, those who had been inside had managed to escape before the whole thing had fallen. Strangely, another shirt factory on the other side of the bridge had burned down a few years before that, with the result that there were now two gaps of rubbled land on either side of the main approach into the city. As part of the City of Culture celebrations, the council had had the areas laid with grass to make a little more picturesque the gaps in the smile the city presented tourists.

'We'll take a drive around,' Fleming said. 'See if we can't spot some of his drinking companions.'

'In that case,' Toner said, 'if either of you should happen to see Sammy Smith, can you tell him he needs to call and get his shots?'

'Shots?'

'Insulin. He's on two shots a day. His pharmacist delivers them to here. I've not seen him the past few days with the good weather. He'd need to get his insulin, especially if he's drinking again.'

'We'll look out for him,' Fleming said.

As they were leaving, Toner addressed Tom Fleming directly. 'I hear Terry Haynes is missing.'

Fleming nodded. 'I only heard last night.'

'I hope he's not had a relapse. The man's been a star; he's done quite a bit for some of our residents to help them get themselves back on their feet. I'd hate to think he'd had a slip himself.'

Lucy felt her mobile vibrate in her pocket. She pulled it out and checked the screen, but did not recognize the number.

'This is All Hallows Crematorium,' a voice said. 'Someone was looking for information about a service here the other day?'

'That was my Inspector, Tom Fleming,' Lucy said. 'I'm DS Black. Who is this?'

'Frank Norris. I'm in charge up here. I believe there was some suggestion that we'd not cremated a body.'

'Not quite,' Lucy said. 'We've found a body in the river which we believed was to have been cremated. Stuart Carlisle.'

52

'Yes. He was definitely done,' the man said. 'I've the paperwork here. Duffy, the undertakers, took the ashes back with them.'

'I know,' Lucy said. 'We've seen them. But we've also seen Mr Carlisle's corpse.'

'Well, we cremated whoever was brought up to us. We don't open the coffin to check who's inside, you know.'

'I understand,' Lucy said. 'And you're sure there *was* a body inside?'

'Certain,' Norris said. 'The ashes …'

'Could that not have been from the coffin?'

'What about the plates and pins?' Norris countered, a note of triumph in his voice.

'Excuse me?'

'There were two metal plates and a few surgical pins removed from the remains,' Norris said. 'We cremate the body in stages. The first part removes soft tissue and that. We then crush the bones. Metal in the body can damage the crusher, so we have to remove it first by running a magnetic plate across the remains.'

'Metal in the body?'

'Tooth fillings and that normally,' Norris said. 'But replacement joints and such things crop up too. The Carlisle cremation produced a number of fillings, long surgical pins and two metal plates.'

'Where are they now?'

'Here,' Norris said. 'We recycle the metal. Unless the next of kin particularly want it. In this case, as the next of kin didn't even bother coming to the service, we thought it highly unlikely they'd want the deceased's fillings. Or his surgical implants.'

'Can you bag those for me?' Lucy said. 'Someone will be up for it shortly.'

'We'll be closing in an hour, so they'd best be quick.'

Chapter Eleven

In the end, the desk sergeant in the Strand Road contacted Belfast and asked a squad car to collect the implants and bring them down the road. A uniform from Derry would drive up and meet them halfway, at the bottom of the Glenshane Pass.

That arranged, Lucy and Fleming drove back through the city to Foyle Street. The old factory, facing the river, had proved to be a focal point for many of the homeless in the area for years. With its collapse, as Toner had said, their groupings had become more dispersed. Despite that, Tom Fleming's work in the soup kitchens at the weekends meant that he had some ideas of the common hangouts.

Even as they drove down the Foyle Road, a girl in her twenties staggered out onto the roadway in front of them and picked her way across to the opposite pavement. The space between the pavement and the river beyond housed the Foyle Valley Railway Museum.

Though now only one train line ran into Derry, from Belfast via the Antrim Coast, at one stage, four different railway systems had connected the city to the rest of the North as well as neighbouring Donegal. The museum, which had been built in the late eighties, was actually the recreation of an old railway station and platform, overlooking the river. A track ran from the museum for three miles, along the site of the original Great Northern Rail line which connected Derry and Strabane, running up the Donegal side of the river, then cutting over the Foyle just north of Strabane, across an island known as Islandmore. Lucy remembered, as a child, her father taking her on the old diesel railcar that had shuffled back and forth along the track when the museum first opened. It had long since stopped. Two original locomotives remained, one inside the building and a second, rusting model, positioned outside.

The drunk girl picked her way across to the low wall outside the museum and, swinging her leg, managed to step over it. They watched as she meandered past the building, then turned in left behind it, to where the platform was.

'We'll try here first,' Fleming said.

Lucy pulled in and parked outside the museum, which was already closed for the day. She and Fleming got out and followed the girl's path, around to the platform.

There were about a dozen people gathered there, most of whom were female. One old man sat in their midst, a bottle of White Lightning cider in his hands. The others were sharing cans of lager. The warm breeze, carrying down the Foyle Valley, seemed to strengthen here, as if the structure of the platform roofing created a wind tunnel of sorts. A second man sat with his T-shirt removed and tied around his head to protect his scalp from the sun, his trunk milky white against the livid red burns on his arms and face. He glanced up at Lucy as they rounded the corner and made to struggle to his feet.

'It's OK, Sammy,' Fleming said. 'Don't stand up.'

'Inspector Fleming,' Sammy said, exposing his gums in a toothless smile. 'Come on and sit,' he added grandly, patting the concrete ground on which they sat with the flat of his hand.

'How are you keeping, Sammy? You've taken a scalding.'

'I'm watching my head,' Sammy said. 'Don't want to get sunburn on me ears.'

'Niall Toner is looking for you. He says you need to call in and get your shots.'

Sammy winked broadly at Fleming. 'I'll call round later,' he said. 'He's an awful worrier.'

'Someone needs to worry about you, Sammy.'

Lucy glanced at the others gathered there who were following the exchange. She recognized a few of them, though not by name. She was struck by the number of women there. Many of them were relatively young. One appeared to be still in her teens. She wore skinny jeans and red trainers. She had her hair scraped back in a ponytail.

'Should you be here?' Lucy ventured.

'Where else should I be?' the girl asked, sharply.

'Leave her,' Sammy said, though Lucy could not tell whether he was addressing her or the girl. 'She's crabbed.'

'Piss off,' the girl said, kicking out with her foot, missing Sammy and striking the older woman who sat next to him.

'I'll slap your arse,' the woman said, with such conviction, the young girl's reply died on her lips.

'We're looking for someone,' Fleming said to Sammy. 'Kamil Krawiec.'

Sam shook his head. 'Never heard of him.'

Fleming handed him the picture that Toner had given them. Sammy took it, studying the picture. After a moment, his face lit with recognition.

'Crackers? Why didn't you say?'

'Crackers?'

'Aye. Crackers. Who the fu—' He glanced again at Lucy. 'Who can say that, whatever it is?' He pointed at the man's name on the licence with a thin, grimy finger. 'Camel?'

'*Kam-eel*,' Fleming pronounced. 'Have you seen him?'

Sam shook his head. 'Not in a while. What's he done?'

'Nothing,' Fleming said. 'We just wanted to find him.'

'Is this about the bin?' a woman to Lucy's left asked.

Lucy glanced down. The woman looked to be in her forties, though Lucy knew that meant little if she'd been living rough. She had thin, pinched features and auburn hair with a single patch of grey above her left ear. 'What bin?'

'The body in the bin? They were talking about it at the soup kitchen. Was it Crackers?'

'We don't know,' Lucy said.

'He used to be about a lot,' the woman said. 'But I've not seen him for months.'

'Can you remember when exactly?'

'What month is this?' the woman asked, as those around her cackled with laughter.

'It's the summer, sure the bloody sun's beating down,' Sammy said.

'Before Easter,' the woman said. 'Earlier maybe. Not for ages.'

'Thank you.' Lucy smiled. 'If you hear anything about it, will you try to get in touch with us?'

She offered the woman her card, but she didn't take it.

'Like I have a phone, love,' she said, joining the others in laughter. However, the girl in the red trainers reached across and took the card from her.

Sammy swallowed a mouthful of cider and passed the bottle to the girl next to him. 'We'll let someone know if we see him.'

'The fella in the bin? Was he sleeping in there?' the woman asked, her laughter fit passed. 'Is that what happened?'

'We don't know,' Lucy said.

The girl in the red trainers snorted derisively. 'Of course he wasn't.'

Lucy examined her a little more closely. 'Why do you say that?'

'Sure why would you sleep in a bin in this heat?' the young girl said. 'You'd be baked.' She lifted the cider bottle to her mouth and gulped down a mouthful while trickles spilled from the corners of her lips.

Lucy nodded agreement. The girl watched her and smiled.

'I could be a cop,' the girl said, offering the bottle out to Lucy. 'If I wanted.'

'No, thanks,' she said, to the proffered drink. 'And I've no doubt you could have been.'

'Could be, I said,' the girl corrected her, sharply.

Chapter Twelve

Lucy didn't speak as they got back into the car.

'What's up?' Fleming asked as she started the engine.

'I don't get it,' she said, aware that she needed to tread carefully in the conversation with Fleming. 'I understand alcoholism is a disease; I get that, I do. And I have every sympathy for someone struggling with it. But I don't see the appeal in ... in that,' she said, nodding towards the museum. 'Sitting there, drinking all day.'

Fleming said nothing and, for a moment, Lucy was worried she had offended him.

'Like, that girl? With the red shoes. Why would she choose to spend her days like that?'

'Street drinkers are a special breed,' Fleming said. 'To everyone else they're the lowest of the low, and they know that. There's only one place they can go where they won't be judged. Among others like themselves.'

'But she must have a home—' Lucy began.

'That question you asked; why would she choose? Over there's the one place she'll not be made to think of an answer to that. The other drinkers all know what they are. There's no denial. And they'll accept her so long as she sticks to whatever rules they operate by. That's a home by somebody's definition. Or an approximation of one at least.'

Lucy wasn't convinced but thought better than to pursue the discussion. She was relieved when her phone rang as they made their way down the Strand Road towards a second spot where the homeless congregated in a local car park. It was Burns.

'Any luck on a name?' he asked, without preamble.

'Possibly,' Fleming said. 'Kamil Krawiec. We've been asking round and no one has seen him in a while. We got a picture of him.'

'Great,' Burns said. 'The PM is being done at the minute. Can you take the picture up to the hospital, see if they can compare it with him on the slab and get a positive ID?'

The pathologist, Martin Kerrigan, was finishing up when Lucy and Fleming arrived at the morgue. The remains of the man lay on the metal table while Kerrigan's new assistant sewed him back up as best she could, considering the damage that had been done. Kerrigan was studying her sewing technique.

'This is Caroline O'Kane,' Kerrigan said, when they came in. 'Caroline; Tom Fleming, an old friend and veteran officer, and ...?'

'Lucy Black,' Lucy offered.

'Ah!' Kerrigan said. 'You're younger than I'd imagined.'

Lucy resisted the temptation to ask him how he'd heard of her, or indeed why he'd imagined her to be older than she was. He smiled lightly as he regarded her, as if daring her to do so.

'So, you're here about the binman?'

'Sort of,' Fleming said. 'The Chief Super asked us to bring this up to you.' He handed Kerrigan the photocopy of Krawiec's driving licence.

'The features are a little difficult to distinguish,' Kerrigan said. 'And I'm not talking about on the photocopy. Try your best.'

Lucy and Fleming approached the table. Lucy tried hard not to look lower than the dead man's face, but could still see, from her peripheral vision, not just the dark stitched Y on his chest, but the livid injuries of his whole body. She noticed his arm sat out at an angle and that his four fingers were missing from his left hand.

Fleming crouched beside the body, staring at the face, which lay sideways, as if looking towards the door in expectation of someone's arrival. He studied the image in the photocopy that Kerrigan held towards him. As Lucy approached, she noticed that one of the eyes hung loose from its socket.

'Could be him,' Fleming said.

Kerrigan moved up and angled the head. 'Yes, I'd say it's him all right. You can imagine how he should have looked when his head was ... well, the right shape.'

'Did he die in the bin lorry?' Lucy asked, moving away from the body.

'Ah, that's the question. Indications are that he was crushed to death by the compactor. Part of his sternum entered his heart as well as significant cranial damage to the back of the skull.'

Lucy understood now why the head had been angled the way it had.

'But ...?' Fleming said.

'But … there are also indications that he was severely beaten in the hours prior to his death. I suspect he would have died anyway from those injuries. In the end, the compactor could have been an act of mercy.'

Fleming shook his head. 'Only you, Martin. Euthanized by a bin lorry.'

Kerrigan laughed. 'There are significant injuries over his body, including to his skull. The older injuries show vital reaction consistent with the man having lived for over twelve or fourteen hours after receiving them before he died.'

'So someone beat him almost to death.'

'Essentially.'

'He couldn't have been hit by a car? Fallen down a set of stairs?' Fleming asked.

'Only if the point of impact with the car was in over seventy different spots on his body all at the same time. He also has defence wounds on his hands.' He lifted the right hand and held out the palm. A series of red scars slashed across it.

'Those are different again. They've healed quite a bit already, so I'd say he probably gained those a few days before his death. Possibly he got into a fight with someone who pulled a blade on him. Having said that, it must have been a very fine blade, considering the width of the cuts. I don't see any other lacerations of that type anywhere else but his hands, so far as I can tell. The beating came between forty-eight and seventy-two hours later.'

'Could he have climbed into the bin unaided, bearing the injuries which you say he had from the beating?' Lucy asked.

'She *is* a bright one,' Kerrigan said. 'No, he probably couldn't have. I'd say both his fibulas were shattered deliberately before death. He'd not have been able to stand up.'

'Shattered?'

'Various impact points. Small, about yay big.' He made a circle with his gloved hand. 'Increased pressure to the lower edge.' He mimed someone swinging something, made a tocking sound with his tongue to mimic impact.

'A hammer?'

'Ball-peen, considering some of the other circular impacts on the body.'

'So someone beat him ...'

'Looking at the legs, I'd go for kneecapped him first, then beat him.'

'Then dumped him in a bin.'

Kerrigan nodded. 'Leaving him to die. Or be crushed in the compactor when the rubbish was emptied.'

'Either way, he was murdered,' the assistant, Caroline O'Kane, offered.

'That's not for us to say,' Kerrigan said, correcting her. 'We simply examine and report. It's up to the good officers here to make conclusions such as murder.'

'He was murdered,' Fleming said to the woman, frowning at Kerrigan.

Chapter Thirteen

'And now,' Kerrigan continued. 'For the dead man who didn't drown himself. That one's yours, DS Black, is that right?'

'He is,' Lucy said. 'Apparently.'

'Well, the good news is that he was much easier to identify. After I unglued the mouth again, we were able to compare with dental records for Mr Stuart Carlisle. They are one and the same person.'

They heard a knocking at the door and a young uniform entered. 'DS Black? I was told to drop this up with you.'

He held a small parcel in his hand. He smiled sheepishly at them, then glanced at the table where Kamil Krawiec lay, his eyeball now touching the metal surface.

'Jesus,' the uniform said, his face contorting. Despite himself he kept staring, then suddenly retched, as if to vomit.

'In the sink,' Kerrigan shouted. 'Or you'll have to clean up yourself.'

Lucy went across to the man and took the parcel from him. 'Thanks,' she said.

The man wiped his mouth with his hand, as if in attempt to stop himself being sick.

'Some things you just can't unsee, Constable,' Kerrigan called as the man turned and left.

'Will I get him some water?' Caroline offered.

'Leave him,' Kerrigan said. 'He'll be fine. What's the special delivery?'

Lucy unwrapped it and pulled out a small, curved square of metal, about the size of a credit card. 'From All Hallows Crematorium. Taken from Stuart Carlisle's coffin.'

'Now that's interesting,' Kerrigan said. 'Can I see it?' He took the piece and brought it across to the light above Kamil Krawiec. 'What's this?' he asked Caroline.

'A surgical plate,' the woman said. 'Skull, maybe?'

'Why?'

'The curvature?'

'Perfect,' Kerrigan said. 'And this came from Carlisle's coffin?' he asked, turning to Lucy.

Lucy nodded. 'As did these.' She held out her hand. A second plate, longer and much narrower than the first, with four holes in it, rested next to four long metal pins and four shorter ones.

'Someone else was cremated in his place,' Kerrigan said, hooting with laughter. 'That's quite brilliant, in its own way. The perfect crime.'

'Not quite,' Fleming said. 'The only perfect crime is the one that no one knew even happened.'

'Perhaps,' Kerrigan said. 'But someone obviously had a body to get rid of. Cremate it in someone else's coffin, and no one will ever find it.'

'But you have to dump the body originally in the coffin first. So someone will find *that*. We did.'

'That was bad luck,' Kerrigan said. 'Or good luck, from your point of view. Once Carlisle's body went in the river, it should never have resurfaced. Embalming would have slowed the decomposition inside him right down. The organs are punctured, there's no gas build up; the body should have sunk like a stone. They can't throw in the unembalmed body they needed to get rid of, because that will come back up at some stage, once it fills with gas.'

'Then why *did* Carlisle come back up?'

'The embalming job might not have been a great one. And the heat, of course. The heat in the water would have been like a greenhouse for whatever bacteria were working inside him. It just took a little bit of gas and up he popped.'

'He was snagged on a tree branch,' Lucy said.

Kerrigan nodded. 'Had he not come back up, you'd never have been the wiser. Or if they'd thrown him into the river in the winter.'

'That doesn't bring us any closer to who actually *was* in the coffin,' Fleming said.

'Of course it does,' Kerrigan countered. 'We know that whoever it was had had surgery for a skull injury and, judging from the collection in DS Black's hand, a broken leg too, I think.'

'So we just phone every hospital and ask for anyone who's had skull and leg surgery, then start whittling them down?' Fleming said. 'That should only be a few thousand for Ireland.'

Kerrigan had been examining the skull plate. He smiled, then handed it to Caroline. 'Let me see the leg plate.'

Lucy handed it to him and he glanced at it, turning it over, then lay it to one side. 'Oh ye of little faith. Luckily, the cranial plate was manufactured in the US.'

'That *is* lucky,' Lucy said dryly. 'Their population is so much smaller than ours. It will be, quite literally, like finding one of these in a haystack,' she added, holding aloft one of the pins.

'Very good. I like that,' Kerrigan said. 'No, you see, here, plates have no markings on them. In the more litigious USA, every surgical implant has to have a logo and batch number, so that if it's faulty, you can trace back to the supplier. So, while that leg plate has no identifying markings on it, and is of no use to you, the cranial plate, on the other hand, has a logo and, if I'm not mistaken, a serial number that will tell you the batch from which it came. Get the batch number, contact the implant company and they'll be able to tell you which hospital the batch went to and when. They keep a database of every patient who receives a prosthetic or implant in America, but not here, sadly. So, while it won't identify the individual patient, but it will give you a place and approximate year of treatment. Your haystack has just become so much smaller.'

All this time, Caroline had remained quiet, studying the cranial plate, examining it through the magnifying glass positioned above the table. At first, Lucy thought she was looking for the markings Kerrigan had mentioned.

'I think this one was murdered, too,' she offered suddenly.

Kerrigan rolled his eyes. 'As I've told you, Caroline, that's not our call to make.'

Caroline straightened and offered him the plate. 'There's a small nick in the side. It looks to be wider at the top than the bottom. Like something cut into it. The metal's shiny at the cut, so it looks like it's a recent thing.'

Kerrigan took the plate and moved across to study it under the glass as she had done. Lucy wondered how he would react to having missed it himself. She was pleasantly surprised when he glanced up at Caroline, smiling. 'Indeed! Well done, you. It looks like the edge of something cut into the side of the plate.'

'Something?'

'As Caroline said,' Kerrigan replied. 'The cut's wider at the upper edge than the lower. My bet would be a hatchet or axe. To the head,' he concluded.

Chapter Fourteen

Using the magnifying glass, Kerrigan managed to retrieve the logo and batch number of the plate. The logo was the letter U with two snakes, one wrapped around each of the main letter's uprights.

'That's the symbol for doctors, isn't it?' Lucy asked. 'The serpents wrapped around something.'

'Nearly,' Kerrigan said. 'You're thinking of the caduceus, the staff of Hermes, the messenger of the gods, in Greek myth. The two snakes were entwined to represent peace. It's often used as a symbol of medicine. God knows why, because there's absolutely no connection between the two. Maybe it's their way of saying, "Don't blame us, we're only the messengers", when you're imparting bad news.' He chuckled softly at his own comment. 'What they should actually use, which this company seem to have realized, is the staff of Asclepius, which has a single snake entwined around a staff. Asclepius was a Greek doctor about whom Homer wrote. The Greeks eventually worshipped him as the god of healing.'

Lucy glanced at Caroline, who raised both eyebrows. *Welcome to my world*, she mouthed.

Lucy smiled sympathetically. She was beginning to appreciate being partnered with Tom Fleming. There were days he barely spoke, but better that than being lectured to all day.

'USS stands for United Surgical Services,' Kerrigan said, angling the plate against the light as he examined it through the magnifier. 'The batch number is—' He glanced around to see that both Lucy and Fleming were standing watching him.

'Are you planning on remembering it, or are you going to write it down?' he asked, looking from one to the other.

'Sorry,' Lucy said, pulling out her notebook.

'Serial 8756943-132,' Kerrigan said. 'They should be able to trace that to a batch and tell you where it went and when. After that, it will be up to you to identify the recipient.'

Lucy dropped Fleming home, then cut across to Tesco to get some groceries. The house was empty of food, a fact she'd realized when, the previous night, Dermot had made tea for her, Jenny and Fiona and been able to provide a variety of biscuits with it. Lucy doubted if she'd have been able to provide sugar if someone had called to visit her unexpectedly. Or indeed, even tea. Then again, generally people didn't visit her, unexpectedly or otherwise.

She was making her way to the car, still debating with herself whether she'd been wise to buy two family-size tubs of ice cream, when her phone rang. Initially, she thought it was work but, when she pulled it out, she did not recognize the number on the screen.

'Lucy?' A female voice.

'Yes?'

'This is Jenny. From across the street.'

'Hey, Jenny.'

'Look, I'm really sorry about this. I told Fiona last night that we were planning on going swimming this evening if she wanted to come along. I wanted to make it sound casual, like we were already planning on doing it anyway, so as not to put her under too much pressure. The thing is, she's said yes. I know you've probably other things on, so don't worry if it doesn't suit. I can tell her you had to cancel at the last minute, but I thought I'd check if you wanted to come? I understand if it doesn't suit, honestly. I really appreciated you calling over, I know it was a bit, you know ...' she gabbled nervously.

Lucy hefted the bag of frozen food to her free hand. The idea of going swimming with two strangers didn't appeal to her, but she didn't want to not help Jenny either. Plus, if she didn't go, she'd end up sitting in the house, alone, eating ice cream. She could, she reasoned, always do that afterwards, anyway. 'Why not?' Lucy said. 'That would be nice.' After a swim she'd have earned the ice cream, she decided.

'Great. We're going to Lisnagelvin. Is half past seven OK?'

Lucy glanced at the time on her phone. It was 5.45 now. That would give her just enough time to go home, grab a quick bite and shave her legs before heading back out. Not enough time to leave the hour before swimming, though.

'Can we make it eight instead?' Lucy asked.

'No problem. We'll see you there, then. Thanks.'

'Look, are you sure you want me to come?' Lucy added. If Jenny was attempting to repair her relationship with her sister, Fiona might not appreciate a third party being present.

'No, please. I don't want Fiona to think I set her up. It'll look more casual if she thinks we were planning on going anyway. You'd be doing me a big favour.'

'See you at eight, then,' Lucy said, then hung up.

As she pulled out of the car park, her phone rang again and Lucy assumed it was Jenny with a changed arrangement. This time, though, it was the Strand Road station.

'DS Black? A Mrs Doreen Jeffries from Bready has been in contact. She's been burgled.'

'That's a uniform call-out,' Lucy said, glancing across at the bags of groceries sliding around the footwell of the passenger seat. 'I'm finished for the day.'

'She's asked specifically for you, said she knew you. She's in a very bad state, apparently.'

Chapter Fifteen

Doreen Jeffries was in her late sixties and lived in a small cottage on the roadside in Bready, a village along the A5, about six miles past Prehen. It was technically in Tyrone rather than Derry, but, as Jeffries had claimed, she did know Lucy, which is why, presumably, she had called the PSNI in Derry rather than Strabane.

Lucy had first met the woman the year previous. She volunteered in a charity shop in Derry, four days a week, sorting through donations to find anything that the shop could actually sell. She'd proudly told Lucy, the first time they met, that she was the one who'd spotted a first-edition Harry Potter, which the charity had sold at auction for several thousand pounds.

The shop in question was one of a number that had agreed to take some of the children from the Social Services Residential Unit in the Waterside as volunteers. The programme had been organized by Robbie, Lucy's boyfriend. One of the kids, a youngster called Helen Dexter, had been working with Doreen, sorting out clothes, in the storeroom of the shop. Doreen had begun to suspect that Helen was stealing from the shop and passed word up to the manager, who had insisted that she report it to the police, in keeping with their zero-tolerance policy on theft. With a significant degree of reluctance, Doreen had contacted Robbie, to inform him that she would have to report Helen to the PSNI. Robbie had suggested Doreen speak with Lucy, which is how the two had eventually met.

When Lucy met Doreen, the woman revealed that she had already spoken with Helen herself and the girl had admitted taking clothes from the storeroom. They were, she revealed, for her younger sister; her mother refused to buy clothes for the child, preferring to drink it. The stock she had taken amounted to £45. In the end, the shop manager had agreed not to press charges so long as Helen paid for all that she had taken and was removed from the volunteer programme.

The money was repaid within the day. Helen denied ever having paid it back, nor would she admit where she had gotten the additional hundred pounds with which she had bought her sister a new school uniform, but despite the considerable age difference, she and Doreen had been firm friends ever since.

Doreen began weeping the moment she saw Lucy standing at her front door. Without warning, she hugged her, her body shuddering. Lucy embraced her lightly, could feel the thin bones of her shoulder blades through the brown cardigan she wore in spite of the heat.

'Thanks for coming,' the woman said, when they separated. 'I'm sorry for bothering you. I'm sure you were on your way home.'

'It's fine,' Lucy said. 'You were burgled, is that right?'

The woman nodded, holding the balled tissue in her fist up to her eyes to stem a renewed flow of tears. Lucy glanced around the living room, which appeared to be undisturbed. Normally, with a burglary, the place would be overturned.

'What was taken?'

'Bennie's watch,' Doreen said, then began to cry again. Bennie, Doreen's husband, had been an accountant in Derry for years. He'd died of a heart attack five years earlier, long before Lucy had even come back to Derry, so she'd never known the man, save for what Doreen had said about him, which, depending on her mood, ranged from his being a saint to her expressing gratitude for peace now that he was gone.

'He bought me a watch for our silver wedding anniversary. It had diamonds in the face, one for each hour. It was far too nice to wear, but I kept it in my room. It's gone. And a lot of the jewellery he bought for me over the years.'

Lucy glanced around. Doreen's television set still jabbered away in the corner, she noticed, though having said that, it was an analogue set and probably too heavy for someone looking for a quick snatch and run.

'Anything else?'

Doreen glanced around the room, as if taking a mental inventory for the first time. 'Nothing obvious,' she said.

'How did they get into the house? Any signs of a break-in?'

Doreen shook her head. 'I didn't notice anything.'

'How about I take a quick look around, eh?' Lucy said.

Lucy moved through the house, checking each window and examining the jambs of both the front and rear doors. In the main bedroom, the drawer of the wardrobe unit was lying on the floor, empty. A musical box lay upturned on the bed, again empty. By the time she came back downstairs, Doreen was sitting on the sofa, cradling herself.

'You wouldn't have left a window open, would you? On account of the heat?'

The woman shook her head. 'I always close the windows,' Doreen said. 'Force of habit since Bennie was here, God rest him.'

'Were you in the house all day?' Lucy asked. A creeper burglary was a possibility if there were no signs of forced entry, though Lucy was reluctant to mention it lest the woman had not considered the possibility that someone had been in her house while she was there, without her realizing it.

'No. I've been away on holidays for the past week. To Blackpool with the WI. I only got back half an hour ago. I phoned as soon as I saw.'

'Does anyone else have a key to the house? Someone maybe who was going to check on it while you were gone?'

Doreen hesitated, staring from the TV screen to Lucy.

'Who has the key, Doreen?'

'Helen has a copy,' the woman said quietly. 'I don't believe it was her who stole from me, though.'

'Helen Dexter?'

Doreen nodded.

'Why has she a key?'

'She does some light work around the house for me,' Doreen replied. 'I pay her for it.'

'Since when?'

'Since the whole thing last year. She offered to do it.'

'To pay you back for the money you gave her?'

Doreen nodded again. 'Did she tell you about it? I asked her not to.'

'No: I guessed. She'd not a penny to her name to pay off what she'd taken. I knew someone had given it to her, and it certainly wasn't her mother.'

'She offered to do some work to pay me back. I let her do it for a week, then told her I'd pay her for it. A few pounds to help her through. A girl at that age needs something to keep her going.'

Lucy smiled gently. 'I hope your kindness wasn't misplaced.'

'I don't believe she'd have stolen from me,' Doreen repeated. 'I don't believe it for a moment.'

Despite that, Lucy reflected, Doreen had still called her, and had still revealed that Helen had access to her house.

'I'll have a word with her,' Lucy said. 'See what she has to say.'

'Don't,' Doreen said. 'She'll think I don't trust her.'

Lucy considered a moment. If Helen had managed to build a proper, healthy stable relationship with an adult, the last thing Lucy wanted to do was damage it unnecessarily. Then again, if Helen had progressed from stealing second-hand clothes to stealing jewellery, then that would need to be dealt with.

'What was the value of your jewellery? Ballpark figure?'

Doreen shrugged. 'The watch cost Bennie over eight thousand when he bought it and that was fifteen years ago.'

'Look, don't touch anything upstairs. I'll have someone come out and see if they can find any fingerprints on the jewellery box and that. How about I hold off on speaking to Helen until I get word back on that first? OK?'

Doreen smiled, gratefully.

'Have you anyone who could stay with you tonight? Keep you company?'

Doreen shook her head, smiled apologetically. 'Helen would have been the obvious one to call.'

'Best not, eh?' Lucy said. 'Lock the doors. If you've any problems, call me directly rather than the station. Here's my mobile number,' she said, handing Doreen her card.

'Do you think whoever did it will come back?'

Lucy shook her head. 'Is there anything else in the house worth taking as much as your jewellery?'

'No.'

'Then I'd say whoever it was won't be back. Can you make out a list of as many of the stolen items as you can remember? Mention any distinctive features. Someone will be out with you to collect it and to take prints.'

The woman looked around the room as if seeing it for the first time, her lower lip shivering.

'I have to go out to the shops. The fridge is empty with my being away,' she explained. 'I've no dinner in. Will the house be OK if I go out?'

'I'm sure it'll be fine,' Lucy said. 'Look, any problems, let me know. Otherwise, I'll be in touch.'

She pushed the key into the car's ignition, then, looking back towards the house, made up her mind.

Doreen looked surprised to see Lucy again so soon, not least because she bore the bags of shopping she'd got in the supermarket.

'We can't have you not getting your dinner, now, can we? How does spaghetti bolognese sound?' Lucy asked, stepping back inside.

Chapter Sixteen

Fiona and Jenny were in the changing room of the pool by the time Lucy arrived. She'd just had time to shave her legs and grab her swimsuit and towel on the way back from Doreen's. Her legs stung, spots of blood reddening the skin.

Fiona smiled when she came in, fixing the straps on her suit. She was thin, small-breasted, with an erect carriage that reminded Lucy of an Irish dancer's. Jenny, though not heavy, did not have the same slim build, no doubt as a result of having three children. Or four. Lucy couldn't remember how many she had.

'Sorry I'm late. Work,' Lucy explained.

'No problem.' Jenny smiled. Lucy sensed she was relieved, perhaps that her sister would believe that they had been planning on swimming anyway.

'This must be a busman's holiday, then,' Fiona said. 'The last thing I'd feel like after training all day is swimming.'

It took Lucy a beat to remember that as far as Fiona was concerned, her work was as a fitness instructor.

'It's a warm down,' she said, smiling. She pulled off her tracksuit bottoms.

'Oh,' Jenny said. 'That's a nasty cut.'

The comment, though clearly directed at the shaving cut on Lucy's leg, below which a stream of blood had crusted, elicited an instant reaction from Fiona who grabbed her towel and clasped it in front of her, causing both Lucy and Jenny to turn and stare at her. Lucy could see her redden with embarrassment.

'I made a bit of a mess, all right,' Lucy said quickly, keen to save Fiona further scrutiny. 'Shall we go?'

The pool was relatively quiet. A few kids splashed around at the shallow end, while towards the deep end, two earnest swimmers pounded back and forth, parallel to each other, completing length after length.

Lucy eased her way in, then did two breaststroke lengths at an easy pace. She hadn't been swimming for a while; after work she was normally so knackered, she stopped at the chippie, then fell asleep on the sofa.

She turned onto her back and kicked a length, keeping her arms still by her side, then flipped and did a final few lengths using the front crawl. She felt the muscles across her chest and back tightening against the stroke, felt the tension knot across her shoulders.

Finally, she stopped along the pool's edge to rest. Fiona was completing a breaststroke length. Jenny was in the deep end, crossing back and forth with a furious front crawl, which seemed more splash than swim.

Fiona paddled over to where Lucy sat, treading water.

'I wouldn't want to be whoever she's using that water as a substitute for,' Lucy said, nodding towards Jenny's thrashing.

Fiona laughed. 'Probably her kids. I don't know how she does it.'

Lucy nodded, keen not to get too involved in the conversation lest she reveal not only not knowing the children's names, but not even being sure of their number. She glanced across towards the seated area at the edge of the pool. A man, perhaps in his thirties, was sitting alone at one of the tables. For a moment, Lucy assumed that he was the father of the children in the shallow end but, glancing across, she saw that their father was with them. The man sitting at the table was drinking from a Coke can as he returned her stare.

'Voyeur at six o'clock,' Lucy said to Fiona. 'Dodgy bloke with Coke.'

Fiona twisted her head to see, pulling her goggles up onto her forehead. She turned suddenly, her face ablaze.

'Do you know him?' Lucy asked, suddenly regretting the 'dodgy bloke' comment.

'He's my partner,' Fiona managed.

'Jesus, sorry,' Lucy said. 'I didn't mean anything.'

Fiona shook her head. 'It's all right,' she said, pulling on her goggles again, as if to resume swimming.

'Did you know that he was here?' Lucy asked.

The girl tossed her head lightly, as if flicking her hair from her face. 'I wasn't ... he must have come afterwards.'

It was such a strange syntactical construction; Lucy guessed she was hiding her embarrassment.

'Does he not trust you to go swimming with your sister?'

Fiona turned suddenly. 'He doesn't like being on his own. He feels safe with me around.'

'And how do you feel?'

Fiona dipped her head beneath water then stood. 'What about you? Have you a boyfriend?'

'Kind of,' Lucy said. 'On and off. It's complicated.'

'Is he married? That kind of complicated?'

The blown-up-in-a-car-bomb-intended-for-me kind of complicated, Lucy thought. Instead, she said, 'Something like that. I don't like being hemmed in. Controlled. That's not me.'

Jenny pushed in beside them, the wake of water moving between them. 'What's not you?' she asked, nervously.

'Being controlled. Fiona's partner is here.'

Jenny looked across to where the man sat. Aware that he was the topic of conversation, he raised his Coke can in salute. Something about the man was vaguely familiar, but Lucy couldn't place it. She ran the flat of her hand over her face to wipe the pool water from her eyes.

'Wanker,' Jenny spat. 'What does he want? Apart from a good slap in the nuts.'

'Don't, Jenny. He's my partner,' Fiona said. 'There's a reason I stopped visiting you.'

'Yeah,' Jenny retorted. 'Because you're not allowed.'

'Fuck!' Fiona cried. 'You're just as bad as him.' She pushed over to the edge of the pool, then, using the edge tiles, pulled herself from the water.

'Fiona,' Jenny said, moving to follow her.

'Leave her a minute,' Lucy said. 'Let me speak to her.'

Lucy turned and lifted herself out of the water too, then padded after Fiona into the changing room.

It was empty inside. The girl had already gone into the shower and was angrily scrubbing at her hair.

'Leave me alone,' she said, when she saw Lucy watching her.

'Are you OK?'

'I want to be left alone. No one leaves me alone. I can't even have a bloody shower without ... I just want to be alone,' she pleaded.

'Jenny's just concerned about you,' Lucy said. 'Try not to be angry at her.'

'What has any of this to do with you? You're not family.'

Lucy shrugged. 'I know. Family just nag at you and tell you what to do. Trust me, I know. You should meet my mother. I'm not going to tell you anything. I just wanted to know if you were OK.'

Fiona stared at her. 'I'm just fed up,' she stated. 'I'm sick of people treating me like I'm weak. Vulnerable. Like I'm stupid.'

'You're not stupid,' Lucy said. 'Or weak.'

'Jenny was always like that. Ever since I met John, she's been nagging at me. That's why we don't visit. He doesn't like her.'

'Just because he doesn't like your sister shouldn't stop *you* from seeing her.'

'It's not ... it's complicated,' she echoed. 'John likes being with me. He likes going with me wherever I go.'

'Everywhere?'

Fiona shrugged.

'What if you want to go out with friends for the night?'

'I, ah … I don't …' She cleared her throat. 'I don't really have friends. My friends are his friends.'

'Were they yours first or his?'

Fiona stared at her. 'I know what you're doing. You're the same as Jenny.'

'Jenny's concerned for you, Fiona. She cares about you.'

'So does John.'

Lucy waited a beat. 'Did he tell you that before or after he split your lip?'

The girl stared at her, the water running down her face, dripping from her chin onto the rise of her chest. Lucy noticed something at the curve of the top of her costume. She moved towards the girl, who backed away slightly.

'I'm not going to hurt you,' she said. 'You have a bruise showing on your chest.' The mark was still partially red at the centre, purpling around the edges. It was no bigger than a ten pence piece, the tip of a finger. Lucy guessed there would be four corresponding concentric marks around it where John had gripped her. She worked hard to keep her tone even, so as not to betray the building anger she felt at the sight of the injury.

Fiona glanced down, then tugged at the collar of the swimsuit, pulling it over where the upper edge of the bruise had shown.

'I walked into the wardrobe door, at home,' she said, quickly.

'You know that's why they choose places like that,' Lucy said. 'Somewhere that no one will see the injuries.'

'I don't know what you're talking about,' Fiona said. 'I had an accident. I'm clumsy. John tells me that all the time. I'm so clumsy I'd fall down the stairs if he wasn't there to look out for me.'

'Is that what he says? They do that. Make themselves feel big, powerful. Disempowering you to make themselves feel in control.'

'I don't know what you mean,' Fiona said, turning and grabbing the towel from the hook where she had hung it.

'There are people who can help, Fiona. If you want. You don't have to put up with anything.'

'I'm not putting up,' she said. 'You're imagining things.'

'I can help you,' Lucy said. 'If you want help, I can help you. Not because I think you're weak, or vulnerable. But because I don't like seeing people being hurt.'

Fiona stared at her. Her mouth worked silently, as if she was trying to formulate some objection or denial, but could find nothing adequate to convince either herself or Lucy.

'I'm not telling you what to do,' Lucy said. 'I'm offering you help if you want it. I don't really have many friends either, so I'm in no position to comment on anyone else.'

Chapter Seventeen

Lucy ended up waiting in the foyer for Jenny to get showered and changed. Fiona told her that she had to go on and to tell her sister that she would call her later, something which they both knew was untrue even as the girl said it.

She waved and smiled mildly as she moved through the automatic doors out into the car park. Only then did John appear. He'd been leaning against the outer wall, speaking with someone on his mobile. Or at least having given the impression that he had been, perhaps to justify hanging around outside, waiting for Fiona.

As the couple walked to the car, he spoke earnestly at her, his head turned towards her, her own bowed. At one point he draped his arm across her shoulders, but she sidestepped out of his embrace.

Jenny appeared from the changing room. 'Has she gone already?' she asked, the flush rising from her throat into her face.

'She said she'd call later,' Lucy said.

Jenny snorted disparagingly. 'She will, my arse. Is Sleeping with the Enemy with her?'

Lucy nodded, trying not to smile at the name.

Jenny cracked a brief smile of her own at Lucy's discomfort. 'Listen. Sorry you've been dragged into

88

all this. Dermot thought he was being helpful last night calling for you. She was in such a state when she arrived. I should have known it wouldn't last for long.'

'Has he hit her before?' Lucy asked, shouldering her bag. They moved out into the evening air. The few scraps of cloud in the sky were high and thin, reflecting the lowering sun along their gilded edges. The air felt cool compared to the humidity of the leisure centre.

'I don't honestly know,' Jenny said. 'As you can probably tell, we've lost contact a fair bit.'

'Since he came along?'

'Fairly much. At first they would visit us together. They were inseparable, the way you are in the first flush of love. I could tell our kids annoyed him, but he tolerated them. Then she started to cancel visits, always with some excuse: she wasn't feeling well; John was tired after work; he'd an important meeting that had overrun.'

'What's he do?'

'He works for the Council.'

'He looked familiar,' Lucy said. 'I can't place him, though. What's his name?'

'John Boyd. He was in all the papers at the start of the year. As part of the City of Culture celebrations, the council had promised to clean up the city centre. All the abandoned buildings?'

Lucy nodded.

'The recession has closed down so many businesses there were all these empty buildings, making the place look run-down. He came up with the plan to put false fronts on them. Barricading up the old broken windows with wooden boards with nice bright windows painted on them.'

Lucy laughed. 'I've seen those.'

'In fairness, they do work,' Jenny admitted begrudgingly. 'The place looks better. Even if a dick like him was behind it.'

'Does he not trust her to go out on her own?'

'She doesn't go out on her own. She'd her phone off last night when she was in our house. Do you know how many missed calls she had from him when she turned it on again? Ninety-three!'

'Maybe he felt guilty,' Lucy reasoned.

'He felt out of control,' Jenny retorted. 'She was out of his control for an hour and it must have driven him nuts.'

Lucy nodded. 'Look, I'm not sure what good I can be. The pattern is so familiar it's infuriating. Unless she presses charges, though, we can't touch him. And if we tried to, you can be sure she'd back him up. She had ...' Lucy paused, unsure whether telling Jenny would do any good. In the end, she reasoned that Fiona's sister had a right to know. 'She had a bruise on her breast. A grip mark. I'd bet there were more. When I asked her about it, she said she walked into a wardrobe.'

'Bastard! A wardrobe this time? It was the cupboard last night. She'll be running out of doors to walk into soon,' Jenny hissed. 'Why doesn't she—? How can she be so weak?'

Lucy held up her hand. 'I understand how you feel, Jenny. But, much as I'd love to nail his balls to the wall myself, there's nothing you can do, except be there for her and support her. It's all part of the pattern. She's not being weak; he will have systematically made her feel that she needs him to be worthwhile. What she really needs is someone to be non-judgemental with her. When she starts to see through his bullshit, she'll maybe look to break away from him a little more.'

The house was quiet, the rooms dark when Lucy got home. Increasingly, she found herself creating excuses to stay away from home in the evenings. She found the silence oppressive. She'd friends at work, Tara being the obvious one, but none of them visited her at home, nor she them. She'd always tried to keep work separate from home life, not least having seen the impact it had on her own family growing up. The problem was, more and more she was beginning to wonder if she had much of a life at home. Even with Robbie, her partner, she realized that she went to his rather than him coming to her home. And even those visits were becoming further and further apart.

She turned on the television in the living room, if only to create noise in the house, a pretence of activity. The news was full of images from Belfast where loyalist protestors continued to riot after a parade was refused permission to pass a nationalist area of the Ardoyne. First flags, now parades. The newscaster was commenting on how it was a return to the bad old days, that these issues had been reignited. Lucy shook her head. The issues had always been there, just below the surface. Like love, the first flush of peace was idyllic, such a contrast to what had gone before, that you were prepared to overlook the flaws; indeed were blind to them. The real test was always going to be the long haul; the ability to face the imperfections and still decide that it was worth sticking with; that the good outweighed the bad.

Strangely, the trouble had not reached Derry. In fact, as a result of local dialogue and accommodation, the twelfth of July parades had gone through the city without incident, as part of the bigger Culture celebrations of the year. While the bonfires burned across the rest of the North, Derry had danced to its own unique tune.

Thursday, 19 July

Chapter Eighteen

Lucy woke just after eight, feeling rested for the first time in months. Her arms ached pleasingly from the exertion of swimming the night before.

She'd nothing for breakfast in the house, having left the groceries she bought with Doreen, so stopped at a café, before heading on to the Strand Road station where she and Tom Fleming were to meet Chief Superintendent Burns to update him on the developments with Kamil Krawiec.

Burns sat back in his seat as they explained the process by which they had identified the man, pushing his hand through the loose sandy curls of his hair as he listened.

'So, we know that the victim was in the Foyle Hostel years back. Where has he been since?'

Fleming shrugged. 'No one seems to know. He may have crossed the border, he may have gone over to England looking for work. We'll continue to ask around.'

'And you have a positive ID on the man from the river?'

Lucy nodded. 'Stuart Carlisle. Our difficulty now is that, while Mr Carlisle didn't make it to his own cremation, someone else did. We need to identify who it was and why they were cremated in that manner.'

'Hugger-mugger,' Fleming said, smiling to himself.

'How were the bodies swapped?'

It was Lucy's turn to shrug. 'Presumably, it was something to do with the Duffys, but they're denying it. The son was the one driving the body to Belfast. It might be worth checking when the service ended here and what time he arrived in Belfast for the cremation. See how much of a gap there was between the two. If we can show that there's an unusually long lag between his leaving Derry and arriving in Belfast, we can put some pressure on him.'

Burns nodded. 'Very good. Look, I know your hands are full enough, but we need help processing interviews over this bin death. We put out a request for information last night and we've had hundreds of calls. The team is stretched beyond breaking.'

'Can uniforms not help out?' Fleming asked. 'We've our own work to do.'

'With all due respect, Tom, neither of your guys are going anywhere – either the one who wasn't cremated, or the one who was.'

'The one who was cremated had a mark on one of the plates recovered from his ashes. The pathologist reckoned he'd been struck with a hatchet.'

'Jesus!' Burns held up his hand. 'Look, don't tell me. When you have a name, we'll open a case. Most of the uniforms have been drafted up to help police this nonsense in Belfast. Derry's so quiet at the moment, we've a skeleton force working.'

'We're victims of our own success,' Fleming added. 'I blame the heat; it's making people fractious. If it was pissing down, half of them would stay off the streets.'

'Regardless,' Burns said. 'DS Gallagher will pass you on names and numbers of callers. Maybe do a quick first interview over the phone, see if any of them are worth following up on with a face-to-face. We can handle those interviews ourselves.'

Lucy knew that, considering the time difference, it would be unlikely that United Surgical Specialists would be open. However, when she checked their website for a contact number, she saw that their European offices were based in Dublin.

Part of the reason that the Celtic tiger had been so ferocious was the policy of the Irish government to offer huge corporation tax incentives for American firms to use Ireland as their European bases, bringing with them thousands of jobs. It had been claimed that some major American companies had paid only 2 per cent tax in Ireland. It was no huge surprise, then, to find that USS were based there, too. However, it took three calls before the receptionist in United Surgical Supplies finally answered the phone and, when she did, she put Lucy on hold.

Despite the earliness of the hour, the heat was building and opening the windows in Lucy's room offered little respite. Maydown station, where she was based, had been built during the Troubles. The windows in the rooms had been designed to sit high up on the walls, well above head height, to reduce the opportunity for a sniper outside the compound to target anyone in the rooms beyond. Their size, no more than one foot from sill to frame, also meant that, in the event of a rocket attack or explosion, there would be a reduced chance of being injured by falling glass. The drawback to such security measures was that it created a heat trap in the rooms. She opened her polo shirt collars as wide as they would go and leaned back in her chair, the phone resting between her chin and chest, stretching her arms above her to ease the aching she felt from her swim the night before.

Eventually, she began flicking through her notes from Tony Henderson regarding his great-uncle's funeral service. Henderson had said that it started at 1 p.m. He'd had a hospital appointment that afternoon, so hadn't gone to Belfast with the remains. Ciaran Duffy had said he went straight from the funeral parlour to Belfast, stopping only for a few minutes in the shop at the foot of the Glenshane. She knew the place, a petrol station with a restaurant attached, positioned just as the road began the incline up through the mountains, then back down into Dungiven and on to Derry.

'Sorry for keeping you. Your call is important to us. How can I help you today?' the woman at the other end of the phone intoned suddenly. Lucy imagined her sitting at the other end of the line, reading a magazine or surfing the net as she spoke.

Her enthusiasm waned as Lucy explained the purpose of her call.

'If he was cremated, how can you not know who he was?' the woman asked, her voice nasal.

'We believe someone swapped the body that was to be cremated with one that wasn't. We've identified the man who was meant to be cremated but wasn't. We've yet to identify the man who wasn't to be but was. If that makes sense?' she added.

'Uh-huh,' the woman said, unconvinced. 'Well, I don't see how we can help. We simply provide the implants. We've no idea who the intended recipients are. You'd need to contact the hospital who used it.'

'I hope to,' Lucy said. 'If you could tell us which hospital the implant was sent to. I have the batch number, if that's any use.'

She read the number off twice, having to repeat it the second time to allow for the broadness of her Northern accent.

'I'll have to come back to you, Sergeant,' the woman said. 'I'll be quick as I can.'

She hung up. Lucy lifted the receiver, then dialled Tony Henderson's number. She explained that she needed to know when the service for his great-uncle had concluded.

'It started at one o'clock,' he said. 'I had an appointment at half past two and I was just on time, so, allowing for the travel time to the hospital, I'd say it was two when it ended.'

'Perfect,' Lucy said. 'Thanks.'

'Listen,' Henderson said. 'Just when you're on the line. Will this whole business screw with the will and that? The sharing of his, you know, his estate and that?'

'I wouldn't have thought so,' Lucy said. 'So long as the death certificate was issued, his burial, or lack of, is irrelevant, I'd imagine.'

'Brilliant,' Henderson said.

Lucy called All Hallows again and asked to speak with Frank Norris. After a moment, she recognized his voice when he answered.

'Mr Norris? DS Black. We spoke yesterday about the Stuart Carlisle cremation.'

'I remember. I've been thinking about it all night. You know, we could get shut down if people think we cremated the wrong body. People here are squeamish enough about the whole cremation thing without something like this.'

'Maybe it's a fear of being burned alive,' Lucy suggested.

'Because that's so much worse than being buried alive, is it?' Norris snapped.

Lucy laughed. 'That's true. Mind you, there's always a chance of getting out if you've been buried alive, I suppose.'

'What I'm saying is, I'd appreciate it if anything that needs to be done about this can be done, I suppose, discreetly.'

'I'll do my best, Mr Norris. The reason I'm calling is, you wouldn't happen to know what time the Carlisle coffin arrived with you, would you? I'm trying to ascertain when exactly the swap was made.'

'Swap?'

'The person in the coffin was obviously not Stuart Carlisle. All I can think is that someone swapped the body.'

'Why? To avoid funeral costs?'

'To hide a murder, possibly.'

Norris groaned. 'Jesus, it just gets worse by the minute. No offence, DS Black, but every conversation I have with you is taking years from my life.'

'Have you a record of the time the body arrived?' Lucy persisted.

'I should have it here,' Norris said. 'I pulled the file yesterday when you called.' She heard his breath echoing on the line as he read through the paperwork, could hear his lips softly mumbling the words he read. 'At 5.45 p.m.,' he said. 'I have it here. The cremation started at 6.15 and we were completed at 9 p.m.'

'You're sure of those timings?'

'Absolutely.'

Lucy jotted them down. She'd have to trace William's van, but didn't want to have to contact the undertakers to ask for details of the van he drove, for to do so might alert them to the angle the investigation had taken.

'You wouldn't happen to know what type of van the body was brought up in, would you?' she asked.

'It belongs to Gabriel Duffy,' Norris said. 'It's his van.'

'I understand that. I was just hoping you might remember something about it.' Like the registration plate, she wanted to add.

'No. You don't understand. It's the Duffys' van. Their name is written up the side of it. "Duffy and Sons, Undertakers". It's unmissable.'

'Perfect,' Lucy said and, thanking Norris, hung up.

Ciaran Duffy had claimed he left after the service at 2 p.m. yet he didn't arrive in Belfast until 5.45 p.m. He said he stopped for only a few minutes. Allowing for traffic, it would take, at most, two hours to travel from Derry to All Hallows, probably less. Taking into account rush-hour traffic, even though most would be coming out of Belfast rather than going into it, and the fact that he stopped at the shop, it would still be a stretch to have taken more than 2 hours 30 minutes. That being the case, there left at least 1 hour 15 minutes unaccounted for.

Lucy looked up, staring absently at the noticeboard opposite her desk. The picture of Mary Quigg stared down at her. Mary was a child with whom Lucy had had some dealings when she'd first joined the PSNI's Public Protection Unit. Mary's mother's partner had murdered both her and her mother, when he set the house alight and took off with as much money as he could steal. He had never been charged with the killings, having fled to the Republic. Notices, posters, bulletins had come and gone from Lucy's noticeboard, but Mary Quigg's picture remained and would do until her killer, Alan Cunningham, finally paid for what he had done.

The ringing phone startled her and it took her a moment to place the English-accented woman who spoke as the one who had taken her call to United Surgical Specialists.

'I've tracked that batch for you,' she said. 'It was part of a large shipment which went to Beaumont Hospital, right here in Dublin, in October 2007.'

'Great. How many were in the shipment?'

'One thousand. Beaumont is a specialist centre for cranial injuries, so they're a big buyer for us.'

Lucy thanked the woman and, hanging up, sighed. One thousand plates. She could ask the hospital to provide her with names of those who'd had cranial and leg surgery, but there was no guarantee that the two injuries had occurred at the same time, or had been treated in the same hospital. That meant someone would have to sift through each one of them, set against Missing Persons reports, hoping for a match. And, as Burns had already pointed out, there were no spare uniforms to help with it.

Chapter Nineteen

She Googled the name of the shop on the Magherafelt side of the Glenshane, where Duffy claimed to have stopped on his way to All Hallows, then phoned through to it. If the shop had CCTV, there was a good chance it would have recorded the arrival of the van in the forecourt.

The person who answered the phone sounded harried, as if the call was an added inconvenience that she didn't need. In the background, Lucy could hear the low murmur of conversations and the metallic clattering of cutlery. She realized, too late, that the number she had dialled had taken her through to the adjoining restaurant rather than the shop. The waitress to whom she spoke gave her the right number and, on her second attempt, she finally got to speak to someone she wanted to.

'When was this?' the manager asked, after he'd introduced himself as such, though without giving his name.

'Monday afternoon. At some stage between 2.30 and 4.45,' Lucy said, allowing for the travel time required between there and both Derry and Belfast.

'What type of vehicle?'

'A van with an undertaker's name on the side. "Duffy and Sons, Undertakers". There would have been a youngish man driving it; thin, late teens to early twenties, dark hair. He bought a can of Coke, if that's any help.'

'Let me see,' the man said. 'This thing is digital now, so it's very easy to use; you can just rewind and fast-forward with the touch of a button.'

Lucy considered that that was always how you'd rewound or fast-forwarded, even pre-digital, but the man was being helpful, so she said nothing.

'I'm checking the forecourt video first. That will pick up everyone coming into the front area of the shop ...' His voice petered off as if even he realized the banality of his small talk. He clicked his tongue a few times, to fill the silence, then said, 'Bingo. "Duffy and Sons, Undertakers". White van.'

'That's it,' Lucy said. 'What time did he get there?'

'You weren't far off: 4.33.'

'Four thirty-three? You're sure?'

'Totally. It's printed here. I can send you the image on email.'

'That would be great,' Lucy said, giving the man her address.

'Oh, just one thing. You've got it wrong. It wasn't the young man who bought the Coke. It was the girl. A blondie.'

'A girl?'

'Well, a young woman. She came out of the van at 4.34. Let me check the till cameras for that time.'

Lucy heard tapping, heard the man clear his throat. 'There we are,' he said. 'Nice-looking girl, too. I'll send you her picture as well, shall I?'

'If it's no trouble,' Lucy said.

'Oh, none at all. That's the beauty of this system. One click and it's away. Because it's—'

'Digital?' Lucy offered.

The images pinged in her inbox seconds later and Lucy was grudgingly forced to admit that the man's CCTV system was impressive. The girl appeared to be in her early twenties. She had short blonde hair, shaved in at the sides. She wore a white top, and jeans over outsized trainers. She bought two cans of Coke and a packet of cigarettes.

'Why did Ciaran not mention you?' Lucy asked, printing the image off. And where had he been from the end of the service until 4.33. The shop was, at most, forty-five minutes from Derry.

'Have you a minute?' Tom Fleming asked, sticking his head around the door jamb. 'I've been skimming through this list that Burns gave us of the phone interviews about the Krawiec death and I know one of the names: Colm Heaney. He's a barman in Spice nightclub. Very reliable he is too.'

Perhaps Lucy's expression betrayed her thoughts. Spice nightclub was the haunt of teenagers. That Fleming knew the barman was a little strange. Even when he had been drinking, he didn't seem like the typical clientele of Spice.

'I know him through the soup kitchen,' Fleming said. 'He stops off every Friday for chicken soup on his way home from work and has a chat. He's a decent sort.'

'So long as we can speak with Ciaran Duffy afterwards,' Lucy agreed.

Chapter Twenty

Colm Heaney was in his forties, but dressed as if twenty years younger. His skin was swarthy and, despite his age, in such good condition that Lucy guessed he must have a more rigorous facial routine in the morning than she did. Admittedly, she thought, that wouldn't be hard.

'How're you, Tom?' he asked, leading them into his living room. He lived in College Terrace, just off the Strand Road, his house facing into the lower grounds of Magee University.

He had two bookcases against the far wall, both laden with CDs and DVDs, though no books.

'Not bad, Colm. Are you working these nights?'

'Run off our feet,' he said. 'Plus we've the Fleadh coming up in a few weeks. They're expecting four hundred thousand extra people in the city for that.'

The Fleadh was an annual celebration of Irish music, held in a different city or town in Ireland each year. This would be the first time it was to be held north of the border.

Lucy stood in front of the shelves, glanced at the contents, realizing with some surprise that the CDs were stacked according to artist, who in turn seemed to be arranged alphabetically.

'You called in about the body found in the bin?' Fleming asked, sitting.

'Can I get you a tea? Coffee? Soup?' he added, nodding at Fleming with a smile.

'I'm good, thanks,' Lucy said.

The man nodded. 'Yeah. I was walking home on Monday night and came down through Sackville Street. The alleyway there behind Mullan's pub? There was a silver Toyota parked in it and two guys were throwing something into the big metal industrial bins that sit there.'

'Right?' Fleming said. 'Could it not have been someone from the bar?'

'Well, I thought that,' Heaney agreed. 'Only, I used to work in there and I know a lot of the staff. I stopped to say hello and that, but the two guys got back in the car and scarpered. They reversed out the other way rather than coming past me.'

'Reversed out where?'

'Onto Great James Street. They pulled out there and then took off up past the post office.'

'What time was this at?' Fleming asked.

'It must have been, like, 3.30 in the morning. The place was dead, like. I just thought it was a bit odd.'

'Did you get a look at either of the men?'

'Not really. It was dark. They were big guys, heavy, you know. The driver especially. Not fat. Big build.'

'You don't happen to remember the registration number of the car, do you?' Lucy asked.

'I'm not Rain Man,' Heaney said, smiling. 'Sorry.'

'Your CDs are arranged alphabetically,' she observed. 'I just wondered.'

'The artists are alphabetical,' Heaney corrected her. 'The CDs are chronological, from date of release, within each artist.'

'That's ... impressive,' Lucy managed.

Heaney blushed. 'They thought I was on the spectrum when I was at school.'

'Did they now?' Lucy asked, attempting to appear surprised.

They drove down Great James Street to get a sense of the whereabouts of any CCTV cameras that might have picked up the car. Derry had its own city-wide CCTV, but it was operated by the City Centre Initiative rather than the PSNI. This was, at the time of its installation, the only way to make its presence palatable to the city's residents, who feared it was another form of police surveillance. The images were monitored by the CCI and, if the police needed to see any images, they had to lodge a request through the Chief Super. The CCI would feed through footage to the Strand Road station and would only provide copies of specific frames from the footage. While the system was working well, it was slow. If they could find a shop nearby whose own external security cameras had picked up the car, it might speed things up a little in identifying the registration number of the vehicle.

'Nothing,' Fleming said, glancing at the various building fronts around the alleyway where Heaney had seen the car. There were, as he had said, two large industrial bins against one side of the alley, their lids gaping open. 'Best get someone out to seal off the alleyway, so forensics can take a check through it.

I'll put in a request to CCI, too. We know what we're looking for, so they can go through it themselves and pull an image of the car if they can find one.'

'Speaking of images, I want to call in with Duffy. The boy claimed he went straight to Belfast. The shop he said he stopped at checked and pulled this picture of a girl who was with him. He was only at the other end of the Glenshane at 4.33. Two and a half hours to make a one-hour journey.'

When they reached Duffy and Sons, Undertakers, a service was taking place. A family was sitting in the service room while a vicar led them in prayers. Fleming lowered his head reverentially as they passed the window of the room, while Lucy glanced in, blessing herself instinctively.

Gabriel Duffy was standing at the back of the room, dressed in the black suit of his trade. He had his head bowed, his hands clasped lightly in front of him, his mouth moving along to the responses of the prayers. He glanced up and acknowledged their presence with an almost imperceptible nod.

'The boy won't speak with his father around him,' Lucy said. 'I'll maybe try to get him on his own.'

At the end of the corridor was a series of doors. One was clearly marked with WC. Of the other two, one was marked PRIVATE, which Lucy assumed to be an office, and the other bore a sign reading NO ENTRANCE: STAFF ONLY. It was this door that Lucy tried first. The plush carpeting and pine veneer of the corridor and service room gave way suddenly to a set of concrete steps with a metal handrail. The walls were unpainted, the lights garish and bright after the softened glow of the upper floor. Lucy could hear an echo of dance music coming from below.

She picked her way down the stairs, which, in turn gave way onto two rooms. The music was coming from the room on the left and it was into this room that she went.

But for the corpse lying on the covered table at its centre, the room could almost have been a dental surgery. The walls were painted white and lined with white wooden kitchen units. Several metal trays of implements sat on the black worktop. Above the body hung a wide metal shower head, attached to pipes running the length of the ceiling. The body itself was attached, via further pipes, to a machine next to it, which thudded mechanically every few seconds as it pumped fluid into the body.

Behind the chemical stench of the room, which burned at Lucy's nostrils, she could smell iron.

'You're not to—' Ciaran Duffy appeared behind her, obviously having been in the other room. Lucy turned to see the man, wearing an apron and face mask, carrying a long, T-shaped metal object. Involuntarily, she raised her hand, stepping back.

Duffy looked at the object in his hand and quickly put it on the table next to the body. 'It's a … don't worry, it's only a trocar. We use it for … well, you don't want to know. You shouldn't be here. Did my father tell you to come down here?'

'Your father's upstairs,' Lucy said. 'I want to speak to you again about Stuart Carlisle.'

Duffy moved past her, his voice sullen. 'That again? I told you, I don't know what happened. I left here and went to Belfast with him. They must have made a balls-up with the bodies in All Hallows.'

'You left here at 2 p.m.? As soon as the service was finished?'

'Yes.'

Lucy took out the picture of the girl. 'Who is she?'

'I don't ...' Duffy glanced at the stairs beyond, his expression hard to read behind the mask he wore. 'She's a friend. My girlfriend.'

'What's her name?' Lucy asked.

'Why? What difference does it make?'

'She was with you when you took the remains of Mr Carlisle to Belfast, is that right?'

Duffy nodded.

'You left here at 2 p.m.?'

'I told you that already.'

'You reached the other side of the Glenshane at 4.33 p.m.,' Lucy said. 'Which means it took you two and a half hours to make a journey that should have taken one.'

Duffy reddened, but still did not remove his face mask.

'That would have given you plenty of time to swap over one body with the other.'

'I don't know what ... Look, I honestly ... I don't know what happened.'

'Where were you for that hour and a half?' Lucy persisted, moving closer to Ciaran who, in turn, backed up against the table, inadvertently putting his hand on the shoulder of the remains which lay there.

'I was ... we were shagging, all right?' Duffy said. 'I stopped at Lisa's house and we had sex. I'd told her I was going to Belfast and she said she wanted to go shopping. I said I'd pick her up. I called at the house, we went to bed, had a shower and then left. That's it.'

'What's her name?' Lucy asked, taking out her notebook.

'Lisa Kerns,' Duffy said.

'Where was your van while you were in her house?'

'Parked in her drive,' Duffy said.

'Which is where?'

'Clearwater, over in the Waterside.'

Lucy knew it. It was a housing development that ran down to the river's edge.

'Would anyone have had access to it?'

Duffy shrugged. 'I locked it, so they shouldn't have had. I wasn't keeping an eye on it to be honest so, you know ...' His voice trailed off as he looked at Lucy.

'I'll have to check that story with Lisa.'

'You can't tell her I said we were ... you know. She'll be angry at me telling.'

'I'll be discreet,' Lucy said.

'OK,' he said without conviction, seemingly unsure what 'discreet' meant.

'Why didn't you tell us this the last day? You could have saved us a lot of time.'

'My dad would have gone nuts.'

'What age are you?' Lucy asked.

'I'm twenty-two,' Duffy said.

'You're old enough to have sex.'

'I met Lisa here. We handled her father's burial a few weeks back.'

Lucy suppressed a shudder. She didn't know which was creepier: Duffy picking up someone in a funeral home, or the girl having sex with the person who had buried her father. Both seemed strangely inappropriate.

'I see,' she said, impassively.

Chapter Twenty-one

'Duffy senior wasn't happy to hear you'd gone downstairs,' Fleming told her in the car after they'd left.

'He'll be even less happy to hear that his son is having sex with one of their client's children,' Lucy said.

Fleming grimaced. 'With a dead body out in the driveway, too,' he added.

'I never took you to be squeamish,' Lucy joked.

'Sex and death,' Fleming said.

'What?'

'I remember I had an English teacher who told us that all poetry is about either sex or death. Or sometimes both,' Fleming said, glancing out the window. 'Maybe it's that primal urge, attempting to create new life in the face of death.'

Lucy glanced across at him, her eyebrow raised. 'That's very deep.'

Fleming nodded. 'Or maybe it's just that most poets are perverts.'

'Or most English teachers are,' Lucy joked.

They drove in silence for a few minutes, then Fleming spoke again. 'I remember the poem, too. "My Son, My Executioner".'

Lucy nodded, unsure what else to say.

'Bloody good poem,' Fleming concluded. 'And that's saying something. One of those things you only understood after you'd left school and had your own kids.'

'How is your daughter?' Lucy asked cautiously. Fleming's ex-wife and daughter had moved to Australia the year before and, in doing so, had precipitated his first slide back into drinking in years. It had taken a suspension from work to get him back on his feet.

'Great,' he said. 'She seems to like it over there. I might go over and see her at some stage.'

Lucy nodded.

'How's all with you?' Fleming asked, in reciprocation. 'How's Robbie doing?'

'He's OK,' Lucy said, realizing that she'd intended to call with him to speak to Helen about Doreen's burglary. 'He uses a walking stick to get around sometimes. He still has a limp.'

'He's lucky it's only a limp he has,' Fleming commented.

Robbie had borne the brunt of a small explosive device attached to Lucy's car during a previous case she had worked. The device had not detonated properly, but had still caused damage to Robbie's leg. In addition to the walking stick, he was increasingly relying on pain relief to help him function.

'And what about you and him? Still going strong?' Fleming added.

Lucy hesitated. 'I'm not sure "strong" would be quite the right word for it. I still call to visit him, but things are complicated.'

'*Things* aren't complicated,' Fleming countered. 'Being a cop screws with every relationship you

115

have. Dealing with horrible stuff and death all day, then trying to have a relationship. Civilians can't handle it.'

'Death and sex again,' Lucy reflected. She realized she'd described their relationship twice as 'complicated'. The complication was her: the guilt she felt at what had happened to Robbie, and the nagging worry that she continued to stay with him primarily because of that guilt. Rather than dealing with it, Lucy hoped that sidelining it would give her space to think it through more clearly. So far, that strategy hadn't proven too successful.

'So, what's your thinking about Duffy then? Is he telling the truth?' Fleming asked to fill the silence in the car.

'Duffy claimed he was in her house for almost an hour and a half, with the van in the drive. If they were having sex, or in the shower, as he claims, then perhaps someone could have swapped over the bodies in the driveway without his knowledge. Or maybe he was set up by this girlfriend, Lisa Kerns.'

'It would need to be a secluded driveway for someone to swap a body without it being seen by the neighbours,' Fleming commented. 'You'd imagine someone would have reported it otherwise.'

It transpired that it was, indeed, secluded. The house was set back from the neighbouring ones, the garden enshadowed by thick fir trees, which formed a solid hedge the whole way around the perimeter, hiding the driveway completely.

Lisa Kerns looked slimmer than the CCTV image suggested, though she was undoubtedly the girl in the image. Her face was drawn in panic as she opened the door and saw Lucy and Tom Fleming standing there, Lucy with her warrant card on display.

'Is it Cathy? Has something happened to Cathy?' she asked in response to Lucy asking if she was Lisa Kerns.

'Who's Cathy?'

'My sister,' she said, pleadingly. 'Is she OK?'

'I'm sure she's fine,' Lucy said. 'It's nothing like that, Miss Kerns. We need to speak to you about your boyfriend, Ciaran Duffy.'

'Ciaran? What about him?'

'Can we come in?' Lucy asked, motioning to step forward.

'Of course. It's definitely not Cathy?'

'Definitely not! Look, is your mum or anyone about?' Lucy asked, reluctant to broach the subject of how she and Duffy had spent Monday afternoon, without first checking that there were no inappropriate ears listening.

'My mum's dead. And my dad now. It's just me and Cathy.'

That explained her reaction, Lucy thought. The girl was obviously terrified of being alone. Lucy wondered if that explained her relationship with Duffy; was she so scared it had driven her to the first welcoming arms she found after her father's death?

'Look, we're trying to trace the whereabouts of Ciaran on Monday afternoon. You went to Belfast with him, is that right?'

Lisa nodded. 'Cathy's iPhone was broken; she dropped it in the toilet of all places. She was devastated. I wanted to take it up to the Apple Store to get it replaced.'

'What time did you leave at?'

'About 3.30. I made it just before they closed. Ciaran dropped me off on his way to the crematorium.'

'Did you and Ciaran spend some time here before you left?'

Lisa's expression furrowed in thought. 'A minute or two, maybe. I think he asked to use the toilet, that was it. I'm not fussed on having people I don't really know in the house.'

Lucy looked across to Fleming who raised his eyebrows speculatively.

'You're sure Ciaran wasn't here for longer than that?'

Lisa looked to Fleming, then back at Lucy. 'Of course. Why?'

'Ciaran told us he was here from after 2 p.m. He said you and he had sex, then showered, before going to Belfast.'

The girl rose suddenly. 'What?' she exclaimed. 'He said what?'

'It's no crime if you did, Lisa,' Fleming said. 'We're not interested in what you were doing. Only how long you were here for.'

'We did not have—I barely know him. After Dad died, he was very good, calling to check we were OK, sorting out things with the grave. That was it. He called on Sunday to see how we were doing and I told him about Cathy's phone. He offered me a lift; said he had a run to do to Belfast the next day and would be away for a few hours. He'd drop me in town and collect me again after to bring me home. I thought he was being nice.' She sat again, then raised her hands to her face. 'Why would he say that? Asshole!'

Fleming stood and glanced out the window at the driveway. 'Have you other family round about?'

'An uncle and aunt in Dungiven,' Lisa said. 'My dad's sister. Why?'

He shook his head, as if dismissing his own thoughts rather than her question. 'Did you open the coffin on the way to Belfast? Or did you see anyone else interfering with it in any way?'

The girl stared at him with disgust. 'I've seen too many dead people in my life already. Riding in the same van as one was disturbing enough; I'd not have agreed to go up with him if I'd known he'd have a coffin in the back, but by the time I found out, I'd already promised Cathy I'd get her phone fixed. Why would you think I'd want to see a corpse? I've seen two recently, both my parents, three years apart. I don't need to see another fucking body ever again.'

She began to shudder, plump tears dripping from her eyes, though she made no attempt to stymie them.

'I'm sorry for asking, Miss Kerns,' Fleming said. 'It's part of our inquiry. The body that was taken to Belfast was not the one it should have been. Someone swapped the bodies and we can't work out who or where.'

'You're sure it was 3.30 when Ciaran called?' Lucy asked, moving to the girl and putting her arm around her.

She nodded. 'Cathy had band practice. She was collected at 3.15 by her friend's mother. I hung out the washing, then Ciaran arrived.'

119

'What age are you, Lisa?'

The girl looked at her, as if attempting to guess the reason for the question. 'Eighteen,' she said, slowly. 'Why?'

Lucy shook her head At thirty, she was barely able to keep on top of the work in the house and she lived alone. Here was this girl, just an adult herself, acting as both mother and sister to her younger sibling and, seemingly, doing a good job of both. 'Cathy's very lucky she's got someone like you to look out for her. If you ever need anything, give me a call.' She handed the girl her card. 'I mean it. Anything at all. Just call.'

Fleming moved across. 'I am sorry about the questions, Miss Kerns,' he said. 'They had to be asked. I'm sorry if they offended you.'

They did not even have time to discuss what she had told them, for, as they left the house, Fleming's phone rang. Lucy listened to Fleming's responses, unable to fill in the gaps.

'We didn't ... He's ... Are you sure? ... When? We'll look into it.'

He hung up. 'That was the station. Ciaran Duffy has done a runner,' he said. 'His father came down to help him with the embalming and he'd vanished. He's wondering what we said that could have made his son run away.'

Chapter Twenty-two

They returned to the PPU Block in Maydown station. Fleming had agreed to contact the City Centre Initiative about the image of the car Colm Heaney claimed to have seen. Lucy, meanwhile, called Gabriel Duffy to get further details about his son's disappearance. Avoiding making such calls, Fleming said, was one of the few perks of promotion.

Lucy listened to Duffy's complaints without commenting on their suspicions that his son had been involved in swapping Stuart Carlisle's body with whoever had ended up in the coffin. For all she knew, she reasoned, the father could have been complicit in it. Instead she assured Gabriel Duffy that his son had not been missing long enough to warrant too much worry. Still, she took details of the boy's phone number and bank account details and agreed to watch both if he hadn't reappeared by the following day.

Having done so, she remembered she'd promised Doreen Jeffries that she'd get someone to come out to her house. She knew if she put in an official request, it could take days to process, considering Burns's frequent complaints about being understaffed. Instead, she called through directly to a Forensics technician, Tony Clarke, with whom she had worked on an earlier case, and asked him to fit it in.

'We're up to our neck in crap, Lucy,' Clarke protested. 'Literally. We've been shifting through all the rubbish that was pulled from the compactor to make sure we've not missed any of the evidence in the "Bin-man killing" and I've two more out sifting through bins in an alleyway, thanks to your boss.'

'I know,' Lucy said, recognizing that the protest was more to elicit sympathy than a prelude to refusal. 'I'm sure you're stretched thin. I'd really appreciate it, though,' she added. 'She's a lovely old woman. It was her life's collection of jewellery. From her late husband,' she added. 'She's terrified to stay in the house alone and I'd really like to be able to get the place cleaned up and back to normal for her.'

There was silence for a moment, then Clarke agreed. 'Enough with the guilt trip,' he said. 'I'll get someone out. Or I'll do it myself.'

'You're a star, Tony. Can you send the results to me rather than going through the system?' Lucy added. If, as she expected, Helen Dexter's prints were found on the jewellery box, she wanted the opportunity to try to deal with it without it being processed and someone in CID picking up on it as a quick and easy case to close. Besides, Burns would wonder why *she* was handling a burglary.

She heard her phone beeping to indicate she had another call coming in. She glanced at the number but did not recognize it. Thanking Clarke, she ended his call and answered the other.

'DS Black,' she said.

'Is that the woman cop from the railway museum?' a girl's voice asked.

'Yes,' Lucy said. 'Who is this?'

'I think I know where Crackers died,' the voice said.

The building, located in Waterloo Place, had housed a bank at one stage but, several years earlier, when the market collapsed, they'd closed up a number of their branches and relocated out of town to a single unit where the rent was cheaper. Many of the high-street businesses were closing down or cutting back, and the Poundlands and Quick Cash shops which had replaced them were operating on too tight a profit margin to be able to afford the rental for the whole block, meaning that on many streets, only a handful of units would be active in any row. Besides, much of the city centre trade had shifted to the industrial parks and supermarket complexes out of town.

Despite that, from a distance, the abandoned building looked to be in state of good repair. It was only as Lucy and Fleming drew nearer that they realized that it was one of the buildings that had been given a false frontage. The windows had been boarded up with sheets of wood, painted to look like windows, showing through to blackness. The main door was, ironically, another solid sheet of wood, painted to look like a large, green wooden door.

'Maybe Jim Lowe designed it,' Fleming nodded, then glanced at Lucy's unresponsive expression. 'The song? "Green Door"? I'm wasted on you, you do know that,' he said.

'I only know the Shakin' Stevens version,' Lucy said. 'That's not something I'm proud of.'

'Understandably,' Fleming agreed. 'So, where's your caller?'

Lucy stood outside the building and, turning, surveyed Waterloo Place itself. It was, Lucy realized, shaped like a capital A, with one upright leading up from the Strand Road and up Waterloo Street, an incline lined with pubs. The other leg ran across towards the Guildhall. The triangular space in between was a pedestrian area, at the centre of which was a seating area. Above it, dominating the far end, was a large LCD screen which had been erected during the London 2012 Olympics and which remained, silently relaying images of great sporting achievements over the heads of those shuffling beneath, trying to get their shopping and get home. Lucy knew there had been statues of emigrants in the Place for some time, to mark the multitude who had had to leave Ireland for a new life somewhere else during the Famine years. She realized with some surprise that the statues were gone.

'Were there not statues of kids and that here?' she asked Fleming.

'They moved them to Sainsbury's along the river,' Fleming said. 'To the point from which they would have departed.' He scanned the area for the moment, then added, 'You could say they've emigrated.'

Lucy smiled, if only to keep him happy. She'd known him long enough to know that his good humour was a facade itself. He'd not mentioned Terry Haynes since, but she wondered as to the effect the loss of an AA sponsor might be having on him.

'There we go,' he said, pointing. Lucy followed his gaze and spotted someone she recognized. Sitting on one of the benches outside Supervalu was a girl, pretending to watch the silent footage of an athletics competition playing out on the screen above her. However, every so often she would glance across at Lucy and Fleming. She smoked a tight roll-up cigarette and sat, one leg tucked under her bottom, the flash of the red trainers unmistakable.

When she saw that Lucy had spotted her, the girl straightened, nipped off the tip of her cigarette and stood. She wore a light vest top, which accentuated the narrowness of her frame and the thinness of her shoulders and upper arms. She stuffed her hands in her pockets and began walking towards the Guildhall, passing the bank building on her left without glancing at either Lucy or Fleming.

'Let's go,' Lucy said. 'She doesn't want to be seen helping us.'

They followed her alongside the city's Walls, as if towards Guildhall Square, past the lines of stalls set out by street traders hoping to capitalize not just on the good weather, but on the influx of tourists they hoped the City of Culture year would bring. Then she cut suddenly to her right, in through Magazine Gate. Lucy and Fleming followed, realizing that the girl had, just inside the gateway, climbed onto the steps to her right, which would take her up onto the Walls. In doing so, she was now standing at the portion of the Walls against which abutted the rear of the old bank building.

When she saw them approach, she moved across to one of the rear windows on the first floor of the bank but actually at chest level to the girl in her elevated position on the Walls, and she pulled back the board on the window. Behind remained the glassless frame of the original window, giving way to what would, at one stage, have been an office but which was now in considerable disrepair. The girl glanced at Lucy, then climbed in.

'Jesus, I'll never fit in there,' said Fleming.

'I'll go in with her,' Lucy said.

'I'll go in through the front,' Fleming protested.

'It'll be fine,' Lucy said. 'I'll call if I need support.'

Using the stonework at the top of the Walls for leverage, she hoisted herself up, then dropped down in through the open window frame. 'Don't stray too far, please,' she added.

'Pull the board closed again,' the girl said. 'Leave a gap for light.'

'You called me?' Lucy said.

The girl nodded. 'I'm Grace.'

'Lucy Black. You think Kamil was killed here?'

The girl nodded. 'I found something downstairs. Look.' From her back pocket she pulled out a folded picture. The light was so meagre, Lucy could barely make out what was on it, until the girl pulled out her phone and, turning on the flash on the camera, illuminated the image for her. It was a picture of a man, woman and two children. It was badly worn, as if through years of being handled. She was fairly certain that the man in the picture was Kamil Krawiec.

'It's Crackers, isn't it?' Grace asked.

'I think it might be,' Lucy agreed.

'I told you I could be a cop,' the girl said. 'Follow me.'

Chapter Twenty-three

As they moved out of the room, Lucy pulled out her own torch and illuminated it. Within its circle, she could see that, regardless of how well the exterior of the building had looked, the bank had been ransacked inside. The fluorescent tube lights had been pulled down and lay smashed on the carpeted floor beneath their feet. The silvered plastic fittings that had housed the lights were shattered and hung from the ceiling. Lucy swept the torchlight across the ceiling above her, examining the polystyrene tiles, stained brown with watermarks, which had been smashed through, the cavity above them empty. As she picked her way down the corridor, she saw that a thick trench had been made in the wall to her left, just above door level. The cement and broken stonework lay on the ground next to her as she walked. They passed a second office, as badly trashed as the other, Grace nimbly picking her way along the corridor in front of Lucy, moving with the ease of familiarity.

'What were you doing in here anyway?' Lucy asked.

The girl didn't turn her head. 'I came in out of the rain.'

'It hasn't rained in weeks,' Lucy said.

'It usually does,' the girl countered, clearly keen not to further explain her presence in the building.

They reached a third office to the left, just before the staircase leading down, and Lucy swung the torch beam in to scan the room quickly. It was tidier than the other two, a lot of the rubble and trash pushed against one wall. A stained mattress lay on the floor, next to which, catching the torchlight in their foil, lay several opened condom wrappers. Lucy guessed at the nature of business conducted in the bank office now.

As she turned to the stairs again, she realized the girl was looking at her, as if daring her to react.

'That's not a Derry accent, Grace,' she said, instead. 'I'd guess Belfast.'

'Lisburn,' the girl corrected her.

'So what brought you to Derry?'

The girl waited a pause, then turned and led her down the steps. 'Watch your feet, the carpet's pulled near the bottom and you can fall. Trust me.'

'Spoken from experience?' Lucy said.

'I was in care,' Grace said. 'In Belfast. My mum couldn't control me and my stepfather made her put me in care in case I infected any of their new kids with my being a fucker.'

'What about your dad?'

'He was killed in a bombing at an army barracks in 1996.'

'I'm sorry to hear that. Was he a soldier?'

'Bread man,' the girl said. 'Delivering their bread for the day. They stopped their ceasefire for one year and that's all it took them to kill my daddy.'

Lucy tried to think of something to say, but couldn't.

'Fuckers. Anyway, when my ma remarried, the new one didn't like me. Thought I had too much to say for myself.'

'Did you?'

The girl twisted to glare at Lucy, then broke into a smile. 'Probably. They put me in care a few years back. Once I was sixteen no one really gave a shit enough to come looking for me.'

'And what age are you now?' Lucy asked. She knew, with all the other demands on Social Services, a child going missing near the age at which they could choose to leave care anyway wouldn't warrant any massive effort in searching. Still, if she was still young enough, Lucy could contact them.

'Eighteen,' the girl said, defiantly, so that Lucy could not tell if she was being truthful.

They reached the bottom of the steps and moved through a doorway from which hung the remains of a door. The space into which they stepped had once housed the cashier area. To one side stood a row of cashier desks behind a security screen of bulletproof glass, spider-webbed now, with cracks where someone had tried their best, repeatedly, to break through. As with upstairs, several trenches ran along the walls, the rubble and cement dust carpeting the reception area.

'That was all recent,' the girl said. 'The holes in the walls. It wasn't like that a fortnight ago.'

'Was that the last time you were in here?'

The girl nodded.

The last time it had rained, Lucy reflected. Grace was evidently plying her trade outdoors in the good weather.

'What is it, anyway?' the girl asked, nodding to the gaping space.

'Someone has stolen all the pipes and cabling, I think,' Lucy said. 'They must have realized that no one would see them doing it, what with the false fronts on the windows. Why do you think Kamil died in here?'

'I'll show you,' Grace said, leading Lucy across. Near one wall was a pile of rubble. 'I found the picture here, last night,' she said. 'Just over to that side.'

Lucy shone her torch across the pile of shattered stonework. Only then did she notice the dark brown splotches among the cement dust, the spatter marks that, in places, had managed to make it as far as the wall several feet behind.

She looked again at the picture in her hand. There was a stain on it, which, absurdly, reminded her of Tony Henderson's paint-encrusted fingerprint on the image of Stuart Carlisle which she had shown him when asking him to identify his great-uncle.

She turned the picture over. The white back still carried the faint outline of several dark brown fingerprints.

'That's blood, isn't it?' Grace asked.

'That's blood,' Lucy agreed.

Chapter Twenty-four

When Lucy called Fleming's mobile, the number was initially busy so she called straight through to Strand Road to tell Burns what she had found. Grace watched her as she did so, waiting.

'I need to split before the cops come,' she said, when Lucy hung up. 'The rest of the cops.'

Lucy nodded. 'I understand.'

The girl waited a moment. 'Is there a reward of something? For finding this?'

Lucy stuck her hand in her pocket and pulled out two notes, a twenty and a five. She hesitated a beat, then handed the girl both.

'Go and buy some food. And a place to stay for the night,' she said.

'Right,' the girl said, without conviction, then turned and took the steps two at a time, holding her phone as a torch.

'And thanks,' Lucy added.

She stopped at the turn of the steps and looked down. 'See you around,' she said.

Lucy's own phone began to ring. It was Fleming.

'What's up?'

'The girl's on her way out. Let her go. I think she's found the kill site down here.'

'We'd best tell Burns,' Fleming said.

'I already have. Your line was busy.'

'It was City Centre Initiative with the registration number we wanted,' he said. 'Wait a mo.' She heard grunts as Fleming, she guessed, helped Grace climb back out through the windows.

'Lucy said there was a reward.' Lucy heard the girl's voice, tinny through Fleming's mobile.

'Tom,' Lucy called, but to no avail. She heard the rustling of movement and Fleming came back on the line a moment later.

'I gave her a few pounds for her help,' he said.

'She already got twenty-five from me,' Lucy said.

Fleming chuckled softly. 'The little shite,' he said, admiringly.

The Forensics team came in through the main doorway on Waterloo Place, after Lucy had helped push out the wooden boards from the inside. The sudden bloom of light filling the room dazed her a little. She could see now the sheer quantity of cement dust motes floating in the shafts of sunlight and realized, with concern, that she had been breathing them in for some time.

With the benefit of the increased light in the room, to which the team added further by removing all the window boards as well, there could be no doubt that the stains she had seen were indeed blood.

Tara Gallagher stepped into the room a few minutes later, accompanied by another DS with CID called Mickey, whose surname Lucy had been told numerous times and had promptly forgotten on each instance. Tom Fleming followed behind, looking a little flushed, the heat, and exertion of climbing up and down the Walls, telling on him.

'Well done, you,' Tara said. 'Scooped everyone to the site.'

'How did you find it?' Mickey asked. 'It's a bit off the beaten track.'

'A tip-off.'

'More like just a tip,' Tara said, glancing around at the state of the place. 'Who would have been in here in the first place?'

Fleming wandered across from where he had been standing examining the holes in the wall. 'Stealing pipes and wiring,' he said.

'Who? The tipster or the victim?' Mickey asked.

'I'd say the victim,' Fleming said. 'Martin Kerrigan said that Kamil had thin cuts on his hands. That would be consistent with pulling out cables and pipes. Kamil was a builder by trade; the trenches cut in the wall are fairly precise.'

'Maybe that's what he's been doing these past few months? Metal thefts?' Lucy said.

Fleming shrugged. 'He'd not be the first,' he said.

Lucy reddened. During a previous case, they'd encountered a metal theft team who had stolen railings off the grave of Mary Quigg. Lucy had broken the fingers of one of the thieves during his arrest. Her only regret was that she'd not managed to stand on his other hand before she'd been pulled off him.

One of the Forensics team padded down the steps, pulling down his face mask, revealing himself to be Tony Clarke with whom Lucy had spoken earlier.

'Looks like some of the local hookers are using the rooms above,' he said. 'The number of used johnnies lying about up there.'

'I'm sure it's not the first time clients got screwed in a bank,' Fleming said. Lucy guessed he had already figured out the use to which the building was being put to by Grace.

'How did they get in?' Mickey asked. 'The front was sealed tight.'

'The window on the upper floor runs level with the City Walls. The board had come loose. You can climb in fairly easily,' Lucy explained.

'Why bring him in here to kill him, though?' Mickey asked. 'It's a lot of effort.'

'It is private,' Tara said. 'No one's going to interrupt.'

'Especially if the beating was prolonged,' Lucy said. 'The PM showed over one hundred impact points. Plus, Kerrigan said he'd been kneecapped.'

Fleming was watching where the CSI team worked. They had cordoned off the area around where the blood could be seen and were following each other's steps across small raised platforms to avoid unnecessary contact with the scene. 'I think he was tortured,' he said, finally.

'Why?'

Fleming looked around. 'Why would he be down here? If he'd been in here for sex, he'd have been in the upstairs room. Maybe he had a falling out with one of the team working with him. Whatever it was, they wanted him to suffer. Breaking both his legs? Beating him with hammers and leaving him in a bin to be crushed? They could have left him sealed in here; no one would ever have known any different.'

'Until one of the whores found him,' Mickey said.

'Girls,' Lucy said sharply. 'Not whores.'

'Regardless,' Fleming agreed. 'It means they didn't want him found near here.'

'Not while he was still alive at any rate,' Lucy said.

Fleming's phone began to ring and he took the call. At first Lucy thought he was unable to hear what was being said, that perhaps the mobile signal inside the building was poor, for he asked the person at the other end to repeat themselves three times.

'You're sure of that,' he said finally. He listened to the response then, thanking the caller, hung up. He stared at Lucy, his expression bewildered.

'I got them to check the registration number of the car seen in the alley that CCI pulled off the CCTV cameras for me,' he said finally. 'It belongs to Terry Haynes.'

Chapter Twenty-five

Fleming was unsettled the whole way back to the PPU, tapping out an impatient rhythm on his knee with his fingers as they drove.

'Are you OK?' Lucy asked, looking over at him.

He shook his head, then turned and looked out the window. 'Terry helped me the last time I dried out,' he said, finally. 'He had slipped himself years back and gave up sponsoring until he got himself right. I knew he'd taken on a few recently, supporting newcomers and that.'

'I'm sorry,' Lucy said.

Fleming continued staring out the window. 'It is what it is. If he's involved in some way then ... you know. I just ... Terry *helped* people who were drinking. He knew what it was like himself. Once you've been through that, you know how it feels. He was almost evangelical.'

'So you don't think he could he have killed Kamil?'

Fleming shrugged. 'If he'd slipped and was drinking heavily again, I suppose he could be capable of anything. I've known Provos and UVF men who were great AA sponsors, just not particularly good people. But I thought Terry was one of the good guys, you know.'

Lucy nodded, watching ahead as the traffic thickened and their journey slowed. 'Just because it was his car, doesn't mean it was he who killed him,' she said.

'But it doesn't mean it wasn't either,' Fleming said. 'Lucy, I'm not going to let my friendship with Terry blind me from the evidence,' he added. 'If he did kill Kamil, he'll have to answer for it.'

Lucy said nothing. She'd not wanted to offend Fleming, but at the same time, she needed to be sure that he was looking at the case objectively.

Fleming glanced at the dashboard clock. Lucy was surprised to see that it was pushing 4.45.

'Can you drop me off at home?' Fleming said, finally. 'I'm going to call around a few people and see if anyone knows where Terry might be.'

Lucy nodded. She realized that she had planned to call at the Social Services residential care unit in the Waterside at some stage to speak with Helen Dexter. She could do so now, once she'd dropped Fleming home. That she hadn't before was partly due to Doreen Jeffries not wishing the girl to think that she suspected her in the theft of her jewellery until the fingerprinting had been completed, but, more importantly, Lucy knew it was because she herself was reluctant to face Robbie. They had dated for some time, before she broke off with him over an errant kiss he shared with a colleague of his at a Hallowe'en party. They had made up on the night he was injured after an explosive device went off under her car. While they had slept together on occasions since, Lucy couldn't help feeling that something had changed. Not least, her nagging doubt that what had once been affection for Robbie on her part had now changed into guilt for what had happened to him.

She could see his outline through the frosted glass pane of the care unit's front door as Robbie hobbled towards it, his newly acquired walking stick betraying his identity.

'Oh, hi you,' he said when he saw her, opening the door wide to allow her in. He inclined towards her and pecked her on the cheek. 'I didn't know you were coming up.'

'How are you?'

Robbie nodded. 'OK. Same as usual. Still sore.'

Despite the passage of nine months, Robbie was still experiencing pain in his leg. The surgeon had managed to save it, though the lower half was composed more of metal pins and plates than bone at this point, he'd joked.

'I thought the Bionic Man felt no pain,' Lucy said. 'And he can jump *really* high.'

Robbie smirked unconvincingly. 'Come on in. Social or business?'

'Business,' Lucy admitted. 'Are you sure you're OK? You usually humour even my worst jokes.'

He smiled mildly. 'My leg's sore, is all.'

'How about a massage?' Lucy said. 'Business should only take a few minutes.'

Robbie managed a more sincere smile at that. 'It might help. It depends how long it lasts.'

'Play your cards right and you never know,' Lucy said. 'Is Helen about?'

'She's in her room. What's up?'

Lucy shook her head. 'Maybe nothing. Did you know she was working for Doreen Jeffries?'

Robbie nodded. 'She's been going out to her for a while. I thought it was a good thing for her to do. The two of them have got quite close. I think Doreen likes the company. Helen's thriving on the trust, especially after how the charity shop ended up. Why? What's happened?'

'While Doreen was on holidays someone stole her jewellery.'

'And you think it was Helen?'

'I don't want to. Nor does Doreen. But whoever got into her house did so without having to break in.'

'They had a key?'

Lucy nodded. 'Doreen said she gave Helen her key.'

'She did. It was a really big thing for her.'

'What was a big thing?' a voice said. Lucy looked across to where Helen Dexter stood in the doorway of the corridor leading down to the unit's bedrooms.

'Someone broke into Doreen's house while she was on holiday.'

'What? You're kidding? How is she?' she said, then as she realized the purpose of Lucy's visit, her expression darkened. 'You think it was me?'

'Whoever broke in had a key,' Lucy said. 'I have to check with all the keyholders.'

'Who are *all* the keyholders?'

'You,' Lucy admitted. 'I'd like to take your fingerprints.'

'You bitch,' the girl spat suddenly. 'I don't believe you.'

'Helen—' Robbie began, raising his hand in placation.

'No,' the girl retorted. 'She thinks I did it. Don't you?'

Lucy held her stare. 'I hope you didn't. And Doreen doesn't believe that you did, either. But we'll be taking prints from her room where the jewellery was taken. I know you were doing cleaning and that for Doreen, which means that your prints are going to be all over the place. I need to take a set for elimination purposes so that when your prints are pulled I can explain why they're there. It's not to try to prove that you did it. You'd be helping me catch whoever stole Doreen's stuff.'

The girl seemed somewhat mollified by the explanation, coming into the room and dropping onto the sofa. 'How is she, anyway?'

'She's shaken,' Lucy said. 'The sooner I can eliminate you, the sooner you can visit her. But I think you'll need to wait until we can prove you didn't take the jewellery that's missing.'

'Why would I steal from her? She's my friend.'

Lucy moved across and sat on the sofa next to her. The girl shifted her weight away from Lucy. 'With what happened in the shop? You need to ask? I'm not accusing you, I'm just doing my job.'

'Well it's a shit one,' the girl retorted. 'And you're very good at it.' She glared across at her. 'So what happens now? Are you going to ink me up?'

'Robbie, can you get me a glass or something?'

Robbie limped across to the kitchen, took a glass down from the unit and, lifting a drying cloth, wiped it thoroughly. He came across and handed it to her, holding its upper lip with the cloth.

Lucy took it, gripping the lower end in an evidence bag she'd taken from her pocket. 'Can you grip that tightly,' she said, offering the glass to the girl, who did so. Lucy then pulled the bag up over the glass, careful not to touch it herself.

'This should be fine,' she said. 'I didn't want to have to start bringing you into the station.'

'That was big of you,' Helen said.

Lucy put the glass into her bag. 'If we do get a hit, I'll have to. The only reason I'm doing it this way is to keep you out of the station and off any records,' Lucy added. 'Doreen doesn't think for a minute that you did it. Nor do I. But can you think of anyone else who might have had a key? Meals on Wheels? Any relatives or home help?'

Helen shook her head. 'She doesn't have relatives. The only person who helps her out is me.'

Lucy nodded. 'Anybody new about the house in the weeks before she went away?'

'She had a bunch of guys doing the driveway,' Helen said.

'When?'

'The week before she went. She said the frost from a few winters back had destroyed her driveway. Some crowd came in and fixed it for her.'

'Do you remember who they were?'

Helen shook her head. 'I'm sure Doreen will, though,' she said.

Chapter Twenty-six

Lucy went home to get a change of clothes, picked up a Chinese meal for them both then drove to Robbie's place to meet him once his shift had finished.

She let herself in and unpacked the food in the kitchen. She could hear the shower running in the bathroom. He'd had to get a wide shower installed downstairs after his injury to save him having to go up and down stairs unnecessarily. After putting the food in the oven to keep it warm, she moved through into the bathroom herself, stripped off her clothes and climbed into the shower with him.

The skin on his leg had not healed well, the scarring puckered along its length from his ankle to his thigh. She washed the wound gently, massaging the muscles, her hands moving higher as she stood again and kissed him.

They ate in bed, the tinfoil cartons of rice and noodles resting in the space between them.

'I've not seen you in a week, you know,' Robbie said, angling his head to eat a fork-load of chow mein.

'Things have been busy,' Lucy said. 'We pulled someone from the river the other night.'

'I heard about that.'

'He was already dead and embalmed. Someone else was cremated in his coffin.'

Robbie nodded, though his interest had already waned. Lucy realized that she had shifted straight into her default conversation with him: work.

'I hardly see you at all, what with work and that. For you and me.'

'We've both been busy,' Lucy agreed. 'Things'll get better.'

Robbie nodded. 'Well, I thought one way that might happen, that we'd see one another more often, would be if … if you moved in here. Permanently.'

Lucy felt her stomach twist. 'You mean live together?'

'Yes.'

'I thought we were doing OK as things are,' she said, deliberately picking through her sweet and sour chicken, not looking at Robbie.

'We see one another once a fortnight sometimes,' Robbie said. 'I'd like to see you more often than that.'

'I've my own house to think about too,' Lucy said. 'What would I do with that?'

'You've done nothing with it anyway,' Robbie said. 'It's been the exact same since your dad … since that all happened. It's your father's house, not yours.'

The comment riled Lucy, not least because she knew it to be true. She'd not redecorated her father's house because she still saw it as his house. Part of her, she reasoned, still believed that at some stage he'd return to it and would expect it to be as he'd left it, even as her rational side knew that this would never happen.

'It's a big change, Robbie,' Lucy said. 'Let me think on it.'

'It doesn't need to be a big thing. You already have a key. Just see it as moving your stuff in here. You must get lonely sitting in that house every night on your own.'

'I'm not lonely,' Lucy said.

'Well I am,' Robbie countered, putting his dishes to one side. 'If we're together, we should be together. And if you don't want that, then you need to say so.'

'That's not what I'm saying,' Lucy snapped. 'I don't want to be rushed into something. I said I'll think about it and I will. OK?'

'Fine,' Robbie muttered, throwing back the covers and climbing out of bed. Lucy watched him limping towards the bathroom, the food suddenly tasteless in her mouth.

The next morning, she'd showered again and, once dressed, sat at the breakfast bar in his small kitchen with him while they had coffee and toast. Despite being barely 8 a.m., the heat was oppressive, even with the window open, the air heavy. Lucy pulled at her polo shirt, tugging it away from her skin, which had remained damp from the shower. The discussion about her moving in had set the tone for the night and, though they had slept together, the distance between them was palpable.

'What kind of a day have you today?' she asked.

Robbie sipped at his coffee, his toast lying uneaten on the plate in front of him. 'OK. Helen will be in a mood after last night. I'll have that to deal with.'

Lucy nodded. 'How's your leg since?'

'Sore,' he replied tersely.

Lucy ate her toast, watching him. 'I know you're angry at me—' she began.

'Not everything's about you,' he snapped, then raised a hand, almost as if to stop the words being heard. 'My fucking leg is killing me. That's what's wrong.'

'Why didn't you say something?'

'So you can blame yourself? Make it all your fault?'

'Robbie, it was my fault. It was my car—'

'You see? I can't even be sore without it becoming about you, Lucy.'

Lucy put down her cup, tapped his hand lightly with her own. 'I'm sorry you're sore,' she said. 'Do you need your painkillers?'

'For all the good they do,' Robbie said, pushing back his stool and moving across to the cupboard to get them.

He walked her to the door as she was leaving. Outside, the sky seemed to carry the sheen and hardness of ceramic, a few wisps of cloud overhead. To the east, though, the upper edge of a thick thunderhead bruised the sky just above the horizon. The air was moist, as if intensifying the heat in the expectation of the impending rain.

'I promise I'll think about what you asked,' Lucy said, but Robbie was staring above her, at the clouds gathering.

'A change is coming,' he remarked.

Friday, 20 July

Chapter Twenty-seven

She was one of the first in the incident room for Burns's 9 a.m. briefing. The station was quiet, most of the Tactical Support Units having been diverted to Belfast where the rioting had continued through the night. Since Belfast City Council had voted not to fly the Union Jack above the City Hall every day of the year, in recognition of the conflicting national loyalties of the city's inhabitants, it had been building to this. The Peace Process may have proved a salve to the wounds of the Troubles, but it had not proved as purgative as people had perhaps supposed, and many of the old animosities remained, just below the surface. In the wrong hands, or with the wrong words, any one of the issues was enough to bring people out to the streets, not to protest about the specific issue necessarily, but more to vent their frustrations at enforced compromises.

As the team began to arrive, Mickey made coffee, complaining loudly enough for her to hear that Lucy had not done so despite being first in. Tony Clarke arrived not long after to bring the team up to speed on the findings in the old bank building.

He came across to where Lucy stood. 'I called with that old doll,' he said. 'Took prints. I've not checked them yet because I had to do this for Burns. It looks like three distinct sets, though. Two sets all over the jewellery box, one very clean.'

Lucy took the glass from her bag, still wrapped in plastic. 'Can you check against these?'

'If they're the old doll's, I don't need them. I took an elimination set already,' Clarke said, sounding a little offended at the implication in Lucy's actions. 'I'm not stupid.'

'They belong to a girl who does work for Doreen,' Lucy explained. 'She was a keyholder. I need to know if those are her prints on the box.' Their presence wouldn't prove that she had stolen the jewellery, but she would have to explain why she'd been handling it if she was simply employed to do some light cleaning. More importantly, Lucy was hoping that the prints wouldn't be hers at all and she could set both her own and Doreen's minds at rest that Helen Dexter had not duped them a second time.

'Right, folks,' Burns said, calling the room to attention. 'Shall we begin? Tony?'

The door to his left opened, causing everyone to turn to see who was arriving late. Lucy's mother, Assistant Chief Constable Wilson, stepped into the room, nodding to the assembly in general, but holding Lucy's stare.

'The blood we've taken from the scene is the same type as Krawiec's,' Clarke explained, once the ACC had taken her seat. 'We have taken DNA for comparison, but it will take some time. Based on our analysis though, the splatters are consistent with the injuries on the victim's body. I would say with a fair degree of confidence that it is the locus for the man's killing.'

'We also have the car spotted by the barman, is that right?' Burns asked.

Fleming nodded. 'Terry Haynes's car.'

Burns pointed to an image of Terry Haynes, which had been pinned up on the board to his rear. Haynes was a heavyset man, with a head the size and shape of a cannonball. One of his ears carried injuries Lucy had only previously associated with rugby players.

'Tara, you were to look into Haynes for me. Anything useful?'

'He served time in the South for assault years back. He and another man beat up a bouncer who had thrown them out of a bar. They'd sat waiting for him to finish work and jumped him on the way home.'

'They beat up a bouncer? That's a turn-up for the books,' Mickey asked, raising a ripple of laughter.

'They attacked him with a bottle and a broken brick,' Tara said, trying hard to hide her annoyance at Mickey's comment. 'He ended up in hospital for a fortnight.'

The laughter died down. 'Haynes served eight months,' she said. 'When he got out he was involved in a RTA a year after.'

'Anyone injured?'

'Just himself. He was drunk on a motorbike. He tried to go straight through a roundabout. The central reservation prevented him.'

'Did he do time for it?'

'The guards figured his injuries were enough of a lesson for him. He agreed to dry out.'

'Which he did,' Fleming said, suddenly. Throughout the previous discussion he had been tapping his foot impatiently. 'Terry Haynes has been working with the alcoholics in the city for years now. He turned himself around completely. He sponsors in the AA; he works in the late-night soup kitchens. I've seen him going around in the winter handing out coats to the street drinkers that he bought for them in the charity shops in the city. He's a good man.'

Burns raised his hand. 'I'm sure he is, Tom. And no one would know the work he'd do there better than you.' Lucy sensed Fleming tense almost imperceptibly beside her. She wondered herself whether Burns was referring to Fleming's own work with the city's alcoholics, or his spell as one himself. Her experience of the man suggested the former, but his comments had obviously annoyed Fleming.

'Can someone open a window, please?' ACC Wilson said suddenly. 'Let some air in.'

The comment was enough to relieve the increasing fractiousness, as if the burgeoning heat had been contributing to the tensions in the room.

'But, all his good work notwithstanding, we do know that he has a record for assault and that his car was spotted at the bins where we believe the deceased was dumped. *And* Haynes himself has been in the wind for a few days, is that right?'

Fleming nodded. 'I called around his friends last night, but no one has seen him recently. I don't have a number for his neighbour: I'm going to call out there today.'

'Physical description, Tara?'

'Haynes is five foot eleven, and weighs eighteen stone, three pounds,' Tara said.

'That would work,' Tony Clarke said. 'The injuries on the vic suggested they were made by someone big, with a bit of weight behind him. Some of the splatter hit the wall five feet from where the body would have been lying, suggesting a fairly powerful follow-through on the swing, considering the size of the weapon used on him.'

'A ball-peen hammer?' Lucy asked.

Clarke nodded. 'The other thing is, based on the splatter direction, I'd guess that there were probably two assailants. If one of our killers is Terry Haynes, he had help.'

Burns nodded. 'Terry Haynes is our priority. Locate the car, find out where he was last seen, any known associates. Tom and Lucy, I'd appreciate your help with that; we're drifting into your territory here. Any further news on the body in the coffin, by the way?'

'Ciaran Duffy has done a runner,' Lucy said. 'The son of the undertaker. He lied about the times of his journey to Belfast. We believe he stopped somewhere and swapped the body.'

'Any motive?'

'Not yet. We're watching his bank account and credit cards.'

'Any luck with an ID on the cremated remains?'

'None,' Lucy conceded. 'We believe the plate in his skull came from Beaumont Hospital. I've asked for them to send me through a list of names of those who received implants from the period they got the batch, but I've not been back in the office yet to see if it came through.'

'Very good,' Burns said. 'Keep at it. That's all, folks. Keep me updated.'

As they gathered themselves to leave, Wilson approached Lucy and Fleming. 'Tom, are you OK with where this is going?' she asked, without preamble.

'Fine, ma'am,' Fleming said.

'I understand your feelings may be quite mixed. Would you rather not work the case?'

'Quite the opposite, ma'am,' Fleming said. 'I think it's important that at least one person investigating Haynes should be working from a presumption of his innocence rather than guilt.'

'Very good,' Wilson said. 'Lucy, a quick word?'

Chapter Twenty-eight

She waited until the rest of the officers had filed out of the room, Tara staring back interrogatively at Lucy as she let the door swing closed behind her.

'I visited your father last night,' her mother said.

Wilson had left Lucy with her father when she was still a child. At the time, Lucy had believed that it was simply to allow her to focus on her burgeoning career in the police. More recently, she had discovered some things about her father that, while explaining her mother's decision to leave, did not, to Lucy's mind, vindicate her leaving Lucy with the man. Consequently, when Lucy had joined the PSNI, she had done so under her father's name of Black rather than her mother's name, Wilson, and none of her peers had made the connection between the two women. At one stage Lucy had seen her mother's assigning her to the Public Protection Unit as an attempt to stymie Lucy's career. Latterly, she had come to appreciate having Tom Fleming, the only officer who knew of their maternal relationship, as her mentor and boss.

However, none of these changes in her perception of past events had allowed her to forgive the woman for walking off and leaving her when she was eight.

'And?'

'Have you seen him recently?'

Lucy nodded. 'His face?'

'And the rest. They said they had to restrain him from attacking another patient.'

'So I believe,' Lucy said.

'And are you OK about it all?'

'He didn't attack me,' Lucy retorted.

Wilson sighed. 'You know what I mean. He didn't know me at all when I was there.'

Lucy stopped herself making a comment and felt unusually pleased with her restraint. Despite her acrimony with her mother, she knew it must have been painful for the woman to realize that her estranged husband had forgotten who she was. 'I'm sorry to hear that.'

Her mother's expression softened, the tight line of her mouth relaxing momentarily, almost as if she too had been expecting a very different response.

'I know he's not seen me much,' she admitted. 'But we did have fifteen years together. He had no idea who I was.'

Lucy shifted uncomfortably, unwilling to give any more sympathy than she already had.

'I just wanted you to be ready,' she said, motioning as if to put her hand on Lucy's arm, then controlling herself by folding her arms.

'For what?' Lucy asked. 'I know what's he's like. I visit him every week.'

'I'm not saying that, Lucy. But he'll forget you at some stage, too. I just want you to be prepared.'

'He'll be fine,' Lucy protested, knowing how ridiculous it sounded even as she spoke. She'd found that her feelings about her father, both for what he had done when she was a child and what had happened to him since, were more easily managed by pushing them to the back of her mind. It was like Robbie's raising of the issue of their moving in together. At some level, she'd been aware that something needed to happen in their relationship. But, to Lucy's mind, things were fine so long as she wasn't forced into having to think about them.

'He's not coming back, Lucy,' her mother said softly. 'Once he disappears into that, he'll not come back again. I know you don't want to face that, but it's going to happen sooner than you think.'

Lucy felt her eyes fill, swallowed back. 'I'm ready. I know what's coming.'

'If you need any—'

'I was thinking about the bank building,' Lucy said suddenly. 'If there was someone in cleaning out that building, I wouldn't be surprised if more of those buildings with the false fronts up have been similarly emptied.'

Her mother nodded lightly, taking the message. She smiled. 'That's a very good point, Lucy. I'll have someone look into it.'

'You'd alrcady thought of it, hadn't you?' Lucy challenged, wondering if the woman would patronize her by lying.

'Yes. We've not got the bodies to do searches yet. When things settle down in Belfast and we get officers back, we'll do a sweep. I've contacted the guy in the council who organized the fronts to see if they can get someone out for us.'

'Was that John Boyd?'

'You know him?' Wilson asked, surprised.

'I've come across him. I've met his partner, Fiona. I think he's abusive towards her.'

'John Boyd?' her mother said, incredulously.

'What? Is he a friend?'

'Not at all. I've met the two of them out at dinner dances and that. They seemed very … normal.'

'They always do,' Lucy said.

Wilson accepted the comment. 'Has she made a complaint against him?'

Lucy shook her head. 'She's not even admitted he did it.'

'Let me know how it pans out,' Wilson said. 'You better go before someone thinks we're getting on too well,' she added, her expression pained in a manner that caused Lucy's breath to catch.

Chapter Twenty-nine

She felt her phone vibrate as she left the room, glancing back at where her mother was gathering together some papers that had been lying on the table.

'DS Black,' she said, not recognizing the number on the caller display.

'This is the Bank of Ireland on the Strand Road. You'd asked us to keep an eye on the account of a missing person, Ciaran Duffy.'

'Yes,' Lucy said, stopping. 'Has he used the account?'

'He called into the branch just now to try to withdraw the funds in his account.'

'Everything?'

'Yes. He has eight thousand in there. We've a policy that we can't give out that size of a cash withdrawal on the spot. We require twenty-four hours' notice usually. He told us he's buying a car and needs it this afternoon, so we've agreed to have it ready for him at 3 p.m.'

'So he'll be calling into the branch?'

'Yes. I just thought you should know.'

'Great. Thanks,' Lucy said, then, before hanging up, added, 'Eight grand? Has that been in his account long?'

The speaker laughed lightly. 'That's the thing. He only put in five of it the other day. If he'd kept it out, we could've given him the other three this morning without a problem.'

Tara was sitting on the edge of her desk when Lucy came out.

'Everything OK?' she asked.

'Great,' Lucy said. 'I've just had word Ciaran Duffy is going to be at the Bank of Ireland at three this afternoon to empty his account. He's obviously planning on running.'

'I meant with your mother.'

'No, she was—' Lucy began before realizing what Tara had said.

'I knew it!' Tara hissed. 'I knew there was something between you and her.'

Her reaction was enough to rouse the curiosity of one or two of the other officers nearby, though Lucy guessed she had said it quietly enough that they wouldn't have clearly heard what she had said.

'Tara, look, I can—'

'Don't,' Tara said, moving back from her. 'That explains *so* much.'

'Tara, look, I'm sorry I didn't tell you before. I can explain. Just not here.'

Tara stared at her, then turned on her heel towards the toilet. Lucy followed behind.

She checked the stalls were all empty before she spoke.

'She left us when I was only a kid. We hadn't spoken in years. I grew up with my dad. She put her career before her family. Trust me; there's nothing between us.'

'Yeah, right! Apart from her helping you along in your career.'

'Really?'

'How come we both started together and I'm making coffee in CID while you're working cases with Tom Fleming.'

'Child abuse and domestic violence cases? Do you want to swap? Be my guest! She put me in the unit she thought would break me. She didn't want me in the police and she stuck me somewhere working cases that would drive me straight out of it again.'

Tara leaned against the sink.

'You don't believe me? She moved me out of CID in the middle of my first big case. To work one about an abandoned child instead. I'm not the only one not telling people about our relationship. She's worked bloody hard to make sure no one knows either.'

'It's not just that,' Tara said. 'It's the fact you didn't trust me enough to tell me. I wouldn't have told anyone.'

'I ... I didn't ...' Lucy began. She paused, took a breath. 'I didn't want anyone to think I was getting preferential treatment.'

'You said yourself, she put you working child abuse cases. According to you, no one would see that as preferential.'

'I just ... I didn't want you to think, I didn't ...'

'Trust me? I thought we were friends.'

'We are friends,' Lucy said.

'No we're not. Friends trust one another.'

'I didn't want anyone to think I was like her,' Lucy said suddenly.

'Well, that I *can* understand,' Tara said. 'Because you're *exactly* like her, as far as I'm concerned – putting your career first!' she added, then turned and left the room.

Fleming was waiting for Lucy in the incident room.

'I was wondering where you'd got to,' he said.

'Tara found out about my mother.'

'How?'

Lucy shook her head. 'Guessed, maybe. I didn't ask. But if she knows, other people will know.'

Fleming shoulder bumped her. 'It's not like she's helped your career or anything, let's face it.'

'That's not how other people will see it,' Lucy said.

'Cross that bridge when you come to it. We'd best get going,' Fleming said. 'I want to see if I can track down Terry. We'll call to his house, have a word with the neighbour.'

Lucy gathered her thoughts. 'Ciaran Duffy's bank has been in touch. He's due in at three to empty his account. He lodged five grand a few days ago.'

'A pay-off for the body disposal?'

'Looks that way,' Lucy agreed. 'If we can get Ciaran, we'll get whoever paid him.'

'And maybe even find out just who was in that bloody coffin,' Fleming added.

Chapter Thirty

Terry Haynes had lived in a semi-detached house on Primity Crescent, at New Buildings, which lay out on the outskirts of the city, a few miles beyond Prehen Park. As they approached the village, Lucy noticed lamp posts were festooned with a variety of flags, including the Union Jack, the Orange Order and the flag of Israel.

'That's quite a collection,' Lucy commented, nodding towards where the flags hung limp in the heated air.

'I counted last year,' Fleming said. 'On a stretch of less than a mile, there were over a hundred flags hung.'

Lucy pulled in on Primity Crescent and Fleming stared out at the houses. 'That one,' he said.

The house was neat, unadorned, the grass fairly freshly shaven, patchy brown in the heat. The curtains were undrawn, the windows carrying venetian blinds which made it difficult to see inside. Fleming knocked twice at the door, then skirted the side of the house and tried the back.

As Lucy waited on the front porch, she heard the click as the door of the neighbouring house opened.

A small bulldog of a woman came out, her arms folded across a chest so ample her hands barely met. 'Are you looking for Terry?'

Lucy nodded. 'Have you seen him recently?'

'Is there something wrong?' the woman asked in return.

'Have you seen him recently?' Lucy persisted.

The woman waited, staring at her. Her expression softened suddenly as her gaze shifted beyond Lucy's shoulder.

'There's a face I know,' she said.

Lucy glanced over her shoulder to see Fleming standing there.

'Mrs Hamilton,' he said. 'I was planning on calling with you.'

'Jesus, I've not been Hamilton since last Christmas. Lily. You're Tim, is that right?'

'Tom,' Fleming said.

The woman addressed Lucy. 'Tom here used to visit Terry, a while back.'

Lucy nodded.

'Have you seen him, Lily?'

She shook her head, a movement that rippled through her frame. 'Not in a few days. I was worried when youse arrived that something had happened to him.'

Fleming shook his head. 'We need to find him, just.'

Lily moved across to the fence between the properties and, leaning her hands on top of it, continued. 'I've not seen him since the weekend. He didn't say he was going anywhere. He usually would. I go in and lift his post and that. Put out food for the cat.'

164

'Have you a key?'

Lily nodded. 'Sure I had to go in and feed Tiger, didn't I? When Terry never come back. I thought he'd gone on a bender again. He hasn't, has he?' she added concernedly.

'We're not sure,' Fleming said. 'You've not noticed anything unusual going on, have you?'

She shrugged. 'How would you tell? There *is* no usual with Terry. He'd another one of his cases staying for a few days.'

'Cases?' Lucy asked.

Lily nodded. 'Terry would take in people for a few days to help them ...' Her breath seemed to catch in her throat as she tried, too late, to swallow back her words. 'Somewhere for them to stay while they ...'

'Dried out,' Fleming added, as Lucy realized why Mrs Hamilton recognized Fleming and, perhaps also, where he had gone the previous year when he'd been suspended temporarily after falling off the wagon.

'Aye,' Lily said. 'Dried out.'

'Who was it? Anyone you know?' Fleming asked.

Lily shrugged. 'He wasn't here long. Rough-looking character, but then, it is Terry we're talking about. Do you know him?' she asked Lucy.

Lucy shook her head. 'Only by reputation.'

'I'd not be taking him on,' Lily said. 'The size of him,' she added, pulling herself to her full height.

Looking at the woman's hefty frame, Lucy knew how she felt.

'Maybe we can take a look inside,' Fleming said. 'Just to check he's not had an accident or something.'

'I've been in and fed Tiger already,' Lily added. 'He's not there.'

'Maybe he's upstairs,' Lucy said. 'Did you check those rooms?'

The woman regarded her. 'I'm not a snoop. Of course I didn't.'

'We'd best then,' Fleming said. 'Has his latest case been back?'

Lily shook her head as she gathered herself then came down her own path, rounded the fence and up Haynes's. 'Not since Terry went.'

The house felt airless inside, the heat of the past days having been trapped in the closed rooms, the windows all shut. A scattering of post lay unopened on a small table in the narrow hallway.

'Did you lift the post for him?'

Lily nodded.

'You'd best wait down here, Lily,' Fleming said. 'In case we find something upstairs you'll not want to see.'

Lucy knew that they wouldn't. Had someone been dead in the house, particularly in such heat, they'd have smelt it at the front door. Lily would get in the way and Fleming wanted a chance to look around.

Lucy and he took the stairs. There were three rooms above. The first to the left was a small, neat bathroom. The next was the big bedroom to the front.

'This is Terry's,' Fleming said. 'I'll take a look around. The small room is for his guests. Check it.'

Lucy crossed to the box room, which overlooked the small scrap of land to the rear that constituted

Terry's garden. The bed was made, the room tidy. Over a chair in the corner lay a pair of trousers which looked freshly pressed. Despite that, they still carried tears and black staining on the knees. Beside the chair sat a plastic bag, folded in on itself.

Lucy lifted the bag and glanced in. Inside were a shirt, some underwear and a small black plastic wallet.

'It looks like the guest left their stuff here,' Lucy called. She pulled on a pair of gloves, then took out the wallet and opened it. It contained five pounds and a small card, which Lucy initially took to be a bank card but which, it turned out, was a driving licence.

Ironically, her first impression was that the driving licence belonged to Prawo Jazdy. It took a second for her to see Kamil Krawiec's name below it.

Chapter Thirty-one

Before leaving Haynes's house, Tom Fleming lifted a photograph from the mantelpiece in the living room. In the picture, Haynes was standing with another man, their arms around the other's shoulders, their heads inclined towards each other, beaming at the camera.

'Boyfriend?' Lucy asked.

Fleming shook his head. 'Brother,' he said. 'He died a few years ago in Galway.' He weighed the frame in his hand. 'We'll need a picture if we're putting out an alert.' He glanced around the walls, as if looking for further pictures.

'Looking for a better one?'

'Looking for any at all,' Fleming said. 'Besides this one.'

Lucy nodded. 'I ... ah ... I want to call with someone,' she said. 'Have we got a few minutes?'

'I've got all day,' Fleming said.

It took Doreen Jeffries a few minutes to answer the door. While they waited, Lucy saw, for the first time, that the short driveway at the front of Doreen's property had been resurfaced. The edges were rough and globules of hardened tarmac marked the concrete path leading to her house. Already, the tarmac had erupted to reveal a profusion of serrated dandelion leaves near the gate. Lucy heard the door lock click then Doreen peered out. She wore a floral pinafore over her clothes and a pair of yellow Marigold gloves.

'Spring cleaning?' Lucy asked, after Doreen had invited them in.

'Trying to clean my room,' Doreen replied. 'I'm scrubbing at the place but it still feels dirty.'

Lucy put her arm around the woman. 'Do you want me to have a go at it?'

Doreen shook her head, tapping her lightly on the hand, then moving out of her embrace. 'You're very kind. I need to do it myself. So I know it's all gone.' She turned to Lucy, worriedly. 'You're not offended, are you?'

'Of course not,' Lucy said. 'I understand completely.'

The woman hesitated a moment. 'How's Helen?'

'Let's sit, shall we?' Lucy suggested, guiding the woman to the sofa. Fleming followed behind, closing the door.

'I spoke with her yesterday,' Lucy explained. 'She says she didn't take anything from the house. She said she never touched your jewellery.'

Doreen nodded, watching Lucy's lips as if reading the words, her mouth forming the echo of the words as she followed the conversation. She smiled briefly as she reached the end of the sentence.

'But,' Lucy cautioned, 'we found three sets of fingerprints on your stuff. One will be yours presumably. If the thief wore gloves, there are two other sets to account for. Even if he or she didn't, that still leaves one set which might be Helen's.'

Doreen shook her head. 'I told you before, I don't believe she stole from me,' she said, her mouth tightening.

'We'll know soon enough,' Lucy said. 'Helen did mention you had workmen here before you went on holidays. Is that right?'

The woman raised her eyes to heaven. 'Them!' she snorted.

'Who were they?'

'The man come round a month or so back. Just landed at the door. He said he'd been looking at the drive and pathway and it needed work.'

'Did it?'

'The frost a few years back had cracked the concrete at the back, but it would have done. He asked to come in and talk through my options.'

'Did you let him?'

'Of course not,' Doreen said. 'I told him I was on my own and didn't want strangers in the house.'

'And?'

'He said he understood. He said they could resurface the drive and the back path for me. He wouldn't take no for an answer.'

'How?'

'He said he knew by looking that the crack in the path would leak water into the foundations of the house. When it rained, it would run down and cause damp. He said it would cost tens of thousands to fix then. It would be too late.'

Fleming glanced at Lucy. 'How much did he charge you for doing the work?'

'Two thousand pounds.'

'Did he give you his name?'

Doreen shook her head. 'I can't, I don't remember what it was.'

'But you said yes?' Lucy asked.

'I wanted him to go away. He wouldn't take no for an answer,' she explained again.

'So what happened?'

Doreen reddened. 'They were meant to start on a Monday and they didn't arrive until Wednesday afternoon. A squad of them pulled up in a blue van. I told him it needed to be finished for Friday because I was going away on holidays and wanted it done. They didn't manage to get the path at the back fixed. I'm still waiting.'

'You've not paid him, though?' Fleming asked.

The pause before Doreen spoke was enough response. 'He said he had to buy materials and pay the men,' she explained, as if trying to convince Fleming.

'That's OK, Doreen,' Lucy said, aware that Doreen felt foolish at admitting that she'd paid for the job before it was done. 'That's understandable. Did you pay the whole amount?'

The woman nodded.

'Cash?' Fleming asked.

She nodded again. Fleming glanced at Lucy and shook his head. They would have no chance of recovering her money.

'Do you remember what the company was called?' Lucy asked. 'Maybe their name was on the van,' she added, thinking of Duffy the undertaker's van.

Doreen stared at her, her lips moving silently as if she was willing herself to speak the name but couldn't. 'I ... I can't ... I'm not sure. It *was* blue, I think.'

Lucy took the woman's hand as tears welled in her eyes. 'I've been made a fool of, haven't I?' Doreen said.

'Not at all,' Lucy replied softly, putting her arm around her and giving her a gentle squeeze. 'Not at all.'

'He scared me,' Doreen managed. 'The man scared me. I wanted him to go. I want to see Helen.'

'Give me a minute,' Lucy said. She stood and, taking out her phone, moved to the front of the house, as if to get a better signal. In the background she heard Fleming ask Doreen to describe the man who had called at the house.

'Clarke.'

'Tony? Lucy Black here. Any luck with the fingerprints from Doreen Jeffries?'

'Jesus, Lucy,' Clarke said. 'Give me a chance. I've not even got to the toilet yet today.'

'I'd make that a priority,' Lucy joked. 'We don't want any accidents now, do we?'

She heard Clarke laugh, then the rustle as he shifted the receiver from one ear to the other.

'Let me check where it's at,' he said. She heard the tap of his keyboard. 'Right. Three sets. One belonged to the old doll herself. No surprises there.'

'What about the glass I gave you? The prints on that?'

'I'm checking,' he replied with exasperation.

'They belong to a friend of the old doll,' Lucy said. 'And she really wants to see her. I'd like to be able to eliminate her as a suspect.'

'Consider her eliminated,' Clarke said. 'No match.'

'You're sure?' Lucy asked.

'Certain. I'm running the other two through the system now, but neither belong to her.'

'Great,' Lucy said, preparing to end the call. 'I owe you one for doing this so quickly for me.'

'Jesus, that *was* quick,' Clarke said.

'What?'

'The results ... Jesus,' Clarke repeated. 'You'll not believe this.'

'Try me,' Lucy said.

'We've a match on one of the sets of prints already. The bin man.'

'Kamil Krawiec?'

'That's the one. Hit on the other set now, too,' Clarke added. 'Aaron Moore. DOB 24.9.84.'

'You're sure about the first set?' Lucy asked, phone clasped between her shoulder and jaw as she jotted down the details Clarke had given her.

'The computer is,' Clarke said. 'That's good enough for me.'

'And me,' Lucy agreed.

She moved back into the living room. 'Good news, Doreen. Helen's in the clear. You can give her a call, if you like.'

The woman's restraint failed her and the tears ran brightly onto her cheeks.

'Doreen was just giving me a description of the man who sold her the tarmac job. Big man, red-haired, heavyset. Ear pierced on one side,' he said.

'We have hits on the fingerprints,' Lucy said. 'Kamil is one of them.'

Fleming stared at her. 'Krawiec?'

Lucy nodded.

'Give me a minute,' Fleming said, standing and going out to the car.

'Doreen?' Lucy asked. 'Is there anyone else with a spare key? Or did you give the workmen a key?'

Doreen shook her head.

'Have you a spare key anywhere in the house?'

'There's one in the back, under the garden gnome. I left it there for Helen in case she forgot her own.'

'Is it still there?'

'I don't know,' Doreen said, rising. 'I'll check.'

Lucy followed her through the kitchen and out the rear door. A small gnome pushing a wheelbarrow stood at the centre of the main flower bed.

Lucy crossed and lifted it. The ground beneath held no key. At that moment, Fleming reappeared with the picture he had taken from Haynes's house as well as an image of Kamil Krawiec.

'Doreen,' he said, offering her both the pictures still in the frame. 'Do you recognize either of these men?'

Lucy could guess where he was going. Kamil had been living with Terry Haynes. Haynes was a big man himself. Both had been missing for some time. It seemed a reasonable question.

Doreen took the pictures and, after wiping her eyes with the edge of her pinafore, studied the image of Krawiec first.

'I know him,' she said. 'He was one of the men working on the driveway. I remember him. He asked to use the toilet. He had an accent.'

'He was Polish,' Fleming said. 'What about the other picture? Do you recognize him?'

'Which one?' she asked.

Fleming pointed to Haynes.

Doreen angled her head, as if in thought. 'No,' she said finally. 'I don't think so.'

Fleming straightened, releasing the breath he'd held since she'd taken the picture from him. 'He wasn't the man who convinced you to get work done? The heavy man who called at your door?'

She shook her head.

'You're sure?'

'I can't ... I don't *think* it's him,' the woman offered, handing him back the picture.

Chapter Thirty-two

They returned to the Strand Road at the request of Burns.

'And you were investigating a burglary because …?' Burns asked, sitting behind his desk while Lucy and Tom Fleming stood before him, having offered neither a seat. He leant forward slightly, his hands restless on the wooden surface beneath them.

Fleming moved across to where two chairs sat against the far wall and dragged one over for Lucy, then returned and brought a second for himself.

'The woman whose house was targeted is a friend. She has given some light housework to a teenager from the care unit in the Waterside. They'd become quite close. She was afraid the child had stolen from her, but didn't know whether she wanted to press charges. She asked me to look into it.'

'That's not PPU business,' Burns said irritably.

'Anything involving children in care is very much our business,' Tom Fleming said. 'Always has been.'

'What about the body in the coffin? Has that reached a dead end?'

Fleming chuckled lightly at Burns's irritability, which just served to fuel it further. 'We're still working it.'

'You might have been working it quicker if you'd not been chasing up burglaries.'

'And following up phone tip-offs in a murder investigation,' Fleming added. 'As it's transpired, all of them have crossed over anyway, so it's a result all round.'

Burns stared at Fleming.

'Sir,' he added, finally.

Satisfied with even such a small victory, Burns sat back. 'So, what do we know?'

'We know Kamil Krawiec was part of a gang that laid a drive, badly, a fortnight ago for Doreen Jeffries, got paid and never came back to finish it. Based on fingerprints found at the scene we think that, at some stage during the past ten days, Kamil and another man called Aaron Moore accessed Doreen Jeffries's house, probably knowing she was on holiday, and lifted all her jewellery. We suspect they used a spare key that the woman hid in the garden to get into the house; the key is now missing. We know that, towards the end of last week, Kamil was staying with Terry Haynes. We know that Kamil was also part of a gang, possibly the same one that laid the driveway for Doreen Jeffries, that was stripping copper from the empty bank building in Waterloo Place. He was murdered there, with hammers used by at least two assailants and his body dumped in the bin off Sackville Street. Terry Haynes's car was seen leaving the vicinity of that bin in the middle of the night. Haynes has not been seen since the end of last week.'

'So what're the priorities?' Burns asked.

'Finding Terry Haynes and Aaron Moore, I'd imagine,' Fleming said.

'Doreen's stuff was worth thousands, but Kamil had five quid in his wallet and was staying with someone with a history of providing free accommodation for recovering alcoholics.'

'Was Terry Haynes running the driveway gang?'

'Apparently not,' Fleming said. 'We showed Doreen Jeffries a picture of him. She said she didn't think it was him.'

'Didn't *think*? Is she an older woman?' Burns asked, sceptically.

'She not only recognized Kamil, but she remembered he had an accent,' Lucy said. 'She's not dotty.'

'And you know Terry Haynes, is that right?' Burns asked, nodding to Fleming.

'I think that's common knowledge,' Fleming said.

'So he *could* be running the driveway gang, but you'd prefer not to think that he is.'

Fleming stared at him for a moment. 'I would prefer not to believe that he's involved, yes,' he agreed. 'I also believe that he's not, having shown his picture to the one witness we have who has seen the person running the gang.'

'A witness who happens to be a pensioner, looking at a picture of someone she saw a few weeks ago,' Burns said. 'If you *didn't* know Terry Haynes, would you be convinced he's not involved in this in some way?'

Fleming didn't speak for a moment. Finally, he coughed lightly. 'Probably not,' he said.

'*We'll* take it from here, then,' Burns said with a nod. 'What's the situation with the coffin body?'

Lucy groaned. Again she'd not called at the unit to collect the list from Beaumont. It was such a long shot her heart sank at the prospect of having to work through the list. 'Ciaran Duffy did a runner yesterday, but has lodged a request to empty his bank account at three o'clock this afternoon. A sum of money was deposited earlier in the week, just after the switch of bodies.'

'You'll be keeping an eye on the bank, Tom,' Burns said to Fleming. 'Lucy, the ACC has asked that you accompany me to a meeting with the council this afternoon.'

'Me?' Lucy asked, glancing at Fleming who was clearly smarting from being told to do a bank stake-out.

'Don't ask me,' Burns said. 'We all have to follow orders, whether we like them or not,' he added, looking at Fleming. 'We're meeting some guy Boyd who was responsible for boarding up the buildings around the town, including the bank where Krawiec was killed. ACC Wilson suspects that other buildings may have been targeted for piping and that and wants us to encourage the council to start inspections. See if it throws up any other leads. We've not the men – or women – for it at the moment.'

Lucy nodded. 'I understand,' she said. She also knew that she wasn't there to talk about boarded-up buildings. Her mother was giving her the opportunity to meet John Boyd officially.

'I can't drive,' Fleming muttered angrily. 'I can't stake out the bank if I can't drive.'

'Ask someone in traffic branch to take you down,' Burns said. 'In fact, I'd like a word, Tom,' Burns said.

'I'll see you here at two, Lucy,' he added, dismissing her from the room.

Lucy waited outside the office for Fleming. While she couldn't hear the exact content of the discussion, there was no doubting the acrimonious tone, not least when she discerned Tom Fleming's raised voice tell Burns, 'I don't really care. Suspend me again.'

When he appeared a moment later, he was flustered, his hands balled at his sides, his shoulders hunched.

'Everything OK?' Lucy asked.

'Chief Superintendent Burns has concerns about my respect for his authority.'

'Really?' Lucy asked, struggling not to smile. 'What gave it away?'

Fleming glared at her momentarily, then broke into a smile himself. 'Jumped-up little shit. I have no respect for the rules of line management, apparently.'

'Line management? What an arse!'

'That's what I thought. *What are our priorities?* He's the man in charge, what's he asking us for?'

'Maybe he was being democratic,' Lucy said.

'Democratic? We're the police service for God's sake. Democracy never comes into it.'

He walked down the hallway, out of the incident room, then stopped and waited for Lucy to catch up. The last time things had got on top of Fleming, he'd started drinking again. Lucy was acutely aware that, considering how important Terry Haynes had been in helping him back on his feet then, Haynes's absence now meant a second slip might not be so swiftly reversed.

'You're not thinking of … leaving or anything like that are you?' she asked, as delicately as she could.

'Leaving?' Fleming said incredulously. 'I'm only starting to enjoy my work for the first time in years. Why would I leave?'

Chapter Thirty-three

They returned to Maydown, having stopped on the way to get milk for tea. While Fleming put on the kettle, Lucy went up to her office to check for the fax from Beaumont. She flicked through the various documents lying in the tray – mostly Missing Persons Alerts sent out from other forces – but there was nothing from the hospital. She phoned through and explained the reason for her call. The receptionist with whom she spoke asked her to hold and, a moment later, she was transferred through to a consultant who introduced himself as Niall Horan.

'You're looking for a list of our patients who received cranial implants,' he said. 'There are all kinds of issues with that.'

'I understand,' Lucy said. 'We're investigating what we believe to be a murder. A body was cremated in a coffin intended for someone else. There's no record of who was in the coffin, but we recovered a metal skull plate and leg plate after the cremation process.'

'I see,' Horan said. 'How do you know the victim was treated through us?'

'The skull plate had a batch number. I contacted USS and they said it went to you in October 2007.'

Horan laughed briefly. 'That was lucky. I remember that batch.'

'You remember a specific batch of skull plates? Seriously?' Lucy asked, incredulously.

'Well, not the plates, but the order they were part of. USS had just set up in Dublin. They treated a lot of the neurosurgeons to a conference in San Francisco, with our partners invited along. They took orders for implants from us at the end of a particularly wet dinner.'

'I see,' Lucy said, neutrally.

'That was the only batch I ordered from them. We took a thousand, I believe.'

'So I understand,' Lucy said. 'Which is why I wanted to get the list to start working through it.'

'Look, there are issues with sharing patients' confidential information, especially with a foreign police force,' Horan said. 'What I will do is get one of the girls here to run a computer check and filter the names against leg injuries, too. We'll see how many that leaves us with first. I'll get back to you later.'

He hung up before Lucy had a chance to give him her contact details, necessitating a return call to do so. As she waited to be transferred, her mobile emitted a text alert: *'Hi. Fiona Walsh here. Do you fancy meeting for a coffee later?'*

It took her a few seconds to work out who Fiona was. She wondered whether her looking to meet was connected in some way with Lucy's meeting with Boyd that afternoon, but she thought it unlikely her mother would have told Boyd who Lucy was, or that he could have made the connection between a name and the woman he saw swimming with his partner a few nights earlier.

'Great. Where and when? Working till 6,' she replied.

Within a moment, Fiona replied, suggesting the Everglades, the hotel at the foot of Prehen, at 8.30.

After she'd left her details with Horan's secretary, she went downstairs. Fleming had a mug of tea waiting for her, milk and sugar already added.

'So, you're off to meet some VIP at the behest of your mother?' Fleming said, smiling wryly. 'While I, your superior officer, get to do a stake-out on a bank?'

'My superior officer or line manager?' Lucy asked.

'Both,' Fleming agreed. 'You know, I think that's where I've been going wrong all these years. I've been giving myself the wrong title.'

'Anyone who needs to give themselves a title doesn't deserve it,' Lucy said.

Fleming looked across at her, his mug inches from his mouth. 'That's incredibly philosophical of you, DS Black,' he joked. 'So who's Boyd?'

'John Boyd,' Lucy explained. 'His partner's sister is a neighbour of mine. The partner arrived at their house the other night, out of the blue, with a split lip. Since she started dating Boyd, the family has barely seen her. We went swimming the night before last and Boyd was sitting by the pool, watching.'

'So, controlling or abusive?'

'Both, I think,' Lucy said. 'She had bruises on her chest which looked like fingermarks, like he'd grabbed her breast too hard.'

'It couldn't have been accidental? A bit of horseplay during sex?'

'Not unless that included punching her in the mouth, too,' Lucy said sharply.

Fleming raised his free hand. 'I'm playing devil's advocate,' he said. 'You know that's what he'll claim. Is the partner prepared to make a statement?'

Lucy shook her head. 'Not yet. Though she texted me to ask to meet for coffee later. She thinks he's trying to control her from one side and her family is from the other. She sees me as a neutral space, I think.'

'Neutral?' Fleming asked, sceptically.

'She doesn't know I'm a cop,' Lucy admitted.

'Really! Well, good luck with that,' he said. 'Of course, if she finds out, and thinks you lied to her, she'll not trust anyone again.'

Chapter Thirty-four

Burns insisted on driving to the council meeting, despite the fact that the offices were only a few hundred yards down the road from the Strand Road police station. The council building, a large, grey affair, backed onto the river, having managed to snag one of the most picturesque spots along the water's edge, providing a vista across the Foyle to the dark mass of greenery that demarcated the boundary of St Columb's Park.

As he pulled into the council car park, waiting for the barrier to rise, he looked across at Lucy.

'How do you find working with Tom Fleming?' he asked. 'Everything OK?'

'Great,' Lucy said. 'He's an excellent superior officer,' she added, stopping herself from using the other sobriquet they had latterly discussed.

'How would you feel about a transfer into CID?' Burns said, suddenly. 'We need good people, people who can think on their feet.'

'I started in CID,' Lucy said. 'The ACC moved me.'

Burns nodded, suggesting that this was not news to him. 'That's not a problem. I'm sure I can persuade her around fairly easily. Put it this way, I wouldn't be mentioning it if she hadn't already indicated she'd be supportive of the move if you wanted it.'

'Thank you, sir,' Lucy said. 'I'll certainly consider it.'

Burns glanced across again, as if teasing out the implications of her response. 'Your opportunities for movement in PPU are limited,' he said. 'And I'd imagine working abuse and domestic cases every day would do your head in after a while.'

Lucy laughed uncomfortably. 'That's true,' she said, feeling a peculiar disloyalty to Tom Fleming and thus keen to change the subject. 'Has the ACC given any indication why she wants me *here* today?'

'I'm guessing to give us a chance to have this little chat,' Burns said, smiling. 'Shall we go?'

They stood in the foyer of the council buildings for a few moments before Boyd appeared on the staircase. He wore a black suit with a wide pinstripe over a light-pink shirt and no tie. As he approached he ran his hand through his hair, then extended it in greeting.

'Chief Superintendent,' he said, addressing Burns first. 'Good to see you.'

'Please, call me Mark,' Burns replied.

'John,' Boyd agreed. He turned to Lucy, hand extended, maintaining eye contact. Lucy watched him for any flicker of recognition from the swimming pool, but none was obvious. 'John Boyd,' he said.

'DS Black,' Lucy said, deliberately.

'Tea? Coffee?' Burns asked. 'A pot of each maybe?' He addressed this to the girl sitting behind the reception desk. 'Would you send some up, Linda?' he asked, then turned to Burns without waiting for a response.

They moved up the stairs, Boyd walking with Burns, speaking to him, while Lucy followed behind. Occasionally he would glance back, as if to include her in the conversation.

'It's been a wonderful few weeks' weather, eh?' Boyd asked. 'Though it's to break this afternoon, apparently.'

The river, visible through the windows beyond, already carried a dull grey sheen reflected from the cloud-heavy sky above.

'It'll do no harm. Clear the air,' Burns agreed.

Boyd's office was set to the rear of the building, giving him a view over the river in both directions, to the twisting Peace Bridge to the left and further north, in the other direction, the high arch of the Foyle Bridge.

'Sensational view, isn't it?' he said, taking off his jacket and hanging it over the back of his chair. 'So, what can I do?'

'We wanted to have a word about the buildings with the false fronts on them in the city centre. Particularly the old bank building in Waterloo Place.'

'Right,' Boyd said, a little uncertainly.

'We believe you're responsible for them. Is that right?' Lucy asked, causing both men to look in her direction.

'I wouldn't say that entirely,' Boyd said. 'The Department of the Environment put them up. I led the taskforce that recommended it be done and identified the buildings most in need of being cleaned up. We applied to the DOE and they had the work carried out. Why? Is this about the killing in the old bank building?'

'Tangentially,' Burns said. 'When we uncovered the site, we discovered evidence of what we believe to be copper theft inside the building.'

'Right,' Boyd repeated.

'We believe, in fact, that the man who was killed was a member of the gang that was cleaning out the inside of the building.'

'I see,' Boyd said. 'What was it? A disagreement among thieves kind of thing?'

'Kind of,' Burns said. 'The thing is, if they targeted the bank building, we have to work on the assumption that they may have been stealing from some of the other buildings which have been boarded up in town, too.'

'Of course,' Boyd said. 'Do you need a list of them?'

'We actually need a little help,' Burns said, with some embarrassment. 'All this rioting business in Belfast has us stretched to snapping point in terms of manpower. We've no spare hands. Would there be any chance you might have a team who could do a quick check on the sites to see if any more of them were targeted?'

Boyd pantomimed a wince. 'You've no men; we've no budget,' he said. 'We contract out all the work like that.'

'I see,' Burns said. 'Is there no way that the contract company could check?'

Boyd took a moment, then inclined his head, as if he had considered an alternative approach.

'Look, I've very little authority in these things,' he said. 'But I am authorized to process payments to the one contract company who handles minor repairs for us: a crowd from Lisburn called Dynamic.

Anything under £5,000 doesn't need an individual tender, you see. I could process a small payment to them to do a very quick check in each place.'

'That would be great,' Burns said.

'Do you not need to clear it with someone?' Lucy asked. 'Someone with more authority?' she added.

'Well, my boss countersigns the cheques,' Boyd said. 'But I'm sure it will be fine; we process payments to them all the time. We've an audit going on at the moment, and I'm going to be in working all weekend, by the looks of things, so I'll get it actioned as quickly as I can.'

By the time tea and coffee arrived, they were ready to leave, so it remained untouched. The first fat drops of rain had splattered against the plate glass window of Boyd's office some minutes earlier. He and Burns shook hands on the stairs. As Boyd turned to offer Lucy his hand, she struggled to overcome her aversion to touching the man again. This same hand, she reflected, had left bruises on Fiona's body, had split her lip. The manner in which he had underplayed his authority, his deliberate self-deprecation, served only to make her dislike him even more.

'He's a nice chap,' Burns said, after they had handed in their visitors' badges. Lucy managed a non-committal grunt.

As they stepped outside, they could feel the drop in temperature, the chill of the rising wind on their faces after the heat of indoors. The air smelt of electricity, a scent which brought unbidden to Lucy's mind the smell of fairground rides and thoughts of her father. The raindrops fell heavy and felt warm to the touch.

'There's something nice about the rain,' Lucy commented.

Burns looked at her quizzically, then fumbled in his pocket as his phone began vibrating. He answered it with a simple 'Yes?'

He regarded Lucy as he listened. 'We'll be there in a few minutes,' he said. He hung up. 'They've found Terry Haynes's car. It's on fire on Sheriff's Mountain.'

Chapter Thirty-five

It took closer to three quarters of an hour to get to the mountain, which overlooked the city to the west. The sudden deluge, on top of long dried roads, had left the journey treacherous and one fender bender had blocked the Northland Road for twenty minutes until they'd managed to get the two cars manoeuvred down the side road of Clarence Hill.

Sheriff's Mountain was the site of the city's television transmitter mast, which towered above them now, where they parked, its upper tip piercing the side of low-hanging cloud. The rain had settled into a rhythmic tattoo on the roof and bonnet of the car, which Burns mimicked with his fingers on the knob of the gear stick as they waited for the heavier shower to pass. A number of other squad cars were parked haphazardly, their occupants waiting out the rain in cars whose windows were thick with condensation.

This latter detail, Burns pointed out to Lucy, before adding, 'It's like a dogging convention out there.' He laughed at his own comment, then added quickly, 'Not that I'd know what one looks like.'

'Of course not, sir,' Lucy said. 'The rain's easing,' she remarked.

The site of the car had already been marked out by the first team on the scene, one of whom stood now at the tape, signing through those who were passing. His hair was slick to his skull, his face washed with drips of rainwater falling from the peak of his cap.

'No fire brigade?' Burns asked, as the man signed him in without seeking identification.

'They're on their way. There's no need for them. The rain had put it out for us,' the officer replied. 'It was already dead by the time we got here.'

The car, a silver Toyota Avensis, sat parked on a thin dirt path, which appeared more obviously used by walkers than drivers, the central line running down it high with grass, along which, on either side, streams of rainwater ran. Burns and Lucy stood a few feet back from it so as not to touch anything.

With the exception of scorching around the window frames, and the shattered windscreen, the body of the car was fairly clean, considering someone had tried to burn it. The inside was a different matter. The seats had burned through, the blackened springs beneath the cushioning now visible. The interior moulding above the steering wheel had warped with the heat and melted through in places.

'No body in it,' Burns said. 'So Haynes is still in the wind.'

The sight of the Chief Super standing at the car had forced the other officers parked below to get out of their own vehicles and start working the scene, despite the fact that the wind had risen again and, with it, the rain.

Three forensics officers appeared, in the white suits of their trade, carrying between them the light, expandable cover, which they would set up over the car to shield both it and themselves from the elements.

'Good of you to join us,' Burns called.

'We took a quick recce when we arrived, sir,' one commented. 'The car is clean, inside and out. Literally, cleaned.'

'As in valeted?'

'As in valeted,' the man agreed. 'Before it was set alight. The wind and rain got so heavy the tent couldn't be put up. We had to wait for it to ease.'

Burns stepped back, his hands in his pockets, to give the men space to work. Lucy felt her mobile vibrate in her pocket and, pulling it out, saw Fleming's name.

'Tom?' Lucy asked quickly, assuming he'd spotted Ciaran Duffy.

'How'd your meeting go?' Fleming asked.

'Fine. Have you got Duffy?' she asked, glancing at her watch. It was pushing 3.30, half an hour after he was to collect his money.

'Neither hide nor hair of him,' Fleming said. 'I'm bored out of my mind sitting here. I'm an Inspector for God's sake!' he snapped. 'Where are you?'

Lucy swallowed. 'I'm up on Sheriff's Mountain. Burns got a call that Haynes's car had been found. Someone tried to set it alight, but the rain put it out.'

Fleming did not speak for a moment and Lucy assumed he was angry at having been left watching the bank while other teams had been called to the site. She knew too that it was deliberate; Burns had

194

taken the case from PPU. She was only there by accident. Or because Burns wanted her in CID.

When he spoke, though, she realized that his concern was of a different kind.

'Is Terry in the car?' he asked.

'No one is. It was valeted before whoever torched it did so.'

'Sir!'

Lucy glanced up to where one of the forensics officers, having just opened the boot of the car, was standing calling to Burns.

'I'll call you right back,' Lucy said, hanging up before Fleming could speak. She followed Burns up the final few feet of the incline.

'Oh Jesus,' she heard him mutter. Looking into the boot, she understood why. A body had been forced into the rear of the vehicle, curled foetally, the arms raised protectively over the face and head. It was a futile gesture for the five-inch impact wound to the skull was visible even from where Lucy stood.

'Get some pictures,' Burns said. 'Is it Haynes?'

The officer shrugged.

'DS Black. You know him. Is that Haynes?'

Lucy approached the rear of the vehicle, stepping on the metal plates the forensics officers had set out around the car to preserve the scene. Leaning in, she angled her head, trying to focus on the face rather than the wound to the back of the skull. The fact that the body was slim and carried a full head of hair made it unlikely to be Haynes, but she wanted to see the face to be sure. Fleming would want to know for certain that it wasn't his friend.

The forensics officer lifted the arm of the body away from the head, cautiously, allowing Lucy just enough time to see the face clearly.

Lucy felt her stomach lurch as she recognized the face. She stepped back. 'That's not Terry Haynes. It's Ciaran Duffy.'

Chapter Thirty-six

'A hatchet, apparently,' Tony Clarke announced to those assembled in the incident room in Strand Road, an hour later. The pathologist, Martin Kerrigan, had been called to the site at Sheriff's Mountain and, while still working on the body there, had suggested a hatchet to be the most likely implement responsible for the blow to Duffy's head.

'A hatchet?' Burns repeated. 'Who the hell kills with a hatchet?'

'Whoever killed the cremated body in our coffin,' Fleming said. 'Kerrigan figured the nick on the metal skull plate may have been made by a hatchet too. Again to the head, obviously.'

'Where are you on that?' Burns asked.

'No further,' Fleming said. 'DS Black was with you all day and I was staking out a bank waiting for Ciaran Duffy to appear. As you told me to.'

Lucy was aware that all eyes in the room had turned towards her, not least Tara's. All eyes but one, she realized. Her mother stared fixedly at Burns in a way that suggested she had not been as fully aware of the afternoon's division of labour as Burns had claimed.

'Beaumont are filtering the patient list for us,' Lucy said. 'We know the victim had both skull and leg injuries. They're trying to match both as a starting point. There are a thousand patients to go through otherwise, and we've not the bodies to work through a list that length.'

'There can't be many with both skull and leg injuries,' Burns conceded.

'They might not have been suffered at the same time,' Tara said, suddenly. 'Filtering like that might miss someone out.'

'See what it brings up. Chase them again,' Burns said. 'What was the story with Ciaran Duffy?'

'We believe he was responsible for the body swap,' Fleming said. 'He deposited five grand in his account a few days ago, so our assumption is that he was paid to get rid of whoever was actually in the coffin.'

'Why would someone go to that effort?' Mickey asked. 'Why not just dump the body? Or burn it, like Duffy himself, in a car?'

'Whoever tried to burn Duffy knew we were onto him by this stage; there was no need to hide his death. We have to assume, on the other hand, that whoever was put in the coffin and cremated was someone they *didn't* want us to know about.'

'Duffy was found in Terry Haynes's car, the same car used to dump Krawiec's body, Krawiec was last known to be in the company of Aaron Moore, whose prints you found at a house burglary along with Krawiec's,' Wilson said. 'Have I got all this so far?'

'So far, ma'am,' Burns said, smiling.

'So, what about Terry Haynes? Are you any closer to locating him?' Wilson asked, directed this time to Burns.

'Nothing yet, ma'am,' he conceded.

'And Aaron Moore?'

'We called at his flat, but there was no one home. We spoke to some of the neighbours, but no one has seen him for the past few weeks,' Tara said.

'His flat? He's not homeless then?'

'He may as well be,' Mickey answered, then added a differential, 'ma'am.' 'The flat looked deserted. Piles of newspapers everywhere, everything in bags.'

'You searched it without a warrant?'

'We looked in the window,' Tara said, quickly. 'One of the neighbours said he's a hoarder; holds on to everything. They complained to him a few times about the smell, said they think he doesn't even dump his rubbish.'

'Why did we have him on the system?' Fleming asked.

'Shoplifting,' Burns said. 'He was caught stealing soap of all things from a local chemist's.'

'Soap?' Fleming repeated over the laughter rippling through the room.

'Fifteen bars of soap,' Burns replied, not containing his own amusement now.

'He didn't manage a clean get away then,' Mickey said. The ripple grew now, with even Wilson cracking a brief brittle smile.

'Tom, you and Lucy keep up the pressure on the coffin body,' Burns said. 'Aaron Moore is our focus. Tara, you stay on that. Mickey, you and Ian are to follow up on Ciaran Duffy's movements. Report back on the PM when it's done.'

'People,' Wilson said, calling the room to attention. 'I know we're all stretched at the moment. Unfortunately, events in Belfast are beyond our control and until someone starts to exert some form of political leadership, I don't believe we'll see much of an improvement on the ground. Use your time wisely. We do still have uniform support available when it's needed, so maybe Inspectors shouldn't be staking out banks, eh?'

She smiled as she nodded at Tom Fleming who returned both. From his expression, though, it was clear that the intended recipient of her rebuke, standing just to her left, had got the message.

Chapter Thirty-seven

'So, how was your afternoon with the Chief Super?' Fleming asked as he strapped himself into the car.

'Wonderful,' Lucy said. 'He's a bundle of laughs. Caring and understanding.'

'Just what you need,' Fleming said.

'He seems to think so. He mentioned my applying to CID,' she added, not looking across at her boss.

'Did he indeed? And what are your thoughts?'

'Are you kidding?' Lucy asked. 'What was your comment? I'm only beginning to enjoy my work. Why would I leave?'

Fleming smiled. 'I'm glad to hear it,' he said. 'How was Boyd?'

'Plausible,' Lucy said. 'Friendly, welcoming. Playing down his importance in things.'

'What was your sense of him?'

Lucy shook her head. 'I went in there looking to not like him,' she confided. 'I didn't come out persuaded I was wrong. Fiona has asked to meet me later, so it'll be interesting to hear what she has to say about things.'

Fleming stared out the side window, tracing the progress of a raindrop along the glass with the tip of his finger.

'So, Aaron Moore?' Lucy said. 'We know he was with Kamil but how did they connect?'

Fleming shook his head. 'I was just thinking the same thing. What have they got in common?'

'Moore's not a street drinker, or homeless,' Lucy said. 'But, if he actually is a compulsive hoarder, like the neighbours claim ... maybe they met through the Community Mental Health team?'

Fleming nodded. 'Try the team. See if they had dealings with Moore at any stage. If he is compulsive hoarding, he may have been referred on to them, OCD or some such. Check Krawiec as well.'

Lucy glanced at the clock on the dash. It was already past six. 'They'll be closed now. I'll try Noleen Fagan in the morning.'

Fagan was the unit psychiatrist with the Community Mental Health team. If Moore had been referred to the team, she would have assessed him at some stage. While the unit would be closed, Lucy knew that Fagan ran emergency clinics on Saturday mornings.

Fleming nodded softly. 'Their paths crossed somewhere.'

Fleming waited in the car while she ran into the PPU block. The time it took her to cover the distance from her parked car to the door, extended by her having to enter the key code at the door, meant that, when she finally made it inside, her face was slick with rainwater.

She went up to her office and turned on all the lights to dispel the still greyness that had gathered in the room.

A ream of sheets sat in the tray of the printer. Flicking through them, she found the list faxed from Beaumont. Despite having filtered down the names, there were still twenty pages, which consisted simply of lists of patients, the dates of their treatment and their dates of birth. She realized that the names were listed, not alphabetically, but by date of treatment.

She stuffed the pages into her bag, took a last glance across at the picture of Mary Quigg, pinned to her noticeboard, and flicked off the lights.

Chapter Thirty-eight

Lucy got home, changed and showered. She'd planned to walk down to the Everglades, the two sharp inclines which she would have to climb on the way home sufficient exercise for the day, but the rain still pounded outside, the sky blooming with lightning occasionally, the boom of thunder reverberating along the Foyle valley in the wake of each flash so, in the end, she drove down.

Fiona was already sitting in the foyer, waiting for her, when she got there, despite Lucy being ten minutes early. She smiled nervously when she saw Lucy, her shoulders hunched a little, her hands worrying at the handle of the umbrella she held.

'Hey,' Lucy offered. 'Are you here long?'

Fiona glanced at her watch absently, though so quickly the time could hardly have registered. 'A while,' she said. 'John goes to the gym at seven so I had to leave before he got home.'

The silence was punctured by the urgent beeping of a phone. 'That'll be him now,' she continued, blushing. She pulled the phone from her pocket and held it up to show Lucy the image on the screen. Lucy reached, took the phone from her and turned it off.

'We should all be non-contactable sometimes,' she said. 'Tell him you went over to Donegal for a run and lost network.'

Fiona smiled briefly, the smile dying just as quickly on her lips.

'Let's eat,' Lucy said. 'I'm starving.'

They were finishing the curries they had ordered when Fiona finally broached the subject.

'How did you know?' she said. 'The other night? The bruises. How did you know?'

If there was going to be an opportunity to tell her the truth about her job, this was it. But Lucy suspected that, having built the courage to contact someone, to talk, learning that she was a police officer would scare Fiona away before she'd even begun to speak.

'It's not the first time I've seen those type of injuries,' she said.

'Right. In the gym and that,' Fiona explained. 'I forgot.'

'Not just that,' Lucy said. 'I've come across people in abusive relationships before. They always hide the injuries. And the abusers always injure in places where it's easy to hide.'

'John's not abusive,' Fiona said quickly.

'He bust your lip,' Lucy said.

'It was an accident. He's under pressure in his work.'

Lucy reflected on the man she had met that afternoon. He did not give the impression of someone under pressure in his job. Quite the reverse, in fact.

'They're doing some sort of audit of the whole department. He handles a lot of the money so they're going through his stuff with a fine-tooth comb. There'll be no mistakes, I told him that. He's so careful, so good with money. He handles it all for us.'

'All?'

Fiona nodded. 'I was a bit useless with my money, he said, so he looks after my account for me.'

Lucy raised an eyebrow. 'What if you need money?'

Fiona blushed. 'There's never a problem.'

'Do you ask him for your own money?'

'He's looking out for us both,' Fiona said, defensively. 'What about you? Doesn't your partner look out for you?'

'Not in that way,' Lucy said, stopping herself from saying she didn't need looking after, lest it appear implicitly judgemental. 'Something happened a while back that changed things.'

'What?'

'He was injured while he was working on my car. I feel guilty about it. He's suggested we move in together but ... I'm not sure that I'm ready to do that quite yet. I need to be certain I'd be doing it for the right reasons, not just out of a sense of guilt and obligation.'

'Is that why you're staying with him?'

Lucy shrugged. 'It's too strong a feeling at the minute for me to be able to work out what else is in there now, you know?'

Fiona nodded. 'I rely on John so much; I couldn't leave him. I'd not be able to manage.'

'Bollocks,' Lucy blurted suddenly, causing the elderly couple at the table next to them to glance across.

'I do,' Fiona protested. 'When we started going out it was … he was so attentive. So focused on me. Wanting to be with me all the time. He hated sharing me with anyone, even family. It was … it was intoxicating. Someone loving you that much that they couldn't be apart from you.'

'That's understandable,' Lucy said. 'At the start. But you need to have your own life. Your own identity.'

Fiona stared at her, her mouth working, trying to form the words to adequately express the situation in which she had now found herself.

'I didn't see it changing. I got so used to it, so used to being the centre of someone's life. I never noticed it getting suffocating. He used to be hurt when I visited someone without him, like it meant he wasn't important to me any more. I was *so* important to him, he said, why would *I* need other people? Now he gets angry instead of offended. He seems to be angry all the time.'

Lucy nodded. 'So, how do you deal with that?'

'I do what I know will keep him happy.' Fiona raised her chin slightly, staring at the wall beyond Lucy, as if considering what she had just said. 'Did you ever … do you ever feel like you're watching yourself just … disappear?' She looked directly at Lucy to gauge her response, then lowered her head again. 'I feel like such a coward. Such a weakling, like Jenny says.'

'You're not a weakling,' Lucy said. 'You have to stop letting other people define you.'

'You see?' Fiona said, laughing helplessly.

'That's not what I'm saying. You've been conditioned through years of control into believing what people say about you, because it's being said by someone you love. But just because you love someone doesn't mean that they're right about everything. I think you're being braver than you give yourself credit for.'

Fiona snorted derisively. 'Yeah, right!'

'You came here tonight,' Lucy said. 'You admitted some things to a stranger that I'd have difficulty admitting.'

Fiona lowered her head, studying the beer mat that she was tearing into pieces between her hands.

'It's easier than telling someone who knows me!' Fiona smiled, sheepishly.

'And you've left your phone turned off since you arrived.'

She looked up suddenly. 'Oh, Jesus, I forgot,' she said, fumbling with the phone.

Lucy reached across, laying her hand on top of Fiona's. 'And that was the right thing to do. The Donegal excuse will be good for at least another hour.'

Fiona regarded the phone in her hand moment-arily, as if physically weighing up the consequences of her action, then pocketed it again without switching it on.

'Feels good, doesn't it?' Lucy asked.

She nodded uncertainly in response. 'He'll go mental when I get home.'

'If he does, turn and walk straight back out again. Jenny will be happy to put you up for the night. Or I will, if you're stuck. Would you speak to the police? Or a counsellor?'

'God, no! I couldn't face all … that. Besides, I can't afford to leave him; I've no money,' Fiona said.

She flushed suddenly as she saw Lucy reach for her purse. 'No, not like that. I mean in general. If I did want to leave. He has my bank card and everything.'

'No one will see you stuck if you do,' Lucy said. 'But it needs to be *your* decision,' she added. 'Don't do it because you think other people want you to.' Lucy had seen too many times, women, and men, encouraged into leaving abusive partners by their families who, at the first moment of missing their former partner, blamed those same families for forcing the decision on them, for being more controlling than the abuser whom they had left. Oftentimes, they ended running back into those same waiting, abusive arms. If Fiona was going to leave John Boyd, and stay away from him, the decision needed to be her own.

'Text me and let me know how you are,' Lucy said, as they parted company under the canopy of the porch. 'And don't be afraid. Lift the phone if he does anything. I'll come and get you.'

Fiona nodded, then reached suddenly and kissed Lucy lightly on the cheek. 'Thanks for listening,' she said. 'And for not judging.'

Lucy smiled, gripped the woman's hand once encouragingly, then watched as she turned and stepped out into the unrelenting rain and ran to her car.

Chapter Thirty-nine

The brief text arrived an hour later: *'All OK.'*

The thudding of the rain increased through the remainder of the evening, the windows shuddering in the frames, both with the thick buffeting of the wind and the occasional reverberations of thunder.

Lucy went to bed early, then slept fitfully, waking before 1 a.m. The thin material of the curtains did little to hide the regular flashes of lightning. The rain had increased, both in tempo and ferocity. She had been thinking about Robbie's proposition. Since her father had been committed to Gransha, his house, *this* house, had not changed. It was almost as if she had been holding her breath, waiting for him to come back. But she knew, even before the conversation with her mother, that her father would never be coming back and that she felt she had reached a liminal point. Either she had to make this house her own, or else leave it and, perhaps, move in with Robbie. Yet the thought of the latter made her feel like she could not quite breathe.

She thought of all the others she'd recently encountered who lived alone: Terry Haynes opening his doors first to Tom Fleming and, more recently, Kamil Krawiec; Doreen Jeffries welcoming Helen

Dexter into her home. Lucy could not decide whether their reasons had been altruistic or an attempt to avoid the loneliness of single living. Or, in Haynes's case, something more sinister still.

Unbidden too, she thought of the girl, Grace. The bank building in Waterloo Place had been sealed off as a crime scene, meaning she would not be able to shelter from the storm in there. She might have nowhere else to go.

She reached across the bedside cabinet, feeling her way to her phone, then picked it up and dialled.

It rang four times before it was answered.

'Who is this?' the girl asked, without preamble.

'Grace? It's Lucy Black. DS Black. Where are you?'

'What do you want?' the girl asked.

There was another flash of lightning outside, followed almost instantaneously by a peal of thunder, which Lucy heard echoed in the girl's phone a second later.

'Are you outside in that?' Lucy asked.

'Why?'

'You'll get soaked.'

'I already am soaked. What do you want? Is it about the money?'

'You'll get more— What money?'

'I took from your boss. The guy waiting outside the bank.'

Lucy remembered now that the girl had taken payment for the tip-off about the scene of Krawiec's killing from both her and Tom Fleming. 'No. It's not about the money. I was worried about you.'

'Why?'

'Because you're a teenager sleeping outside in a thunderstorm,' Lucy snapped. 'Where are you? I'll come and get you.'

'The railway,' she muttered, then hung up.

Lucy guessed that she meant the railway museum, beneath the bridge, rather than the city's proper railway station. When she arrived and sprinted round onto the platform at the back, holding on to the edge of her umbrella to stop the wind pulling it inside out, the girl was waiting for her.

She was sitting alone, her back against the metal shutters of the rear doors. The rest of the platform was deserted. The overhanging roof provided little shelter, the direction of the wind running down the river valley carrying the rain in beneath its cover.

Lucy looked at the girl, sitting on the ground, her face slick with rainwater, her hair hanging in strangled curls over her face. Lightning flashed overhead and, in its momentary light, Lucy noticed a darkening below the girl's eye.

'Are you coming?' Lucy said. 'I'm getting soaked.'

The bruise blushed her left cheek, its lower edge ending in a small cut which had started to scab over.

'What happened to you?' Lucy asked, turning off the light in the car again following the girl's protests at Lucy's examination of her face.

'Someone smacked me,' she said.

'Who?'

'A customer.'

'A *customer*?'

212

'He haggled on the price and I made up the shortfall by lifting his wallet. He realized and came after me.'

'He punched you?' Lucy asked, keeping her voice even.

'It happens,' Grace said, dismissively.

'What did he look like?'

'Balding. Middle-aged. Just the usual.'

'Do you know his name?'

'I don't ask if they don't tell. I don't really want to know anyway. As if it matters what they're called.' She sat in silence for a moment, then added, quietly, 'They'd probably just lie about it anyway.'

Lucy turned up the heat a little, causing the windows to mist, then immediately changed the airflow back to cold.

'So, where are you putting me? I'm not an alcoholic, so none of those places will take me.'

'There must be someone you can stay with?'

The girl considered the statement. 'Put it like this,' she decided, 'I've shat in too many nests.'

'Really? You shock me,' Lucy said, earning a smile of pride from the girl. 'That's not a good thing, by the way. Shitting in nests.'

Grace raised her head a little, as if balancing something on her chin, then turned and looked out the window. 'So, where *are* we going?'

'You can kip over at mine till the rain passes,' Lucy said.

Grace stood in the living room, surveying the furniture. She moved across to the TV, an old analogue set, to which Lucy had attached a Freeview receiver.

'No offence, but your house looks like it was decorated by an old man,' she said finally.

'It was. It's my father's house,' Lucy explained. 'I've not had much time to change it.'

'When did he die?'

'He's not dead. He's in a home. He has Alzheimer's.'

'Near enough then,' Grace said, plumping down on one of the armchairs. 'So, what's the deal?'

Lucy raised her eyebrows interrogatively.

'What do you want me to do?' Grace continued, pulling off her coat.

'Nothing,' Lucy said. 'You're welcome to stay for the night. Get a shower if you need one. Get out of the rain. Eat in the morning.'

'Are you a lezzie?' Grace asked. 'I don't mind,' she added. 'I've done it before.'

'Jesus,' Lucy muttered. 'It's pissing down outside, you're a kid sleeping rough. You can stay the night. I don't want anything in return.'

'Yeah, right,' Grace said. 'Nobody doesn't want nothing.'

Lucy tried to unravel the logic among the multiple negatives. '*I* want nothing,' she said. 'There are a few ground rules. No stealing, no drugs, no drinking.'

'I'm not a junkie,' Grace protested.

'I never said you were. I told you the rules of the house. I'll get you some towels and a change of clothes.'

She padded downstairs half an hour later, wearing Lucy's pyjama bottoms and a T-shirt. The bottoms were too long for her, Lucy standing a few inches taller, and she'd rolled up the legs. She rubbed at her hair with the towel, scrunching it in her hand to encourage it to curl.

'Do you want tea?' Lucy asked.

The girl nodded. 'I'll make it,' she said. 'Where's all your stuff?'

They moved into the kitchen, Lucy laying the cups, tea bags, sugar and milk out on the counter while Grace filled the kettle. 'Milk, one sugar,' Lucy said, standing back, allowing the girl the gesture of contributing.

In the light of the kitchen, she could better see the bruising on her face.

'That looks sore,' she observed. 'You sure you don't know who did it?'

'Why?' Grace said.

'Men don't hit women.'

Grace pantomimed an expression of stupidity. 'Duh! Yes, they do,' she said, indicating her own face with her upraised hand.

'Not when I can help it,' Lucy said. 'Who was it?'

'What're you going to do? I won't press charges. I'll be done as a prossie.'

'There are ways around everything,' Lucy said. 'Your name won't come into it.'

The girl held her stare a moment, then turned and padded into the living room. She returned with her phone. She held it out to Lucy. The picture on the screen was of a black Audi, its registration plate just visible.

'That's his car,' Grace said. 'I take pictures of the cars when they approach me. In case anything happens to me.'

'Who do you send them to?' Lucy asked, making a mental note of the registration number.

Grace looked at her quizzically. 'No one.'

'What good will that do? If you're the only one with the picture of the car.'

'If I die. If they do something to me, your lot will find the phone with the car pictured on it.'

'And no idea what it means,' Lucy said. 'And you'd be dead. Fat lot of use that would be.'

'At least the bastard wouldn't get away with it. If you did your job properly, like.'

Lucy sighed, as the girl flipped the phone in her hand, weighing its heft. 'I thought it was pretty smart,' she said.

Saturday, 21 July

Chapter Forty

At first, Lucy had begun to doubt the wisdom of letting the girl stay. She lay awake in bed, listening both to the storm assail the trees bordering the back garden, and for sounds of Grace moving around the house. Lucy had made sure her purse and phone were locked in the cabinet next to her bed.

Despite this, she must have drifted off at some point, for when the girl's shouting woke her, it was 6 a.m. She was out of bed before she even realized she was up and moved quickly into the girl's room, not sure what to expect. In the half-light of the room, dawn light already spilling around the edges of the curtains, she could see that, though the girl was still asleep, her face was wet with tears, her arms flaying as she screamed. Lucy considered wakening her, trying to reason with her, and moved across, motioning to touch her. In the end, though, she moved back and closed the door quietly, leaving the girl to face alone whatever raged in her dreams.

'Did you have a nightmare?' Lucy asked her two hours later, as they drank tea and ate toast in the living room, the television playing quietly in the background. 'You were screaming in your sleep.'

Grace shrugged as she tore the crust off her bread and laid it on the plate resting on the chair arm. 'I don't remember,' she said. 'Did I wake you?'

Lucy shook her head.

'I must have for you to know I was screaming.'

'I thought you were being attacked or something,' Lucy said. 'It was fine.'

The girl chewed open-mouthed. 'So, what are you doing today?' she asked.

Lucy took the hint. 'Looking for someone. A friend of Kamil's: Aaron Moore?'

Grace shook her head. 'Never heard of him,' she said. 'Is he a drinker?'

'I don't think so,' Lucy said. 'He's ... possibly vulnerable.'

'Aren't we all?' Grace observed. 'What's he done?'

'He was involved in something with Kamil. We were hoping he might know what happened to him.'

Grace shrugged, lifted the remote and flicked the channel. 'They might have met at the soup kitchen,' Grace said. 'I know Kamil went there to try it.'

'The Christian one?' Lucy said. Tom Fleming was involved with a soup kitchen which operated at night in the city, as much for youths too intoxicated to find their way home as for the city's destitute.

Grace shook her head. 'There's a different one. It started a few months back, running out of Great James Street. Sammy told me about it. He uses it, too.'

'I've not heard of it,' Lucy said. 'I'll ask Fleming.'

'Is he your boss?' Grace asked.

Lucy nodded.

'He's a God botherer, isn't he?'

'He's a decent person,' Lucy said. 'A good man.'

'He's in a minority, then,' the girl concluded.

Lucy dropped the girl off at the Waterside end of the Craigavon Bridge, as she asked. As she opened the car door, she looked back at Lucy. 'All right,' she offered, by way of thanks.

She got out and waved briefly. As Lucy drove away, she glanced in the rear-view mirror at the girl, standing on the kerb side, as if unsure where to go next.

Lucy called through to the Strand Road and asked the desk sergeant there to trace the registration number of the car that Grace had photographed; a moment later he informed her that it was registered to a Mrs Bernadette Thompson, with an address in Eglinton. She was just jotting down the details and Thompson's phone number, the pages from Beaumont in her bag the only handy source of paper, when her mobile beeped, showing an incoming call. It was Tom Fleming.

Lucy ended the first call and answered Fleming's. 'I'm on my way in,' Lucy said, assuming he was wondering where she was.

'Just to remind you to go to the Emergency Mental Health clinic,' Fleming asked. 'CID have been at Aaron Moore's house in Pump Street several times now and are still getting no answer. Noleen Fagan might be able to help.'

The Community Mental Health team was based in Rossdowney House in the Waterside. Lucy knew the psychiatrist there, Noleen Fagan. Fagan had once worked with a number of the teenagers in the

221

residential unit until changes to the system meant that they were assigned to the children's unit. As a consequence, Lucy didn't see Noleen quite as often as once she had.

It was a surprise then, to see that her once long brown hair was now cropped, with patches of skin visible through the thinning.

'Lucy,' Fagan said, standing. 'How are you?'

Lucy smiled. 'Noleen,' she said. 'Good to see you. You look good.'

'I look a mess,' the woman replied, lightly waving away Lucy's comment. 'I developed alopecia a while back. Stress related apparently.'

'I'm sorry to hear that,' Lucy offered, sitting.

'No massive surprise, working here,' Fagan said, sitting herself. 'And how are you? Still at PPU?'

'For now,' Lucy said.

'You're thinking of changing?'

Lucy shook her head. 'Not unless they force me to,' she said. 'It's beyond my control.'

'So, what can I do for you?'

'I'm trying to get some background on someone you might know: Aaron Moore?'

Fagan nodded. 'I know Aaron. What about him?'

'We think he knew the guy who was found dead in the bin a few days back. We're looking for him in connection with a robbery. '

'Aaron Moore?' Fagan asked incredulously.

'You seem surprised.'

'I am; Aaron doesn't strike me as a thief.'

'We found his prints at the scene of a burglary.'

Noleen shrugged. 'Fair enough. You should try his brother.'

222

Lucy raised an eyebrow.

'Moore and Co., Solicitors.'

'*Seamus* Moore?' Lucy repeated.

'Yes, indeed.'

Seamus Moore ran one of the biggest law firms in the city taking up a sizeable block of Clarendon Street. Lucy had met him only once, following a case in which he'd defended a youth who'd been arrested leaving the scene of a robbery, carrying items stolen from the property. Moore had claimed the youth had found the items on the street and was returning them to the burgled home. He won the case.

'Is Aaron Moore not essentially homeless?' Lucy asked, the implication in her question clear.

Noleen smiled mildly. 'I believe he has a house which his brother paid for, in Pump Street. According to Aaron, having done that, Seamus has nothing more to do with him. He's a sad case, really.'

'Aaron or Seamus?' Lucy asked.

Noleen smiled, though avoided answering. 'I know that Seamus is a keyholder. Maybe you could phone him and ask him to let you into the house, see if Aaron's there. It's actually his house, so he can give you permission.'

'*If* he gives us permission,' Lucy corrected.

Noleen winked. 'I'll call him and tell him Aaron has missed his last appointment, which is true. I'll say I'm worried about Aaron; that I've not been able to get in contact with him. Give me five minutes, then try calling him. He might be more amenable.'

'Thanks,' Lucy said, standing.

Lucy left the call until she'd made it down to the PPU Block in Maydown.

'What was your name again?' Seamus Moore asked, seconds after Lucy had introduced herself.

'DS Black,' Lucy said. 'I'm calling about your brother, Aaron.'

'Why?' His tone was one of practised boredom.

'We found his prints at the scene of a burglary,' Lucy began.

'I am not my brother's keeper, Miss Black,' Moore said.

'DS Black,' Lucy said. 'You are, however, his keyholder, I believe?'

'And who told you that?'

Lucy ignored the question. 'We're concerned for your brother's safety, Mr Moore. We need to locate him as quickly as possible. We've not been able to find him.'

'You're not the only one,' Moore muttered, which Lucy took to mean Noleen Fagan had kept her word and had contacted him. 'I thought you said you were looking for him in connection with a burglary? That's not really out of concern for his welfare.'

'We found two sets of prints at the scene of a recent break in; one from your brother and one from another man called Kamil Krawiec. The latter was beaten almost to death and dumped in a bin. He was crushed in the compactor before anyone knew he was there. Your brother has now also vanished. I think he might know something about who attacked Kamil Krawiec and that, perhaps, he is at risk of harm for possessing that knowledge. I'm with the Public

Protection Unit and I promise you, our foremost concern is for Aaron's safety. We need to check his house.'

Moore did not speak for a moment. Finally, he said, 'Someone will be up at his house in twenty minutes,' then hung up the phone before Lucy could speak again.

Chapter Forty-one

Despite his 'someone' comment, it was Moore's car – a sleek black Jaguar – that pulled up onto the opposite pavement twenty minutes later, despite the roadway being marked with double yellow lines.

He got out and locked the car.

'You'll see me right if someone gives me a parking ticket,' he said to Lucy by way of greeting, then moved past her and, hammering three times on the front door of the building, shoved his key into the lock and pushed the door open.

'You're looking for my brother,' he cautioned as he entered the building. 'That's it. If he's here and he's OK, you ask your questions about the dead guy and then you leave again. And I wouldn't expect much from him. My brother has the mental age of a child. And not a very bright one at that.'

Lucy stepped past him, without response. At first, the smell in the house was so strong, she feared that Moore was already lying dead somewhere in the building. She realized though that the odour was caused more by the pent-up heat of the past weeks inside the building and the dirt of the place than any specific source of decay.

The narrow hallway was made all the more impassable by the collection of black bags slumped against the wall, as Mickey and Tara had mentioned.

'What's in the bags?' Lucy asked.

'*I'll* look,' Moore said, pushing past her before she had a chance to touch the one closest to her. 'My brother finds it difficult to dump things. You never know what you'll find in his collections.'

He pulled open the bag, ripping through it rather than spending the time needed to undo the thick knot into which its handles had been tied.

He rummaged through the bag, pulled out a magazine.

'*Horse & Rider* magazine?' Lucy asked, taking the proffered item.

'Several hundred copies, by the looks of it,' Moore said, pulling open a second bag. 'And this one.'

'Is your brother a horse rider?' Lucy asked.

Moore sighed. 'No. He was a stable hand in the Queen's stables when he was a teenager.'

'Really?' Lucy asked, unable to disguise her disbelief.

Moore nodded. 'He was … troubled when he was in his teens. Our parents sent him to an uncle in London who got him a job in the stables of the Royal Horse Guards.'

'What happened to him?'

'He left after the Hyde Park bombing in '82.'

Lucy knew of it, though it had been before she was born. The IRA had exploded two bombs in London, in Hyde Park and Regent's Park, killing four soldiers, seven bandsmen and seven horses taking part in the Changing of the Guard.

'He left?'

'A mixture of things,' Moore said. 'An Irish stable hand wasn't too popular after an Irish terror bombing. Besides, he had to help put down some of the injured horses. He was never right after it.'

Lucy replaced the magazine carefully in the open bag, patting back the plastic to look undisturbed.

'Aaron,' Seamus Moore shouted. 'Are you here?'

'When did you last see him?' Lucy asked.

Moore glanced at her. 'About six months ago,' he said. 'We're not close.'

'But you bought him this house?'

Moore nodded. 'He'll not be able to say I never did anything for him. Aaron,' he shouted again, angrily. 'Are you here?'

Lucy moved past him, into the living room. The room was dark, the one window facing out into a narrow yard overshadowed by the rear of the buildings backing onto this one from Artillery Street, which ran parallel to Pump Street.

An old sofa sat against one wall, though it was covered in black bags of magazines too, some of which spilled onto the floor. The wall behind it was festooned with horseshoes, of a variety of sizes, each nailed up. In their midst hung a faded picture of the Sacred Heart.

The air in the room was stale with the smell of dirty clothes, which lay in a mound at the other side of the room. Moore moved past her, sharply pulling up the blinds and opening the small window that gave way out onto the yard.

'Excuse the mess,' he offered, stepping over a mound of clothing gathered next to an aged television set and moving into the kitchen area. Lucy realized that the set looked almost as old as her own. No wonder Grace had commented on the decor of her house.

'Jesus,' Lucy heard Moore mutter as he surveyed the state of the kitchen. From where she stood, Lucy could hear the clattering of empty cans on the linoleum floor as Moore kicked them from his path.

'What exactly is your brother's malady?' Lucy asked, diplomatically.

Seamus Moore looked in at her from the kitchen. 'He's a dirty, lazy bastard,' he said.

Lucy negotiated the mound of clothing and stood next to the window in the hope of catching a breath of fresh air. She looked out at the overgrown scrap of yard, the patch of weeds, though no bigger than a living-room rug, almost standing knee high. At its centre was a pile of soil, among which were pieces of rubble, though Lucy, glancing around the yard, could not see its obvious source.

'Is your brother having some work done?' she asked.

'What?' Moore asked, coming back into the room.

She gestured at the mound in the yard. 'It's flattening the grass,' she said. 'It must have been put there recently.'

Moore shrugged. 'Aaron does a bit of handy work. Did. When he's dry. He worked on the building sites after he came home.'

'He's in construction?' Lucy asked.

'He was,' Moore said. 'He's not been in years. On account of being a—'

'Lazy bastard,' Lucy said, completing his sentence. 'You said.'

Moore stared at her, as if challenging her to show more explicitly her disdain for his attitude.

'Kamil Krawiec was a builder too,' Lucy said, instead. 'Maybe that's what connected them? We believe Krawiec was part of a gang laying a driveway for the victim of the burglary. Could Aaron have been part of that gang?'

'I wouldn't have thought so,' Moore said. 'He didn't feel the need to earn for himself. No sense of responsibility. No shame. It would appear he was even getting fed at a soup kitchen.'

'What do you mean?' Lucy asked.

Moore raised a finger imperiously, gesturing for her to follow him into the kitchen.

Lucy squeezed past the piles of bags that cluttered up the entranceway into the kitchen and followed Moore, bristling at the manner in which he had directed her.

The mess of crumpled beer cans on the floor, which had been visible from the living room, was only a small part of the bigger disarray in the kitchen. The units and worktops were covered with rubbish bags, their necks knotted. Through some of the translucent white plastic of some of the bags, Lucy could see the flies crawling inside.

'Jesus' she muttered, echoing Moore's earlier statement.

'Look,' Moore said.

On the windowsill of the kitchen, next to a spider plant whose green fronds hung down into the sink, lay a number of leaflets. Lucy picked the uppermost and saw that, though the leaflets were a variety of colours, they each proclaimed the same information: *Hot Food Available. Mon, Wed, Fri. 11 a.m. Opposite the GPO. Great James Street.*

They searched through the rest of the house, quickly checking each room, but Aaron Moore was clearly not there. Despite that, as she left, Lucy could not help but feel that she was missing something.

It was only as she was driving away that she realized: it was the spider plant in the kitchen, the leaves lush and green, the small plate beneath the pot brimming with water. The heat of the past days would have long dried it out. Someone had been in the house, watering it.

Chapter Forty-two

Fleming's office door was shut when Lucy let herself into the PPU, though she could hear raised voices from inside. She went up to her office and deposited her bag and coat. The rains of the previous day had cleared the air and, through the small window, high up in the rear wall of the room, the fresh blue of the sky was just visible.

She opened her bag and took out the ream of sheets from Beaumont. With the best will in the world, she had intended to work through them the previous evening, but her meeting with Fiona had put it out of her mind.

She began scanning down through the first page, trying to make some sense of the lines of writing, but found herself losing her place as she went. Finally, she pulled over a thin manila folder sitting on the desk and used it as a ruler as she moved down through each name and date. She was just making it to the end of the third page when the voices below grew louder, as if the discussion that had been taking place in Fleming's office had now moved out into the corridor below.

There were two voices, one of which she recognized as Fleming's. The other, also a male's, was shriller, raised in objection as Fleming attempted to calm him. Her interest piqued, Lucy went out onto the stairs and glanced down.

Gabriel Duffy, father of Ciaran, stood in the corridor. 'You drove him to it,' he said. 'You pushed him into running,' he said.

'We just wanted to speak with Ciaran,' Fleming said. 'I understand you're angry, but we simply wanted to know who had paid—'

'No one paid him!' Duffy shouted.

'He deposited five thousand pounds in the bank on the day after the body was swapped.'

'That wasn't our mistake,' William snapped. 'I told you that. You and that girl.'

Fleming must have noticed Lucy standing watching, for he glanced up over Duffy's shoulder at her briefly, long enough for Duffy to, likewise, register her presence. He turned to follow Fleming's glance.

'You!' he said. 'You're to blame, too, for what happened to my son. Skulking on the stairs.'

'I'm sorry for your loss, Mr Duffy,' Lucy said, moving down to them now. 'I understand how you feel.'

'No you don't,' Duffy spat.

'Ciaran got involved with people he shouldn't have,' Lucy said. 'He was paid to swap a body in the coffin. We believe that whoever paid him to do that probably killed him as well.'

Duffy stared at her, his mouth a little agape. 'Was he killed with an axe?'

Lucy glanced at Fleming, who seemed equally unsure what to say.

'I heard that. Is that true?' the man demanded.

'We're still waiting on the results of the post-mortem,' Fleming said.

'You can't even tell the truth, can you?' Duffy said.

'Some things are best not known,' Lucy offered.

'Only someone with no children could say that,' Duffy said, the tears brinking on his eyes.

'DS Black is right, Mr Duffy,' Fleming said. 'You're best remembering your son as he was. I say that *as* a father.'

'How I remember him is hunted to his death by you lot,' Duffy said. 'I curse the pair of you.'

He pushed past Fleming and pulled at the door, which would not open. He turned and scanned the wall, looking for the release catch, thumped it with the soft of his fist, and pushed his way out into the sunlight.

'Are you OK?' Lucy asked Fleming, who had clearly borne the brunt of his visit.

'Fucking Burns,' Fleming said. 'Burns set him on me.'

'Maybe not,' Lucy offered.

Fleming raised his eyebrows sceptically. 'How else would he have known to come here? Or about the hatchet?'

'Why would he do that?'

'Line management,' Fleming said. 'Control.'

Lucy cleared her throat, waited for his anger to dissipate. 'I think I've found a connection between Moore and Krawiec,' she said. 'Moore wasn't home, but I did find fliers for a soup kitchen in Great James Street. Grace, the girl who showed us where Krawiec was killed, told me that she knew he used it, too.'

'When did she tell you that?'

Lucy hesitated. 'This morning,' she offered. 'She said Sammy went to it as well.'

'How did you get into Moore's house?'

'His brother, Seamus Moore.'

Fleming nodded. 'Seamus Moore is his *brother*? Very careless of Burns not to have picked up on that when he was telling us all about the soap theft yesterday. What did big brother have to say?'

'He wasn't the most sympathetic, to be honest,' Lucy said. 'He did tell me that Aaron Moore was looking after the horses at Hyde Park when the bomb went off in '82. Which would explain his current mental health issues,' she added.

'And now he's having to eat in soup kitchens?' Fleming shook his head. 'How we look after our victims, eh? I've heard of the new soup place. Shall we take a visit?'

Chapter Forty-three

While a number of the support centres in the city provided food and shelter for those living rough, the soup kitchen in question was the most recent to open its door. Fleming's was targeted more at those making their way home from the pubs late in the evening; this one, it seemed, was providing for those who needed support during daylight hours. It actually operated out of a prefab building that had been set up in waste ground across the street from the Postal Sorting Office, as the flier had stated. The area had once been used as a car park. The prefab stood against the rear wall of a local pub, which, Lucy reasoned, was either dreadful planning or inspired, depending on the target audience for the kitchen's wares.

When they arrived, the prefab door yawned open and a man, dressed in kitchen whites, stood in the doorway, leaning against the jamb, feet crossed at the ankles, a cigarette in his mouth. As Lucy and Fleming approached, he flicked the cigarette out onto the ground and straightened.

'We're not open yet,' he said.

Lucy raised her warrant card. 'We're with the Public Protection Unit of the PSNI. Can we have a word?'

'Are we in trouble? The guy who owns this land said it was OK for us to be here,' he explained.

'No trouble,' Lucy said. 'We'd just like your help.'

The man stepped down. 'Come in, so,' he said, indicating with his hand that they should go inside.

The interior of the prefab was furnished with a number of white plastic patio tables and chairs. At one end was a set of stainless steel bain-maries, behind which worked a middle-aged woman, again dressed in whites, wearing a cap and hairnet. She was pouring a large pan of soup into one of the stainless steel containers, the sediment from the bottom of the pan slopping in with a soft splash.

'Ellie. Them's police.'

Ellie smiled, put down the pan and wiped her hands on her apron. 'Is something wrong?'

'We're investigating the disappearance of a number of homeless,' Lucy said. 'We believe that they may have crossed paths here.'

'We're not here too long,' the man began. 'We'll not know them yet.'

Ellie moved around from behind the unit and gestured to Lucy and Fleming to sit on one of the plastic garden chairs.

'We only started here a few months ago,' she explained. 'We began in Omagh and then branched out to here too. We open for a few hours over lunch, just, to give anyone who needs it some hot food.'

'What's available?' Fleming asked.

'Soup and bread at the moment,' Ellie said. 'Our funding is limited, so that's all we can manage.'

'Do you charge anything?'

'Of course not,' the woman protested. 'We're a charity.'

'Based in Omagh?'

The woman nodded. She fumbled in her pockets, beneath the apron, and produced a card. 'Here.'

The card carried on it the logo that Lucy had seen on the fliers in Moore's home, above the title 'Helping the Homeless'.

'Do you only help those living on the streets?' Lucy asked. Aaron Moore did not fit into the narrow definition of that term.

'We can hardly ask someone to prove they're destitute,' Ellie said. 'If someone is in such a state that they come to us for food, we'll not turn them away. They're not having to come here for food through choice.'

'Do you know this man?' Fleming asked, handing Ellie a picture of Kamil Krawiec.

'That's Crackers,' the man, who had yet to offer his name, said. 'He's the one they found in the bins. Across the way. It was on the news.'

He pointed out of the small grilled window of the unit and Lucy realized that the alleyway in which Kamil's body had been dumped was indeed directly across from where they now sat.

'What about this man?' Lucy said, as Fleming pulled out a picture of Aaron Moore.

Ellie took it and stared at it, before handing it to the man. 'He was here a few times, wasn't he, Stephen?' she asked.

'Stephen' took the picture and studied it. 'Yeah. Bit of a loner. Keeps himself to himself. But he's been here.'

'His name's Aaron Moore. Was he with Kamil?'

Stephen shook his head. 'He's not with anyone. Sits on his own. Polite, but a bit odd.'

'Oddness is relative,' Ellie offered. 'Crackers *was* here a few times with a big man, greying a bit. Nice man.'

Fleming tapped Lucy on the knee. 'Excuse me a moment,' he said, before getting up and leaving the prefab. Ellie watched after him as he left.

'When was the last time you saw Kamil – Crackers?'

'He came at the start,' Stephen said. 'Then we didn't see him for a few weeks. Then he came back again for a bit.'

'That was when he was with that other man, the older man I mentioned. He told me his name, too, but I can't remember it.'

'We've not seen him this week,' Stephen said. 'Either of them.'

'Do you know where they went?'

Ellie shook her head. 'Apart from Crackers. We all know where he ended up, God rest him.'

'They were chatting outside with a heavyset guy, drives a blue van,' Stephen offered. 'I went out for a smoke one day and they were talking with him.'

Lucy struggled to keep on top of the various people being named as 'heavy guy'. 'The man with the grey hair?'

'Yeah. Him and Crackers.'

'And he was driving a blue van?'

'No,' the man said, as if she was stupid. 'Crackers and Grey-hair were talking to a heavy guy with a blue van. He was a redhead, I think.'

Ellie smiled apologetically. 'As Stephen said, we don't know all the names yet. Sorry.'

Fleming came back into the prefab, a little out of breath, a patio chair skittering across the floor out of his path as he entered.

He handed Ellie another picture. 'Is this the man?'

Lucy could see from the image that it was Terry Haynes.

'That's him,' Ellie said with delight. 'He was with Crackers. Tony? Was that his name?'

'Terry?' Fleming offered.

Ellie clicked her fingers and smiled. 'That's it. Terry. Terry and Crackers were here last week, talking to the redhead in the blue van. I think they headed off with him.'

'Can you tell us anything more about the van driver? Apart from the red hair?'

Stephen shook his head. 'Not really. He'd be younger than Terry. And bigger. He's around every few days. He parks over on Patrick Street and stands at the corner of the pub some days, chatting with the men.'

Stephen's description of the man sounded similar to that which Doreen Jeffries had used to describe the one who'd intimidated her into getting her driveway laid. The man for whom Kamil Krawiec and Aaron Moore were, apparently, working. Lucy glanced at Fleming. 'Maybe he'd been recruiting cheap labour?'

Fleming nodded. 'When was the van driver last here?'

'Last week some time,' Ellie said.

'There was someone different came after that. A younger guy, fitter looking. But in the same blue van,' Stephen added. 'Could be his son, maybe? Similar looking, but much trimmer.'

'You're sure?' Lucy asked. 'When was this?'

'Yesterday? No, the day before. Two days ago. He was chatting with that funny old guy. The drinker. You know,' Stephen said to Ellie.

Ellie shook her head.

'You do! The old guy. Drinker. No teeth.'

'Sammy!' Ellie said.

'Sammy,' Stephen repeated, nodding his head. 'They were out there talking, Sammy headed off with him.'

'Sammy headed off in the blue van?'

Stephen nodded.

'The same van that Crackers and Terry left in?'

Another nod.

'Has Sammy been back here since?' Fleming asked.

Stephen looked to Ellie who shrugged. 'I don't think so,' he said.

Chapter Forty-four

'So, what're your thoughts?' Lucy asked as they crossed the waste ground back to the car. A light breeze fluttered at the scrap of crime scene tape, which remained from when the alleyway opposite had been closed off for a forensics search. She wondered whether there was significance in Kamil Krawiec's body being dumped so close to the soup kitchen.

'So, someone is using homeless people to do construction work for them,' Fleming said.

'And they're recruiting at a soup kitchen,' Lucy agreed. 'It makes sense. The day we saw Sammy, he was the only man among a group of women. Where have all the other male drinkers gone?'

'Sammy'd hardly have been anyone's first choice for building work,' Fleming said.

'I wonder if he's been back to the Foyle Hostel,' Lucy said. 'To get his insulin.'

Fleming nodded. 'I'll check it up,' he said.

'So this red-haired guy turns up at the soup kitchen in a blue van and recruits men, one or two at a time. To do what?'

'Lay driveways? Like Doreen Jeffries's? Over-charging her and probably underpaying the workers?'

'Or demolition work, perhaps?' Lucy said. 'Cleaning out the inside of closed-off buildings for copper piping? We know for a fact that Kamil was in the old bank building.'

Fleming nodded. 'Or maybe they're doing both. Steal the materials from the abandoned buildings and then use them in other jobs. Widen the profit margin even further. Did Boyd come back to us yet on whether any of the other buildings in the city had been hit?'

Lucy shrugged. 'I've heard nothing,' she said. 'We could call round at the council offices.'

'It's a Saturday,' Fleming said.

'Boyd told us the other day he'd be working all weekend,' Lucy said, checking her watch. 'He might still be about. It's worth a try. Keep the pressure on him.'

As they climbed into the car, Fleming said, 'We know Terry wasn't the one running the gang then. If the redhead in the blue van was recruiting people.'

'Unless Terry was working *with* them? Like a Judas goat, bringing them willing hands for hire. Otherwise, why *was* he at a soup kitchen? He wasn't homeless, or in need of low-paid construction work.'

Fleming considered the question. 'We know from the two in the kitchen that Kamil went missing, then reappeared. We know that he was then with Terry for a few days, before vanishing again and this time winding up in the bins over there. We can assume that his first absence was when he was recruited and did the work for the gang with the blue van – we know he was at Doreen Jeffries's house a few weeks back, after all.'

'And that Kamil robbed her, possibly with help from Aaron Moore, who also had a background in construction,' Lucy added. 'Maybe that's why Kamil reappeared in town. Maybe he didn't need to work for a week or two; Doreen's jewellery was valuable enough to keep him afloat for a bit. He stayed with Terry Haynes for a few days. Then what?'

'Maybe he told Terry what was happening to the homeless and Terry wanted to see for himself? He'd have been outraged if he thought someone was exploiting the street drinkers. He goes along with Kamil, pretends to be one of the homeless to see first-hand what's happening.'

Lucy waited a beat, to see if Fleming would continue. When he didn't she said, 'Well, where is he now? We know what happened to Kamil. Where is Terry Haynes?'

'And the rest of the gang working out of the blue van? And Sammy?' Fleming agreed. 'And Aaron Moore? Burns has had people checking his house and keeping an eye out. There's still no sign of him either. Is Moore still with the works gang, or did he leave when Kamil did? He'd have his cut from the Jeffries burglary, too.'

'I think he's been in that house,' Lucy said. 'There's a plant in the kitchen which was watered. Like, the saucer it sat in was full to the brim.'

'Could the brother have done it when he was in there?'

'I don't think so.'

'And you checked the house?'

Lucy nodded. 'Seamus Moore was with me, but we still went through the place. He wasn't there.'

Fleming nodded. 'So, we find Moore. Or we find the red-haired man recruiting homeless into doing building work.'

Lucy started the engine. 'I'll call with John Boyd first and chase up the lists of other buildings hit. We might find something there.'

'What about the Beaumont list of the people with surgical implants? Anyone we know on it? Any Derry folk?'

Lucy shook her head. 'It's in my bag,' she said. 'I've only started working down through it.'

'May I?' Fleming asked, lifting the bag from the footwell. 'We don't want to give Burns anything else to complain about.'

He pulled out the sheaf of papers, on the top of which was scrawled 'Bernadette Thompson, Beech Park, Eglinton'.

'Who's Bernadette Thompson?'

'Different case,' Lucy said. 'I'd nowhere else to write it.'

'Anything you need help with?'

Lucy shook her head. 'No, I'm good,' she said.

Lucy pulled in on the pavement outside the council offices. Fleming remained in the car in case they were ticketed for parking.

Though initially reluctant to bother her boss, the receptionist asked Lucy to wait while she checked if Boyd was free after Lucy commiserated with her having to work on the weekend. While she waited in the foyer, she flicked through one of the City of Culture programmes, which were sitting on the glass table next to the sofa where she'd been instructed to sit.

A moment later, she heard voices and looked up to see John Boyd and another man coming down the stairs. Assuming that he was coming down to see her, Lucy moved across to him. 'Mr Boyd? Thanks for seeing me.'

Boyd stared at her distractedly, trying to place her. 'Sorry,' he said. 'I'm on my way out. Did we have an appointment?'

Lucy shook her head. 'I'm DS Black. I was here yesterday. I'd asked about checking whether any other buildings in the city had been targeted in copper theft.'

Boyd's face lit with recognition. 'Of course. I'm sorry. We're up to our eyes in it. We have an audit going on this week. We're just going out to Claudy to inspect some works, I'm afraid.' He offered the final lines as way of apology and began moving past Lucy, without having introduced the man with whom he had been standing. This second man wore a visitor badge clipped to his jacket breast pocket and carried a high-visibility jacket over his arm. Lucy guessed that he was one of the auditors rather than a fellow council worker.

'I really need the list, Mr Boyd,' Lucy said, riled at the manner in which he had dismissed her request. 'We are investigating a murder, after all.'

Boyd stopped now, turned back towards her. 'A murder?' he asked, smiling nervously. 'You told me it was a copper theft.'

'We believe one of the thieves was murdered on the site of the old bank building,' Lucy said. 'Clearly, if we know the gang has operated in other buildings, we may find something of investigative value.'

'Of course,' Boyd agreed. 'I'll arrange for our works team to check the buildings.' He turned now to the receptionist. 'Linda, will you contact Dan Summers in Dynamic Works and pass on ...' He glanced back at Lucy, as if trying to remember her name. 'Pass on DS Black's request?'

'Is that OK?' he asked, glancing back at the auditor. 'I'll sort the paperwork when I get back. It is a murder investigation.'

The man smiled, nodding his head. 'That's fine,' he said.

Boyd nodded at Lucy. 'Someone will be in touch with you as soon as we get word back from Dynamic,' he said, smiling. Lucy could sense, however, a barely suppressed anger at having to ask permission from the man next to him, especially in front of her. 'Perhaps next time, you'll make an appointment,' he added.

'I'll try my best. Sadly, murders generally don't happen to appointment, Mr Boyd,' Lucy retorted. 'Thank you for your help.'

She turned and left before he could respond.

Her stomach was still twisting with adrenaline when she made it to the car. She climbed into the driver's seat and shut the door.

'That man is an asshole,' she said. 'He's not even started checking the buildings yet.'

Fleming said nothing. She looked across at him. He had the papers from Beaumont on his lap, his face ashen.

'Is everything all right?'

Fleming held out one of the sheets to her.

'I think I've found Terry Haynes,' he said.

Chapter Forty-five

'You're sure it's him?' Burns asked. They were sitting in his office, having returned to the Strand Road station, only a few hundred yards from the council offices.

'No,' Fleming said. 'We'll never be sure, unless he turns up alive somewhere. The cremation will have destroyed all DNA. Someone would need to work through the entire list to be sure that all the others on it are either still alive or are dead and securely buried. But, there is a T. Haynes listed. Date of birth twenty-eight November 1957, which makes him fifty-six, the same age as me.'

'The weight of evidence would certainly suggest it was Haynes in the coffin, sir,' Lucy agreed. 'He was in a motorcycle accident in Dublin; that would certainly explain the head and leg injuries.'

Burns nodded. 'So where does that leave us?'

'If it is Haynes, then he can't have killed Kamil Krawiec, or, at the very least, he certainly can't have dumped Krawiec's body; that happened hours *after* the cremation. It also means he wasn't connected with Ciaran Duffy's killing either, despite Duffy's remains being burned with Terry's car.

'And we can assume Terry was probably killed by the same person; both he and Duffy bore the marks of a hatchet attack, based on the pathologist's comments,' Fleming added.

'So, whoever did kill Ciaran Duffy and Kamil Krawiec used Haynes's car to try to frame him for it, knowing we'd never find him because he'd already been cremated.'

'And you think this connects to this construction scam how?' Burns asked.

Lucy nodded. 'We believe Kamil Krawiec was recruited by a construction-work gang at the soup kitchen in Great James Street. Certainly, we know Krawiec was working as part of that gang in Doreen Jeffries's home a few weeks back, as was Aaron Moore, also a frequenter of the soup kitchen. We know he and Aaron Moore stole from that home. We know that, subsequently, Krawiec was staying with Haynes, which people did when they were trying to dry out. Following that, we know that Haynes and Krawiec turned up at the soup kitchen as customers, despite Haynes not being homeless. We know that they went off with the red-haired guy in the blue Transit van, whose description matches that of the man who first offered to re-lay Doreen Jeffries's driveway,' Lucy said, glancing across to Fleming to see if she had missed anything out.

'And we know that Krawiec was killed inside the old bank building while helping someone steal copper piping. We can only assume that the gang stealing the copper piping might be the same one with which he worked at Doreen Jeffries's. That being the case, he must have rejoined them,' Fleming added.

'Kamil must have confided in Terry Haynes about what the gang were up to and, perhaps, what he had done in Doreen Jeffries's house. Perhaps Haynes went with him to see first-hand the gang who were exploiting homeless people. Perhaps he challenged the gang leader, the man with the red hair, and that's why he was killed. Kamil was punished for having exposed the gang to Terry Haynes. And Duffy, who had helped them dispose of the original owner of the coffin, Stuart Carlisle, so they could cremate Terry's remains, became a liability when Carlisle's body resurfaced and we started taking an interest in Duffy's role in the body swap.'

'Exploited?' Burns said, as if that was the only part of what she had said which had registered with him.

'The gang at Doreen Jeffries's could be stealing building supplies from the boarded-up buildings around the city and using them in other jobs they're doing, using homeless people as labourers,' Fleming said. 'So, yes, exploited is the right word.'

'If they're stealing stuff, that's criminal. If they're using homeless people as slaves, then that is exploitation. But if they're simply offering work to the unemployed, they're not doing anything wrong. In fact, they could be providing a public service, getting the street drinkers off their arses and helping them get on their feet,' Burns said.

'An alcoholic's problem isn't laziness, sir,' Tom Fleming said. 'It's an illness.'

'A self-inflicted one,' Burns said, laughing lightly as he glanced at Lucy, as if seeking her support.

Lucy could sense Fleming's anger growing and stepped in before he said something they'd all regret. 'It's not our place to judge the worthiness of victims, sir. They all need our help, equally,' she said quickly.

'I'm not judging their worthiness, DS Black,' Burns snapped. 'I'm judging whether there's a crime involved.'

'Why would Terry have gone with Kamil to the soup kitchen unless he thought there was something wrong with what the construction team were doing? Something criminal,' Fleming said. 'And what did he discover that was bad enough for them to kill him to stop him revealing it?'

'*If* they killed him,' Burns countered.

'I think it's unlikely that the body cremated in Carlisle's coffin wasn't Terry Haynes,' Fleming said, exasperated.

'All right, Tom; I'm simply playing devil's advocate,' Burns said. 'So, following your logic, why did this construction gang kill him? And, more importantly, why would they go to such lengths to hide Haynes's body, but they just dumped Krawiec in a bin and Duffy in the boot of a burning car?'

'Maybe they knew he'd report it to us ... to the police. I suspect that, knowing Terry, they discovered that he couldn't easily be controlled. Or intimidated.'

Lucy nodded. 'Kamil, we'd write off as a homeless man falling asleep in a bin. Duffy, we already knew he was involved in something by that stage, so maybe they reckoned there was no point in hiding his remains; we were looking for him anyway. They stuck him in Haynes's car, cleaned it out, then torched it, implicating Haynes, whom they believed we would never find.'

'And whose disappearance, if it ever was reported, we would assume was as a result of going on the run after carrying out the killings of Kamil Krawiec and

Ciaran Duffy,' Burns agreed. 'So, what do we know on the blue Transit van driver?'

'Heavy, red-haired,' Lucy said. 'Doreen Jeffries said he had an ear piercing, too. We could send someone out to her to do an e-fit.'

'We asked the two running the soup kitchen to call if he or his son appeared again.'

'His son?'

Fleming nodded. 'They said that the heavy guy hadn't been there in a few days, but that a younger man, slimmer looking, also in the same blue van, had been. We know that another one of the long-term street drinkers, Sammy Smith, a diabetic, went off with this man the other day. And hasn't been seen since. We don't know how much insulin he has with him to keep him going, but he's going to need more at some stage.'

'What about the soup kitchen itself? Is it legit?'

'We'll run background on the group organizing it and see,' Fleming said. 'They are registered as a charity according to the card they gave us.'

'What about Aaron Moore, sir?' Lucy asked. 'Any sign of him?'

Burns shook his head. 'We've called at the house every hour or two. Had teams passing by all night looking for lights or drawn curtains. I don't think he's there. Maybe he's with this construction team, too.'

Lucy shook her head. 'I think he's been in that house. Someone watered his plant in the kitchen.'

'You were in Moore's house?' Burns asked. 'Why? How did you get in?'

'I spoke with the Community Mental Health team and they suggested contacting his brother, Seamus.'

'The solicitor?' Burns blanched, realizing he had missed this detail of Moore's background.

Lucy nodded. 'He let me in.'

'He let you search his brother's house? Without a warrant?'

Lucy shook her head. 'I told him we were concerned about his safety following on from what had happened to Kamil.'

'Aaron Moore is wanted in connection with a burglary,' Burns said, his ire building. Lucy guessed it was a combination of his embarrassment at not making the connection between Seamus and Aaron Moore, and also his annoyance that she had managed to make it inside the house when his own team had not. 'That's not a PPU investigation, Sergeant. This is why we have different teams and units, so that each team can work on its own assigned cases. I have officers assigned to check Moore's house.'

'Noleen Fagan in the Mental Health team asked me to check; Moore had missed appointments with her,' Lucy said, using the excuse Fagan had offered her for Seamus Moore. 'Besides, Moore *is* part of our investigation,' she added. 'We were investigating the body in the coffin, a case which is clearly connected to Aaron Moore, sir.'

'You didn't know that yesterday,' Burns snapped. 'You had no right to go into Moore's house.'

'On the plus side,' Fleming said. 'Lucy managed to do something that appears to have eluded the rest of the MIT: getting inside his house and determining that it appears Aaron Moore is not only still alive, but has been back in his house recently.'

Burns stared at him, clearly weighing up the benefits in pursuing the argument. Eventually, he decided against. 'And what *did* you find?'

'Nothing,' Lucy said. 'The house is almost uninhabitable, it's so cluttered. He hoards stuff, mostly to do with horses.'

'Horses? He steals soap and now he hoards horse memorabilia?'

'He was at Hyde Park on the day the bomb went off in 1982. He worked with the horses. He had to help put a number of them to sleep. He seems not to have recovered from it.'

Burns considered the information. 'Jesus. I suppose that's understandable. Is he not getting help for it? Even from the brother?'

'Beyond buying him the house, no,' Lucy said. 'They haven't seen one another in months. I think Seamus Moore is a little ashamed of his younger brother, to be honest.'

'Seeing the way Moore senior behaves in court, it should be the other way round,' Fleming said.

'Nothing else of interest?' Burns asked, ignoring Fleming's comment.

'Just a plant,' Lucy offered. 'It looked freshly watered, indicating that someone had been inside the house. Seamus Moore claimed he hadn't seen his brother in six months, so we can safely say it wasn't Seamus who'd been going to water the plant. And there was rubble. There was a pile of soil and rubble lying in the backyard, on top of the grass.'

'And?'

'The grass was long, but the pile was on top of it. It hadn't grown up around it yet.'

'Moore has a construction background,' Fleming said. 'The same as Kamil Krawiec. Presumably that's why the gang hired the two of them.'

Lucy nodded. 'This soil and rubble looked like it had come from the house. He'd hardly have brought it there from somewhere else. But, we looked in all the rooms and there was no sign of construction work having been done.'

'We need to get back inside that house,' Burns said. 'I'll speak with the ACC. We'll work together on this now.'

Lucy and Fleming stood to leave.

'You must be happy, Tom? Now that you've proved your friend didn't kill anyone. That must make you feel a little better?' Burns reasoned.

Lucy glanced across at her boss. Terry Haynes had helped Fleming through his own alcoholism, had supported him when he'd reached his lowest ebb. She realized, with a pang, that in addition to the case, he was having to deal with the violent death of a friend. She reached across and, taking his hand momentarily in hers, squeezed it.

He nodded in acknowledgement of the gesture before looking at Burns. 'Strangely, I find no comfort in the knowledge that my friend was killed.'

He turned and left the room, Burns reddening as he did so. 'Tell Tom I didn't mean it like that,' he said to Lucy as she turned to follow Fleming. 'Tell him I'm sorry for his loss.'

Lucy nodded. 'That might be best coming directly from you,' she said before adding, 'sir.'

Chapter Forty-six

DS Tara Gallagher was sitting in the incident room when they came out of Burns's office. She glanced up at Lucy as she emerged onto the corridor, then returned her attention to the screen in front of her.

'I'll be a minute, sir,' Lucy said to Fleming, handing him her keys.

She crossed the room to the desk where Tara sat. 'Hey, you,' Lucy said, nudging her gently on the arm.

'Hey,' Tara said without humour.

'Look, I'm sorry,' Lucy said. 'I should have said something earlier. I've never told anyone about her, about my mother, because, well, because, I never really thought of her *as* my mother.'

'I thought we were friends.'

'We were ... we are, I hope,' Lucy said. 'But because I didn't tell anyone when I first started here, the longer it went on, the harder it was to see a natural way of doing it.'

'You could have told me during any of the times I was bitching about her to you,' Tara hissed. 'At any point, you could have stopped me and said, "She's my mother."'

'I know,' Lucy said. 'I didn't want to embarrass you.'

'Like I'm not embarrassed now?' Tara snapped.

'Listen,' Lucy said, squatting next to her seat, to keep her voice low. 'I really don't care what you say about her. None of it will be worse than what I've thought, believe me. I'm sorry I didn't say anything to you. But it wasn't that I didn't trust you. I just don't admit it to anyone.'

Tara nodded lightly, as if accepting the point. 'Forget about it.'

'Are we friends?' Lucy asked, laying her hand on Tara's arm.

Tara took her hand in hers, holding Lucy's fingers in her own. 'I suppose,' she said.

On the way downstairs, Lucy stopped at one of the free desks to use the phone. She knew that calls from the station would show up as 'Blocked' on a caller ID. She pulled out the Beaumont list and dialled the number she'd written for Bernadette Thompson, the owner of the black Audi that Grace had photographed on her phone before the man driving it had assaulted her.

She began to think that the woman wasn't home until, just as she was starting to reconsider the wisdom in making it, she heard the click as the call was answered. She panicked as she realized she might be best not using her own name either and tried to think of a suitable alternative.

'Mrs Bernadette Thompson? I'm PSNI Officer Jane Wilson,' she said, using her mother's name, though not her rank. 'I'm calling regarding an assault on a young girl in Foyle Street last night.'

'Yes?'

'Your car was seen near where the girl was assaulted.'

She heard a flutter of nervous laughter. 'You've got the wrong number. My husband had the car with him last night.'

'Where would he have been?'

'He was out at a work do. One of the teachers in his school retired before the summer and they had a leaving party last night.'

'Your husband's a teacher?' Lucy asked.

'That's right.'

Lucy considered carefully how best to continue. 'The girl who was assaulted was a teenage prostitute. A man who had just used her services beat her. That man was driving your car. You might wish to discuss the finer details of all that with your husband,' she said, then hung up the phone.

Fleming was sitting in the car waiting for her.

'Everything OK?'

Lucy nodded. 'Yeah, I'm ... just pouring oil on troubled water with Tara, over the whole thing about my mum. She was a little pissed that I hadn't told her.' She saw no reason in telling Fleming about Thompson. Grace had made it clear that she wouldn't press charges and, Lucy suspected, would refuse even to acknowledge that the assault had happened if she pushed her too hard on it. The best she could expect was that Thompson might suffer more at the hands of his wife than he would at the hands of the law. Certainly, he'd have some awkward questions to answer.

'Understandable,' Fleming said. 'The amazing thing is that it's taken this long for word to get out.'

'What about?'

'Your mother,' Fleming said, looking at her quizzically. 'Is that not what we were talking about?'

'Yes. Sorry. My mind was somewhere else,' Lucy said, starting the car and pulling out of the parking bay.

'Burns apologized for what he said, about Terry Haynes,' she said, looking across at Fleming. 'He felt bad.'

'He should,' Fleming said.

'Are you OK?'

Fleming shrugged. 'I'd guessed that the body in the coffin was either Terry or Aaron Moore, simply because they're connected in some way in all this and both are missing, so seeing Terry's name on the list from the hospital wasn't a shock. But I still feel gutted.'

Lucy nodded. She knew there was little she could say.

'The first night I stayed with him, I was in a horrendous state. I was drinking water constantly and bringing it back up. I could see things coming through the walls at me; I thought my heart was going to burst out of my chest.'

He went silent and Lucy glanced across again to see that he was staring out the window now, his eyes glazed.

'Sorry. I shouldn't have told you that,' he said, turning to her. 'And I appreciated you having my back in there with Burns.'

'It's OK,' Lucy said. 'I'm glad you trust me enough.'

Fleming smiled mildly. 'It takes a special kind of person to clean up your vomit and still be your friend, you know? That was Terry Haynes.'

'You're lucky,' Lucy said. 'To have had a friend like that.' As she said it, she reflected on who would do the same for her if she needed it. Robbie, presumably. But that thought simply made her feel even more guilty. Tara? Maybe not now that she knew Lucy hadn't been honest with her.

'I called Niall Toner in the Foyle Hostel while I was waiting for you,' Fleming said, filling the silence in the car. 'Sammy went back on Wednesday after we met him and stayed that night. He got his first insulin shot on Thursday before leaving. Toner gave him a handful to take with him in case he stayed away for a few nights again. He's not been back since.'

'How many shots did he have with him?' Lucy asked.

'Five,' Fleming said. 'His last one will cover him tonight. If he doesn't voluntarily come back himself, or we don't find him soon, he's going to start having very serious problems.'

Just as they waited for the steel entrance doors to slowly draw open, Fleming's phone began ringing. Absurdly, Lucy thought it might be Toner, calling to say Sammy had returned.

'Inspector Fleming,' he said. He listened to the call. In such close proximity, Lucy could hear the tinny sound of the man's voice on the phone, but could not quite distinguish what he was saying.

'We're on our way,' Fleming said. 'Thanks for letting us know.' He ended the call then began dialling.

'That was the soup kitchen guy,' he said. 'Head back up there now. The blue van has just returned.'

Chapter Forty-seven

The traffic was heavier than they had been expecting, not helped by the fact that, as they crossed the Clarendon Street junction, two men dressed as sailors stepped out in front of the car, as if to offer an advertising leaflet from the bunch they held. As Lucy swerved around them, the sheets of the one nearest her dropped fluttering in the wind in her wake.

'Is there a Village People convention on?' Fleming asked. 'They've lost the Indian, Cop and Builder.'

'You know a worrying amount about the Village People,' Lucy said, turning down Patrick Street. 'So, who's here? The young slim guy or the heavy red-headed guy?'

Fleming shook his head. 'He only said that the blue van had pulled up.'

'Great,' Lucy said.

Ahead, to the left, they saw a blue Transit van parked along the pavement.

'Is that it?' Lucy said.

'Looks like the only one here,' Fleming said. 'I'll call in the registration number.'

There were no free parking spaces along the road until, just before the junction with the Strand Road, Lucy spotted the bus bay, which was clear.

'We'll only be a few minutes,' she reasoned, pulling in.

They parked up and, after locking the car, crossed the road and entered into the waste ground, rounding the corner of the bar against whose rear the soup kitchen had been set.

Lucy was struck by the crowd of people using the kitchen as she scanned the area, looking for someone matching either of the descriptions they had been given for the van drivers, but no one stood out. Many of those clutching slices of bread as they sipped from polystyrene cups had come outside and were standing, facing towards the sun as they ate. A group of half a dozen stood at the entrance to the prefab itself, blocking the way so that Fleming had to push his way through, offering excuses and suffering curses as he tried to speak to Stephen or Ellie and ask them to point out the driver of the blue van.

'Oi! Inspector!' someone shouted.

Lucy looked across and there, standing with two others, was the woman to whom she had given her card the day she had first met Grace. The one who had laughed at the suggestion she might have a phone.

'Inspector!' the woman shouted again, waving exaggeratedly to Lucy in a manner that suggested she had already started drinking for the day.

Lucy scanned the others in the waste ground now, looking to see if anyone else had reacted to the public announcement of her profession. One man, near the pavement on Great James Street, talking earnestly to a man so unsteady on his feet that he had to support him with one hand, looked across at her quickly, then averted his gaze. Lucy noticed that he didn't have a cup in his hand, so was clearly not availing of the services of the kitchen.

He turned back to the man, but a moment later, glanced quickly in her direction again, as if checking whether she was continuing to look at him. As Lucy began moving towards him, the man set off suddenly, sprinting across Great James Street, making for the alleyway in which Kamil Krawiec's body had been dumped while the older man whom he had been supporting tumbled to the ground.

Lucy took off after him. She reached the kerb and had to stop while the traffic, already moving through the traffic lights at the lower end, passed. The old man was being helped to his feet by a few of the others gathered near him. Lucy stepped down onto the road, judging the distance of each oncoming car, gauging when best to make a run for it. Ahead, the man had made it through the alley and out onto Sackville Street, turning left towards the Strand Road. Lucy cut down towards the traffic lights instead, rounding the corner onto the Strand.

Ahead of her, Waterloo Place was heaving with Saturday shoppers, the street lined with ice-cream vans and stalls selling inflatable hammers and green, white and orange hats. Lucy could see the slim figure of the man weaving his way through the crowds, pushing his way up towards Waterloo Place itself. Across the street, two uniformed Neighbourhood Policing officers were standing, chatting with one of the vendors as they bought ice creams.

'I'm in pursuit of a suspect,' Lucy called, breathlessly, as she ran across towards them. 'I could do with some help,' she managed. One of the men dropped his ice cream as he moved with her; the other, she noticed, held on to his. Lucy sprinted up towards the pedestrianized area, the two uniforms coming behind. To her left, a boy and girl, dressed as sailors, were dancing a hornpipe, while an appreciative crowd of spectators had moved back to create a semicircle of space around the couple in which to dance.

Lucy pushed through the mass, spilling into the dance area, upsetting the rhythm of the boy, earning, in so doing, complaints from some of those who had been watching. The uniforms behind her edged their way around the circle of spectators, excusing themselves as they pushed by. There was, she reflected, a clear reason why they were community officers.

As she turned the corner into Waterloo Place proper, she realized that the whole area, right up into Guildhall Square, was filled with marquees and tents. The air was heavy with the smell of cooking fish. The shoppers had increased in number now, their space limited by the tents spotted around the square, in such a way that her progress was slowed. As she passed, someone dressed in a bright pink T-shirt handed her a flyer, bearing the legend 'Flavours of the Foyle Seafood Festival'.

The two uniforms had reached her now.

'Who are we looking for?' one asked.

'A young lad. Late teens, early twenties at most,' Lucy said. 'He's wearing jeans and a pale-yellow T-shirt. Short-haired, strawberry blond.'

'Where did you lose him?' the other asked, standing on tiptoe to see above the heads of those milling in the space before them. As he did so, he licked the melted ice cream from around the cone, which he still held.

'I didn't lose him,' Lucy said. 'He's in *here* somewhere. And he's wanted in connection with a murder inquiry,' she added, lest the men thought he was a shoplifter or something. It had the desired effect for the second uniform binned his ice cream. 'Right,' he said. 'Which way?'

They began moving through the square, glancing into the tents on each side, looking for the man. Eventually, they realized, as they stood in front of the old bank building where Kamil Krawiec had been murdered, they would have to split up, for Waterloo Place fed out onto Guildhall Square to the left and Waterloo Street and William Street respectively to the right.

Lucy directed them, one heading towards Guildhall Square, the other to Waterloo Street on the right. She was about to go left herself, towards where the greater crowds had gathered and where, presumably, the young man could best disappear, when something fluttering just ahead of her caught her eye.

The crime scene tape which had been used to seal off the main door of the bank building had been ripped, the boarding over the doorway pulled back to reveal a two-foot gap. If the young man was part of the construction team with whom Kamil had been working, he'd know his way through the bank building. She realized that he hadn't gone left or right: he'd gone into the old bank building itself.

Lucy glanced from right to left, but neither of the uniformed officers could be seen. She pushed through the shoppers ahead of her and approached the newly exposed doorway.

Chapter Forty-eight

She squeezed her way between the board and the existing doorway, snagging her leg on a splinter from the wood. For the young man to have made it through here without being spotted, he would need to be even slimmer than Lucy.

The inside of the bank was as she remembered it. To her left now sat the cashiers' counter. It ran the length of one wall, and measured about three feet from counter to floor. Atop the counter, protective glass panels, which had once separated the cashiers from the customers, dimly reflected among their spiderwebs of cracks, the limited light seeping around the frames of the boarded windows beyond. The whole room smelt of urine, suggesting that some of the street drinkers had, perhaps, been making the most of the space after all, while the boards covering the front door had been down for the Forensics team to work the scene.

Lucy pulled out her torch and, holding it in one hand, her service gun in the other, she moved towards the cashiers' counter, behind which the young man could be hiding. As she approached it, she moved the beam slowly from one side of the room to the other, scanning the space for signs of the young man. The light threw elongated shadows against the back wall, which shifted and banked as she moved across the rubbled floor.

The heat inside the space seemed to build as she walked, her steps soundtracked both by the crunch of broken plaster beneath her boots and the sound of a hornpipe being played to a smattering of applause from outside.

She reached the edge of the counter and directed the torch beam at the protective glass in front of her, hoping to see through to the space behind where the cashiers had once sat. Instead, the light glared back in reflection, the shattered shards of glass spilling it in all directions. She realized that if she wanted to check behind the counter properly she would have to climb over it.

Laying the torch on the counter, she heaved herself up onto the wooden surface, then took the torch and stood on top of the counter, the glass partition atop it now reaching to her waist as she leaned over it, straining to see into the space behind the counter. She lifted the torch and, swinging it round, scanned the floor where the tellers' chairs would once have sat.

She was startled as the torch beam illuminated the man's face. He looked to be in his late teens. His hair was cropped short and looked wet, whether with sweat from the exertion of running or by design, Lucy could not tell. His nose was crooked slightly at the bridge, as if once broken and now healed. He bore a piercing through his right eyebrow. He leapt up quickly onto the counter, knocking her off balance as he clambered back over the glass partition at which she stood and dropped down off the counter on the other side.

267

'Jesus!' Lucy exclaimed, falling backwards, heavily, onto the floor, her torch clattering a few feet to her left. She struggled to her feet and grabbed the torch, turning the beam in time to see the youth make for the stairs that led up to the offices where she had first gained access to the building the day Grace had called her.

She brushed herself down as she set off again in pursuit, making for the staircase, her shoulder aching where it had borne the brunt of her fall. She took the stairs two at a time, pausing only when she reached the uppermost step.

She quickly checked each of the other offices at the top of the stairs, but it was immediately clear the youth wasn't in either of them. By the time she reached the end office, he was already pulling himself through the glassless window frame above her. He slithered out through the space and onto the City Walls.

It was significantly harder to get back out of the window than it had been to drop into the building through it. After putting her torch back into the loop on her belt, she had to wedge one foot against the wall sitting at a right angle from it, then use her other foot against the connecting wall to lever herself up sufficiently to make a grab for the frame. She managed to hold on with both arms, then used her feet to try to propel herself through the opening.

Suddenly, she felt a hand grip hers and felt herself being pulled through the space. She looked up into the face of one of the Neighbourhood Policing officers.

'Did you get lost?' he asked.

'Where is he? Did you get him?'

The man shook his head. 'The Guildhall Square's heaving with people.'

Lucy looked down through Magazine Gate, to the square beyond which, like Waterloo Place, was crowded with tents and exhibition sites. Chefs were standing at small gas cookers, frying up seafood, the saline smell carrying up onto the Walls on the warm breeze off the river.

If the youth had gone down off the Walls into the square, he'd find it much easier to hide. From there, he'd have any number of escape routes into the city.

They trudged down from the Walls and made their way back towards Great James Street, the uniform who'd had to abandon his ice cream stopping to take a proffered sample of seafood chowder as they went.

'What?' He shrugged as Lucy watched him gulp it down. 'Just getting in the spirit.'

Tom Fleming was sitting in the soup kitchen, similarly helping himself to some soup, when she made it back to him.

'He got away,' Lucy said. 'But thanks for your help.'

Fleming looked at her, one eyebrow cocked. 'I knew you were on it,' he said. 'Besides, he's left his van here. There's always that.'

Chapter Forty-nine

'The van is registered to someone called Rory Nash,' Fleming explained as they climbed back into Lucy's car. 'He has an address in Ardmore.'

It took them fifteen minutes to make it to Ardmore, a village lying on the outskirts of the Waterside, just a few miles further along the road on which the residential unit where Robbie worked was situated. Despite its proximity to the city, it lay along a quiet country road, surrounded on all sides by fields, and separated, ultimately, from the main A6 road by the River Faughan. The river, starting in the Sperrin Mountains and running, in total, almost forty miles before discharging into Lough Foyle, followed the path of a glacial valley, skirting round the city.

The house sat along the main Ardmore Road, though set back a little in its own grounds, surrounded by black metal railings sat atop a low red-brick wall. Though initially the address looked dilapidated, once they had made it in through the front gates, they realized that the run-down bungalow which had been visible from the road was unoccupied and that to its rear sat the actual property. It was a two-storey detached house, in red brick, which, Lucy guessed, must comfortably have housed six bedrooms and at least two reception rooms, for the roof carried two chimney stacks at either end.

A Mercedes sat in the driveway, the doors open, perhaps to allow the leather seats within to remain cool in the building heat of the day. A small white and brown terrier came scurrying around the corner of the house, yapping at them, its claws skittering on the brickwork of the driveway. It came to within six feet of them, then followed their progress to the house with short, bounding movements, barking at them continuously, but never coming any further.

'Shut up!' Fleming snapped at it, causing it to retreat a foot or two, then to resume its barking with increased fervour.

The door of the house opened before they had reached it. A heavyset woman stood in the doorway. She wore a white top and denim shorts, the hem of which dug into the skin of her legs.

'Help you?'

'We're with the PSNI,' Fleming said, showing his warrant card. 'Are you the owner of a blue Volkswagen Transporter, registration ZUI 2257?'

The woman nodded. 'What of it?'

'Are you Mrs Nash?'

'What of it?' she repeated.

'Maybe we could do this inside,' Lucy said. 'Out of the sun?'

The woman stood a moment, as if undecided. She glanced towards the roadway, snuffed into her hand, then turned and walked down the hallway, the still open door the only invitation for them to enter.

It was significantly cooler inside the house, not least because the hallway was tiled with marble, their passage along it marked by the alternating slap and slurp of the woman's flip-flops as she led them to the kitchen.

'What's happened to the van?' she asked.

The kitchen was tiled in a similar fashion to the hallway, its centre dominated by an island in which was built a hob, the room to the right filled with a dining table and eight chairs. The space opened out, through two French doors, to a lawn to the rear, bordered by woodland. A quad sat in the centre of the lawn.

The woman held a glass of juice in her hand, but did not offer either of them something to drink.

'Your van has been spotted several times now at a homeless shelter in Great James Street in Derry,' Fleming began. 'We've been told that the driver of the van has been in conversation with some of the destitute men who frequent the kitchen and indeed some of those men have gone with him on occasions.'

'Generally not to be seen again,' Lucy added.

The woman nodded, more as an indication that Fleming should continue than an agreement with what she had heard.

'We believe at least two of the men seen leaving with the driver of your van have been subsequently killed.'

'By us?' the woman asked, incredulously.

'We were hoping you might be able to tell us that,' Lucy said. 'We attempted to speak with the driver of the van today but he fled when we approached him.'

'And?'

'Do you know who has your van today?'

'Probably my son. Did he do something wrong?'

'If it was your son, he ran from us when we tried to question him.'

'I wouldn't know anything about that,' the woman said.

'And your son's name?' Fleming said, taking out his notebook.

'Padraig.'

Fleming noted down the name. 'We believe that Padraig isn't the regular driver of the van. You wouldn't happen to know who is? A man, heavy built, red hair?'

'Sounds like my husband.'

'That would be Mr Rory Nash?'

'That's right.'

Fleming waited for the woman to say something further, but she drained the juice and refilled the glass from a jug sitting on the counter.

'Is your husband here?'

The woman shook her head as she drained the second draught. 'He's working,' she said, then burped softly.

'What does he do?'

'He's a builder. A foreman.'

'Where is he at the moment?'

'Work.'

'Whereabouts?' Fleming asked, exasperated.

The woman shrugged. 'I can't keep up with where he is.'

'Have you any idea why he'd be at a soup kitchen, picking up homeless people?'

The woman finished the drink and placed the glass in the sink, her back to them. 'Sometimes, if some of the workmen he hires let him down or that, he'll need someone quick. A lot of the builders what came in from Europe can't get work no more. They'll work cheap. Saves us money, gives them a job.'

'Did your husband do a driveway for a lady out towards Bready a few weeks back?'

The woman shrugged. 'I told you, I can't keep up with what he does,' she said.

'We'll need to speak with your husband as a matter of urgency,' Fleming said. 'Can you call him and find out where he is at the moment?'

'He could be out of range,' the woman protested, before she'd even lifted her phone. 'If he's working up in the mountains or that, he goes out of range.' She picked up the mobile, pressed the speed-dial button and waited. They could hear the phone ringing through the receiver. The woman waited for six or seven rings, until they heard the call going to voicemail, then she hung up. 'I told you,' she said.

Lucy took out her card and handed it to the woman. 'We need to speak with your husband,' she said. 'We'll be back before the end of day if he hasn't contacted us before then.'

'And we'll need a word with your son, too,' Fleming said. 'I take it he's not here?'

The woman shrugged. Just then, her mobile started to ring. She glanced at the screen, then quickly away.

'Go ahead and answer it,' Fleming said. 'Don't mind us.'

The woman hesitated, but the urgency of the ringing compelled her against her better judgement to answer it.

'Yes? The police are here looking for you ... Something about the van at a homeless shelter ... I told them that. They want to speak to you … Where are you?' She listened a moment, grunted, then hung up.

'He'll meet you at the Strand Road station, he says.'

'No need,' Lucy protested. 'We can go to him. Where is he at the moment?'

'He's going to the Strand Road. He needs to collect the van anyway,' the woman said, folding her arms. 'He'll see you there.'

Chapter Fifty

In fact, it took Nash almost an hour to reach the station, by which stage Burns was threatening to send out a team to pick him up. The desk sergeant who called up for Lucy, as it was her whom Nash asked to see, announced his eventual arrival.

The man was at least eighteen stone, his height and breadth helping him carry it, though still not able to disguise the paunch of his belly, which hung over his trouser belt. His hair, while undoubtedly red, was shaven fairly tightly against his scalp. However, what most surprised Lucy, when she saw him, was Nash's face. His features, naturally pugnacious and squashed, appeared all the worse due to the two black eyes he bore. They were clearly a few days old, the bruising already segueing from purple into yellow. He had a gash below his right eye, which had healed into a scab, though something had caused it to reopen at one side and a thin trickle of dried blood marked his cheek.

'Are you Black?' he asked.

'DS Black,' Lucy said, extending her hand.

He looked stupidly at the offered hand, then wiped his own on the leg of his jeans and shook it. His arm was thick and matted with red curls, his forearm scarred. His hands and knuckles though were particularly bruised, one of them split.

'Were you in an accident?' Lucy asked.

'Perks of the job,' Nash commented. 'A two-by-four in the face.'

Lucy led him into Interview Room 1 where DS Mickey Sinclair was already standing. Burns had made it clear he wanted someone from CID in with Lucy on the interview with Nash. Lucy wondered whether it was just another way to keep Fleming sidelined or to make her feel more part of the CID team.

'Sit down, Mr Nash,' Mickey began when he entered the room. 'We're just looking to clear up a few things.'

Nash glanced from Mickey to Lucy. 'Unless your name's Lucy Black, I'm guessing she's the one I'm here to see,' he said to Mickey, unnecessarily indicating Lucy with his thumb for effect.

'I'm DS Sinclair, with CID. You clearly already know that this is DS Black with PPU. We'll both be sitting in today,' Mickey said. 'Have a seat.'

Reluctantly, Nash lowered himself onto the seat on one side of the desk, while Lucy and Mickey took the other side.

'Maybe you can start by explaining why your son did a runner this afternoon when approached by DS Black here?'

The man grunted. 'Do I need a lawyer?'

'I hope not,' Mickey said. 'As I said, we're just looking to clarify a few things.'

Nash nodded. 'He's doing the double,' he said. 'He's on DLA on account of his back.'

'DLA?' Lucy asked. 'He ran like that because he's claiming Disability Allowance?'

277

Nash nodded.

'In fact, he ran like that *despite* claiming DLA?' Lucy added. 'I couldn't keep up with him. His back wasn't causing him problems today, particularly when he vaulted over the cashiers' desk in the old bank on Waterloo Place.'

Nash scratched the scab on his face, inspecting his fingernail after he did so, then wiping the blood onto his trouser leg.

'It plays up in the winter,' he said. 'Thank God for the good weather. He's like a new fella.'

'What was he doing at the soup kitchen on Great James Street today?'

Nash inhaled slowly, as if readying a prepared response. 'He was there for me. If I'm ever short a hand on a job, I can sometimes pick up someone there who'll work the day for a few pound, cash in hand.'

'Why there?'

'A lot of the good builders who came over from Europe when things were booming are on the skids now,' Nash said. 'It's good to throw them a bit of work if you can.'

'And presumably it's cheaper for you than having to pay someone a full wage?'

Nash feigned outrage. 'They're all paid. I'm a businessman. If I can get work for cheaper, and they can get paid a wage they're happy with, what's the problem? That's capitalism in action.'

'You don't consider it exploitative?' Lucy asked.

Nash shook his head. 'They're offered forty quid for a day's work. If they need it, they'll take it. No one's forcing them into working for me. They choose to come along.'

'And what about how they behave when they're working for you?' Lucy asked.

Nash frowned. 'Meaning?'

'Did you do a driveway for an older woman in Bready a few weeks back?'

Nash raised his eyes, as if trying to remember.

'Jeffries,' Lucy reminded him.

Nash clicked his fingers. 'That's right. Nice old girl.'

'She found *you* intimidating,' Lucy replied. 'You had two men working with you: Kamil Krawiec and Aaron Moore.'

Nash shook his head. 'They don't ring any bells.'

Lucy pushed the picture of Kamil Krawiec across the table. 'That's Kamil,' she said.

'Yeah,' Nash said, uncertainly. 'I think I might have picked him up once. A while back.'

'You picked him up twice,' Lucy said. 'Once, when he was working on Mrs Jeffries's driveway, and then again last week, along with this man, Terry Haynes.' She pushed the picture of Haynes across to him.

Nash studied the picture. 'No. I don't remember him,' he said. 'I kind of remember the other guy. Foreigner?'

'That's right.'

'He was a good worker. I might have used him twice so, if that was the case.'

'He *was* with you on the Bready job,' Lucy said. 'Mrs Jeffries remembers him. We found his fingerprints all over the jewellery boxes in her bedroom after her house was broken into while she was on holidays.'

Nash pointed at the picture. 'He broke into her house? I'll not be hiring him again, so.'

'You'll not be, all right,' Mickey said. 'We found him crushed to death in a bin lorry.'

'Was this him?' Nash asked. 'I heard about that.' He pantomimed a wince. 'That's a nasty way to go. He was sleeping in the bins or something, is that right?'

'He was beaten up,' Mickey said. 'In the old bank building in Waterloo Place. Where we think a construction gang was stealing copper piping. You wouldn't know anything about that?'

Nash shook his head, holding Mickey's stare. 'Nothing.'

'That might be another way to cut corners. Steal building supplies from the empty buildings in the city centre and use them in your own jobs? Capitalism in action.'

'Are you accusing me of stealing?' Nash snapped.

'We're only making inquiries,' Mickey said. 'No need to get aggressive.'

'Trust me, I'm not,' Nash said, his hands joining on the desk in front of him. 'Maybe these two guys were stealing the piping and that themselves. If they were both builders, they'd be well able for it.'

'We didn't say that this man was a builder,' Lucy said, tapping on the picture of Haynes.

Nash stared at her a moment, his mouth slightly open, as if mentally rewinding the conversation to confirm this for himself. 'Well, if you think I hired him, he'd hardly be a brain surgeon, would he?'

Lucy nodded. 'So you know nothing about the burglary?'

Nash shook his head. 'I'm just trying to run a business and make a few pound.'

'By the size of your house, you're making more than a few pound,' Lucy commented. 'I thought the building bubble had burst.'

'It has. But the work's there if you're willing to go out and chase it down,' Nash said. 'Are we done here?'

Lucy glanced at Mickey who shrugged.

'For now,' Lucy said. 'But we might be in touch again. Where are you working at the moment?'

'Out at Claudy,' Nash said. 'We're doing some resurfacing works. I need to be getting back to finish them up for the day,' he added, standing. 'And I'll be needing the keys to my van, too.'

Lucy accompanied Nash to the front desk. Mickey was waiting for her as she came back upstairs.

'Well, what do you reckon?' he asked.

She shrugged. 'It's hard to tell. Maybe the son was worried that what they were doing, hiring the men, was illegal. Maybe it was just that he's been doing the double, claiming benefits while he earns.'

'Or he could be elbow deep in all the killings.'

Lucy nodded. 'The only person who can really tell us is Aaron Moore. Until we find him, we're going to be stuck in the dark.'

Chapter Fifty-one

Before going home for the evening, Lucy drove once more down to Gransha to see her father. Her mother's warning about his condition had served both to make her want to see him, and to simultaneously dread to do so, lest he be so far gone from her that he wouldn't know her any more.

She was relieved then, when she arrived, to find him sitting up in the chair in his room. The bruising on his face had begun to heal, the weals darkened in colour in the folds of skin beneath his eye.

The television was playing in the corner, *You've Been Framed!* parading a series of home videos of people falling into paddling pools. Lucy could tell that, though he was looking at it, the images flickering on the screen were not registering with him. He laughed along with the canned laughter of the show, but without seeming recognizant of the source.

'Dad?' Lucy asked, as she came in.

He turned and smiled at her, mildly. 'Hi, love,' he said. 'Good to see you.'

She moved across and kissed him on the forehead, his skin clammy to the touch, his breath stale and warm.

'How are you feeling?'

'Good,' he said, vacantly, then turned once more to the screen, already smiling in expectation of the next pratfall.

'Your face looks better,' Lucy said.

'Yes,' he agreed. 'I fell.'

'Has Mum been with you?'

He stared at the screen a moment, his brow furrowed with concentration. 'No, but Lucy was here the other day.'

'*I* am Lucy, Dad.'

'I know,' he said, waving away her comment with his hand. 'The other one.'

'Which other one?'

'*Our* Lucy.'

'I am Lucy,' she repeated, leaning down, positioning herself between him and the television, forcing him to focus on her. '*I'm* Lucy.' She could feel her eyes filling as he shifted in his seat in order to see past her. Despite momentary lapses in the past, when he'd confused her for a girl named Janet he had once known, and indeed despite her mother's words of warning, she had not been prepared for this moment when he seemed to no longer know her. He was moving further away from her, she realized.

He nodded. 'She said to say hello. She was looking well.'

Lucy bowed her head, her hands still lightly gripping his shoulders. 'Dad, I am Lucy. Me. Your daughter. Do you not know me?'

She felt him move, felt his hand cup her face. He raised her chin so that she was looking at him.

'I worry about her,' he said, his eyes red and rheumy with tears. 'I don't think she's happy.'

'I'm fine, Dad,' Lucy said, feeling her own eyes flush. 'I am happy.'

'I told her,' he said. 'I told her, look at your mother. Look how she's doing now. Happy.'

'I am Lucy,' she snapped, hoping it might bring him back.

She looked at him as he studied her face, smiling mildly, his eyes alight. But as with the programme he had been watching, she knew that the smile covered his inability to recognize her any more.

'Jesus, please know me,' she pleaded. 'Please try, Dad. Try to remember me.' Lucy stared into his eyes, at the flecks of red which peppered the whites, the shard of blood which had leaked into the eyeball as a result of the fall he had suffered, as if by studying him closely enough, she might be able to find him once more.

'I still love you, you know,' he said.

Then he leaned gently forward and kissed her on her open mouth.

The door opened just as Lucy pulled back from her father in shock. The orderly who had helped her pull the man from the mudbanks days earlier stood, a tray in his hand bearing a plate of stew and a glass of milk.

'Sorry! I didn't know you were here. It's dinner time,' he explained, raising the tray as proof. 'Have you recovered from the rescue mission?' He laughed then, when no one spoke, he added, 'Is everything OK?'

Lucy could not speak, staring at her father as if it was she who no longer recognized him.

Chapter Fifty-two

Lucy showered as soon as she got home around 9 p.m., turning the heat down low and standing beneath the stream until her skin began to numb. She could not easily dismiss the memory of her father's mouth against hers, the sensuality of the kiss.

Pulling on her bathrobe, she went down to the kitchen and lifted a roll of black bin bags, then went up to the room which had been her father's bedroom and which she had not changed since his committal to hospital. She opened one of the bags and began gathering up the small ornaments that decorated the tops of the bookcase and chest of drawers in the room and, one by one, dropped them into the bag. That done, she began clearing the bookcase itself, keeping only a few novels which she had promised herself she would get around to reading at some stage. She continued working until the room was cleared and five bulging bags sat against the far wall. The wallpaper, a fine-striped print, would have to come down too, she reasoned. And the carpet would need lifting. She would need to get someone to do both for her, she decided.

It was only afterwards, as she padded into her room to get changed, that she realized that in all that she had just done, she had given no thought to Robbie's proposal that they move in together. Regardless, she decided, whether she was staying here or selling up, the house needed to be changed, the decor updated to something more reflective of her tastes.

As she pulled on a T-shirt, she noticed that the screen of her phone, lying on the bedside cabinet, was alight and, picking it up, she saw she'd missed a call from Grace. She rang back, but there was no response, nor had she left a message. Perhaps, Lucy reasoned, she was hoping to stay another night. Or, perhaps, she had called the number by accident. Perhaps it was Lucy, not the girl, who had enjoyed the thought of having another person in the house with her, a break from the routine of her loneliness.

She made a dinner for herself of oven chips and curry sauce, then carried the plate and a can of Diet Coke from the fridge into the living room. When she'd finished eating, she tried Grace's number again, but without reply.

She was just hanging up when she heard knocking at the door and, for an absurd second, believed it to be Grace. Perhaps the girl had somehow managed to make her way out to Prehen. She was a little disconcerted then when she opened the door and Dermot, her neighbour, stood on the step.

'It's Fiona,' he said. 'She's across in ours again. She's left him.'

Fiona and Jenny sat on the sofa, again in their respective spots, just as on the night Lucy had first called. The damage to Fiona's face, though, was much more pronounced than on the previous occasion. The old cut on her lip had reopened with the force of the blow, which had left one eye shutting, as if winking against the light, swollen and red and running tears.

When Fiona saw Lucy, she began to cry again, noisily, into the tissue she had balled in her fist.

'How are you?' Lucy asked, unnecessarily, glancing across at Jenny whose expression shifted from concern to anger and back.

'I've been better,' Fiona managed. 'I've left him.'

'Good for you,' Lucy said. 'Is that your stuff?' she added, gesturing towards the small overnight bag that lay on the ground at Fiona's feet.

Fiona nodded. 'I don't even know what's in there,' she managed, the words bubbling out in a half-laugh that dissolved again to tears.

'What happened?' Lucy asked.

'He came home in a mood. He'd had to work today, even though it's a Saturday, because of this audit that's being done, so he'd not been happy with that, anyway. Then something happened at work, one of the jobs wasn't right. And the police had been with him about something this morning, too.'

Lucy nodded, watching Fiona carefully for any sign that she realized that Lucy had been the one who had visited him. Dermot, Jenny's husband, appeared, having put the children to bed.

'I said I wanted to go shopping tomorrow. I wanted my bank card back,' Fiona said.

'Did he give it back?' Jenny asked.

Fiona shook her head. 'He lost his temper and went off on one. We rowed and he … he hit me again.'

Dermot gathered himself. 'I'm going to call over there,' he said.

'No!' Fiona pleaded. 'It'll only make things worse. Leave it.'

'Maybe you should get the police involved now,' Lucy said. 'There are officers trained to handle these types of cases. I know one who's very—'

Fiona shook her head, straightening her back as she did so. She rubbed at her nose with the wad of tissue, then sniffed. 'No. *I* left him. I've taken control of things.'

'You need to get your card back,' Jenny said. 'You need to have access to your money.'

'I'm not asking him for anything. I'll go to the bank myself on Monday morning and close that account. I'll get a new card for a new account.'

'You need—' Jenny protested, but Fiona raised her hand.

'No. I'm not asking him for anything.'

Dermot had just brought in tea and biscuits when the doorbell rang, twice, in quick succession. At the sound, Fiona stiffened where she sat, instinctively grabbing for her sister's hand.

'I'll get it,' Dermot said, laying down the tray and going out, closing the living-room door behind him.

They sat in silence, listening as the door latch clicked open and they heard the low rumble of a man's voice. Fiona was gripping her sister's hand now, her knuckles whitening in the grasp.

Dermot's voice was louder, raised. 'You're not wanted here,' he said. 'Piss off, now.'

Then they heard Boyd's voice. Angry, demanding. 'I want to see her.'

'You'd better leave, John. If she wants to see you, she'll call you,' Dermot said, his voice unsteady, as if with the effort of controlling himself.

'She'll fucking see me if I—'

They heard a thud then, as the two men in the doorway slammed against the wall separating the living room from the corridor. They could hear the sounds of scuffling, the guttural swearing of both men.

Fiona made to stand, but her sister pulled her back to her seat. 'Leave it,' she said.

Another sound now, almost a screech of pain, though Lucy could not tell from which of the men it had come. Unable to control herself, she stood and moved quickly into the hallway. Dermot and Boyd were scuffling in the doorway as Boyd tried vainly to force his way in past the bigger man. On Boyd's final attempt, Dermot grabbed him by the front of his shirt and hoisted him out through the doorway, where he fell onto the path outside. Boyd's face was flushed, the blood from his nose dripping onto the 'Welcome' mat on the front step as he looked up.

'You!' he spat when he saw Lucy. 'You!'

Lucy turned and realized that Fiona and Jenny had joined her now in the hall, both crying out at the sight of their respective partners.

'Fee, I'm sorry,' Boyd said, trying to gather himself from the ground. Dermot motioned as if to go for him again, gaining a pat of approbation on the back from his wife, but Fiona held out a hand to stop him.

'Go home,' Fiona said. 'You're embarrassing yourself. And me.'

Boyd staggered to his feet. 'I'm sorry, Fee. Let's talk about it. Somewhere else. Not here. Not with them here.'

'You need to leave,' Fiona said, stepping forward. She gripped the door and began to close it.

'It was her, wasn't it? Turned you against me. The cop!' Boyd shouted.

The movement of the door stopped as Fiona turned to look at the three figures standing behind her, then back to where Boyd stood.

'What are you talking about?'

'Her!' Boyd said, pointing past Fiona to Lucy. 'Black. Did she make you do it?'

'Lucy's not a cop,' Fiona said, half laughing though without humour.

'Is she not?' Boyd laughed. 'Is that what she told you? And you believed her?'

Fiona stared at Lucy, willing her to deny it. Lucy lowered her head, unable to meet her gaze.

Boyd sensed victory in the gesture, for he said, 'Ask her. Ask her now. Go on. Tell her,' he added, calling to Lucy. 'Tell her the truth. That you're a cop.'

Fiona turned now, her hand still on the door. 'Lucy, what's he talking about? You're not in the police, are you?'

'It's not ...' Lucy began, before finally simply nodding.

'You lied to me too,' Fiona said.

'It's not like that, Fiona ...' Lucy began.

'I want you to leave.'

Lucy looked to Jenny and Dermot, both of whom stared at the carpet beneath them.

Lucy passed them, stopping abreast Fiona, laying her hand on her arm. 'I'm sorry,' she said. 'I didn't mean ...'

'Take your hand off me,' Fiona hissed. 'Just leave, please.'

Lucy stepped out onto the driveway. She could see, in the house opposite, one of the neighbours standing looking across, openly watching proceedings.

Boyd stared at her as she passed, his teeth bloody from his bust nose.

'You'll answer for hitting her,' Lucy said. 'Don't think this changes anything.'

'We'll see,' Boyd managed, spitting blood from his mouth onto the ground. 'Don't count on it.'

'Go fuck yourself, Mr Boyd,' Lucy said.

Chapter Fifty-three

She realized, as she crossed the road towards her own house that, if she went inside, Boyd would know where she lived. Though she had no reason to fear him, she likewise knew that he had cause to bear her a grudge. She'd parked her car on the street, her own driveway prohibitively steep for her to park on. She'd brought her car key with her, the house key being on the same ring.

Consequently, she walked across to her car, climbed in and drove off. She figured that she'd circle for so long as it would take for Boyd to leave now that it was clear he wouldn't be seeing Fiona. If Lucy could take any comfort from what had happened, it was that at least Fiona hadn't walked out and gone back home with Boyd. She'd chosen to take control but, more importantly, she'd chosen to stay with her sister. That resolve might not last too long, but it would, at least, keep her safe for the night. In the morning, Lucy would call with her and try to explain why she hadn't wanted to tell her that she was with the police. Perhaps she might even be able to encourage her to press charges against Boyd.

With nowhere in particular to go, she drove through the town. The streets were busy, even so late in the evening, but as she drove down the main thoroughfare inside the city's Walls, Shipquay Street, Lucy couldn't help but notice the number of premises that lay empty, the shopfronts just painted boards, much like the bank building in Great James Street. The facade of prosperity and business hid a much more sinister truth: the city centre was dying, slowly, hemorrhaging trade out of town.

On the corner of Shipquay Street, just before she passed through the Gate out towards the Guildhall, Lucy spotted a girl who, for a moment, she thought was Grace. She slowed the car as she drew near, which caused the girl to turn and look at her. The girl was much younger, her face fresh and alight with the laughter she shared with her friends.

Lucy raised a hand in acknowledgement of her mistake and drove on. She lifted her mobile and tried dialling Grace one more time. Again the call rang out, going to call answering.

'Grace. Lucy Black here. You called me earlier. Not sure if you meant to or not. Will you give me a shout if you get a chance? Just to let me know everything's OK.'

She did another circuit of the city centre, in the vague hope that she might spot Grace, before cutting back up through the Diamond to head home. As she passed the bottom of Pump Street, she glanced up to see a squad car parked opposite Moore's house. She stopped and, doing a U-turn, went back around the one-way system and pulled down into the spot behind the marked vehicle.

As she approached, she saw that the two officers inside were eating their dinner, a bucket of KFC balancing on the dash. One, a thin man with a goatee and a shaven head, opened the door, the windows of the car being sealed shut. He wiped the grease from his fingers onto the Kevlar vest he wore.

'Everything all right?' he asked, then recognized Lucy. 'DS Black? Hot wing?' He proffered the fast food bucket.

'I'm good, thanks,' Lucy said. 'Are you sitting out here all night?'

The man shook his head. Lucy was fairly certain his surname was Frazer, but didn't want to risk calling him that lest she was wrong. After all, he had remembered her name.

'No. We're to drive past every so often, take a quick check.'

Lucy nodded. 'Any signs of life in there?'

'Nothing. We're here about ten minutes; stopped for a bite to eat and thought we'd sit for a bit and kill two birds with one stone, you know?'

Lucy straightened, staring up at the house. There was something about the rubble in the yard. She wanted to get back into the house again, to check the rooms carefully for signs of activity. The mixture of earth and old bricks she'd seen in the garden had come from somewhere, after all. The only way she'd get back in to search more thoroughly would be if they knew Moore was in there.

'What's that?' she asked suddenly. 'In the back?'

Frazer shifted in his seat to see, unbalancing the bucket of fried chicken from the dash, which spilled onto the floor of the car.

'Shit,' he said, gathering up the food with the aid of his passenger, whom Lucy now saw to be a

294

fresh-faced female officer, her blonde hair pulled back in a ponytail.

'I didn't see anything,' the woman offered.

'I think I saw torchlight,' Lucy said. 'Moving about in the kitchen. Definitely. Look.'

She moved away from the car, approaching the darkened house and peering in the front window. 'I'm sure I saw someone moving about in there.'

Frazer had joined her now on the pavement, his presence marked by the waft of grease and spices. 'Where?' he asked.

Lucy moved next to him, leaning lightly against him as she pointed. 'In there,' she said. 'I'm certain I saw something.'

Frazer peered in where she pointed, not moving away from her closeness. 'You might be right,' he said.

'I didn't see anything,' the passenger said, getting out of the car.

'Best be sure,' Frazer said. 'Eh?' He lifted the radio handset from the shoulder pocket of his vest and radioed through to the Strand Road to report it.

Seamus Moore arrived almost half an hour later, his manner more abrupt than it had been when Lucy had previously met him.

'This better not be a waste of time,' Moore said, flicking through the keys on the ring, then selecting the one he needed. 'I've better places to be on a Saturday night.'

'We appreciate your assistance, Mr Moore—' Lucy began.

'I'm here because the Chief Superintendent asked me,' Moore said. 'That's the only reason.'

295

Lucy nodded. 'I understand, sir.'

He unlocked the door and opened it ajar, then stopped. 'And, as before, this is also on the understanding that my brother, if he is here, will give you any information he might have about the death of the man you found in the bins, but will not answer any questions about anything else he might have done. Is that clear? The Chief Super has already agreed to it.'

Lucy nodded again. 'That's fine. I'm sure I saw someone in there,' she said, already regretting her lie.

The house was exactly as it had been on her previous visit, bin bags still lying on the hall floor. This time, though, Lucy noticed that the papers that Seamus Moore had removed from the bags had been replaced and the torn part of the bag tied up in a knot. Perhaps Seamus Moore himself had done it, she reasoned.

She moved upstairs, while the other two officers searched the ground-floor rooms. There were two bedrooms in the house. One was crowded with bags and boxes of magazines and books all relating to horses, even the bed sagging a little under the weight of the materials piled on top. The second room contained more memorabilia – boxes of trophies and rosettes, many of them tattered with age and frequent handling. A chest of drawers against one wall was covered with statues and toy horses. There was no space for anyone to sleep in either room, or indeed any evidence that Aaron Moore had recently been there. More importantly, Lucy noted, there was no evidence of building work having been done.

Both rooms were papered with fading patterned wallpaper, which appeared to have been on the walls for some considerable time.

She moved back down the stairs, picking her way carefully past the black bags, which lined the staircase.

'Nothing,' Frazer said, blushing a little. 'Are you sure you saw something?'

Seamus Moore stood behind him, arms folded, glaring at Lucy.

'Constable Kerr here tells me that she didn't see anyone moving about from outside,' he said, nodding to the female officer.

'I'm sure I saw someone moving about in here,' Lucy said. 'I saw a torch beam moving about.'

'Why are you even here?' Moore asked. 'I understand that the two officers were passing by as requested. Why were *you* here?'

Lucy shrugged. 'I was on a call-out,' she said. 'Let me just take a last look down here,' she added.

'It's been checked,' Moore called, but Lucy was moving into the living room again where Constable Kerr glared at her.

'We've already looked,' she said. 'He's not down here either.'

Lucy couldn't explain that it wasn't the man she was looking for; it was evidence of what work had resulted in the pile of soil and rubble littering the backyard. Again, though, the kitchen, living room and downstairs toilet showed no evidence of recent work.

'Downstairs toilet only,' Lucy observed. 'That must be a pain in the middle of the night.'

'He's lucky there's one at all,' Moore said. 'These houses didn't have inside toilets. When I bought it there was only the outhouse. We had to get this one installed; that used to be a cupboard.'

'There's an outhouse,' Lucy said. 'Can I check it?'

Moore frowned. 'You think he's living in an outhouse?'

Lucy shrugged. 'It won't take a minute,' she said.

Moore shuffled through the keys on his key ring again until he found the large deadbolt key and unlocked the back door.

'Be my guest. It's the last time you'll be getting inside this house without a warrant,' he said.

The yard was small, boxed in on all sides by the houses surrounding it. A small scrap of grass at its centre had held the pile of soil and pieces of red brick that Lucy had seen on her first visit. As she shone her torch around the yard she saw, for the first time, tucked in around the corner of the house itself, a small cinder-block building, with a corrugated iron roof and an old wooden door.

'Is there an outside light?' she asked. A moment later, the yard was bathed in light from the halogen lamp above the back door.

Lucy moved across to the outhouse, pushing open the door with her foot. At first, she could not understand what had happened, for the torch beam seemed to drop from where she had expected to see it shining against the back wall. Her own shadow, cast by the halogen lamp behind her, fell forward into a hole, about five feet in radius, which had been excavated in the floor of the outhouse where the toilet should have been. Leaning forwards, holding on to the door jamb to prevent herself falling, Lucy could see that a ladder descended down into the hole.

'There's something here,' she shouted, turning and putting her foot on the uppermost rung, her torch clamped in her hand as she tried her best to continue gripping the side of the ladder.

She climbed down twelve steps before she felt the ground beneath with an exploratory prod of her toe. She stepped down onto the ground and, gripping the torch, shone it around where she stood. The space was just large enough to accommodate her height, with a foot to spare above her. The side walls curved around her, joining above her head to create a perfect circle. She shone the torch upwards, noting that the masonry was red brick. In one or two spots, along the curve of the wall, single blocks seemed to have fallen out onto the ground, where they lay, shattered.

Lucy had heard before of the supposed tunnels running beneath the city. Some people had claimed that they stretched right back to the Siege in 1688; others that they were, in fact, Victorian sewer systems. The red brickwork, which Lucy could see, supported the second hypothesis more than the first. She directed the torch beam along the length of the tunnel walls, to where it curved out of sight. Finally, she directed it towards the ground at her feet, worried that she might be about to step into sewage, but the ground was dry, the system long since out of use.

As she heard the clatter of Constable Frazer's steps on the ladder above, she began moving forwards, following the curve of the tunnel.

Chapter Fifty-four

As she moved, she sensed that the tunnel was inclining slightly to the right, though she wasn't sure if this was actually the case, or simply a result of her staring at the ever-receding turn of the wall. The brickwork was damp, mossy in places, though the floor beneath her wasn't as slippery as she'd expected, due in large part to a coating of sediment along its length, which provided her with some grip.

The further along it she moved, she realized that the ceiling was starting to rise slightly above her head and she had a sense that the tunnel itself was widening. Finally, she saw that there was a more definite shift in direction and, having turned the corner, she stepped out into a small chamber.

The ceiling was perhaps fifteen feet from the floor, held up, seemingly, by four arches of red brick which grew from the four corners of the chamber up towards its apex, where they met. The chamber opened out onto two further tunnels, both of which had gullies running the visible length of the floor, evidently, at one time, feeding water into this chamber and then on down the tunnel along which Lucy had just come.

Lucy could hear the persistent plop of water dripping from ceiling to floor, but it was not that which held her attention. Next to the far wall of the chamber stood a small cooking stove, beside which was a sleeping bag lying on the ground. The bag yawned open, its flap thrown back, as if only recently vacated.

She moved across, scanning the rest of the space for signs of Moore, but the room was clearly empty. And, as he hadn't passed her on the tunnel that she'd just walked, she reasoned that, if indeed the sleeping bag was his and he was still beneath ground, he must have taken one of the two tunnels now facing her.

She reached down and felt the cooking stove cautiously, but it was cold. Next to his sleeping bag, she could see now, tacked to the wall, were more pictures of horses, seven in total, their images arranged in a circle. At the centre of the circle was another image, this time a crudely hand-drawn picture of a blood-red flower, at its centre a single black circle. At first, Lucy thought it was a bleeding bullet wound and then, she realized that it was actually meant to be a poppy. She could see the ground beneath the pictures was strewn with the foil of chewing-gum wrappers. As she peeled the corner of the poppy picture back, she could see Moore had evidently been using gum in place of glue to create the shrine on his wall.

'Jesus!'

She turned to where Constable Frazer stood at the entranceway to the chamber, looking around him.

'Did you know this was down here?' he asked.

Lucy shook her head. 'Not here exactly. I had heard of the tunnels before, and the chambers. There were over twenty of them, I think.'

Frazer stared up at the vaulted ceiling and whistled softly through his teeth in admiration of the workmanship.

'I think Moore has been living down here. Sleeping here at least,' Lucy said, training her torch beam on the makeshift bed.

'Is he still here?'

Lucy shook her head. 'I don't know. If he is, he's gone one of two ways.' She nodded towards where the tunnels split.

'Do you want left or right?' Frazer asked.

'Where's Kerr?'

He rolled his eyes. 'Still up top; she's claustrophobic, she says. I'll take left.' With that, he moved off into the tunnel, ducking down to avoid banging his head on the lowering ceiling.

Lucy felt the heft of her torch in her hand, then set off towards the right-hand side.

Again, as she moved, she had a sense that the tunnel was veering slightly to the side and she tried to guess whereabouts she was relative to what was above her. She could hear, behind the constant dripping water now, the low drone of traffic overhead and she guessed that she was moving towards the Diamond. That being the case, Frazer was probably headed towards Bishop's Street. She knew that the Apprentice Boy's Memorial Hall had once had access to the tunnels beneath and wondered if that would be where he would emerge. She also knew, however, that the Army had sealed up the tunnels during the late seventies, after they'd been mapped and had, indeed, confiscated all the maps lest someone try to plant a bomb beneath the road to target passing

Saracens overhead. The thought of being sealed below ground brought her little comfort and she regretted now not leaving markers to allow her to find her way back to the ladder and Aaron Moore's outhouse if she needed to.

Suddenly, she heard something different from the rumble of the cars above and the plop-plop of water from the ceiling. The sound was like a soft scuffling ahead of her. The tunnel seemed to curve towards a bend now and she could only see to the edge of her torch beam, six or seven feet ahead.

The shifting of the light beam along the curvature of the tunnel made everything seem to skew to the left. She could hear the sound more clearly now, the scraping of something against the stonework. She resisted the urge to call for Frazer and instead kept inching forwards, approaching the bend in the tunnel, torch held steady.

As she rounded the curve, a large, fat-bodied rat sat on its haunches, staring at her, the bristles of its whiskers gleaming in the torch beam, the light reflecting off the small black beads of its eyes. Lucy shuddered involuntarily, shivering away the goosebumps as the rat dropped to all fours and bounded away.

Lucy scanned ahead now, moving the torch from side to side in search of where the rat had gone. It was then that she saw the elongating shadows, thrown against the far curved wall of the tunnel, assume a slightly different shape and, bringing the torch around again, she saw, ahead of her, a stooped figure rounding the bend of the tunnel and vanishing from view.

'Mr Moore,' Lucy called, setting off at a run. 'Mr Moore. I'm with the police. I've come to help you.'

There was no sign of the figure ahead, now, as Lucy continued moving along the tunnels. Suddenly, something cold touched the skin of the back of her neck, startling her. Reaching back, she felt it wet to the touch. Bringing her fingertips close to her face, using the torch beam for light, she saw it had been a drip of water. Angling the torch upwards, she saw a second drop falling from the ceiling above.

She could sense, again, that the tunnel was widening now and, as she turned another bend, found herself in yet another chamber, similar to the first, though empty of vestiges of human habitation this time. Again, the chamber opened onto two further tunnels.

Afraid of being lost, she decided to keep going right, as she had done the first time. She jogged across the space of the chamber and up the right-hand tunnel. However, she had only made it about fifty metres when she realized that, just ahead of her, the tunnel had been bricked up with concrete blocks, the hardened overspill of cement curled around the spaces between the stonework. There was clearly nowhere for Moore to hide, which meant that he had taken the left-hand opening from the second chamber.

She ran back along the tunnel and took the second path, all the time wondering if Moore may have already made his way back towards his house unnoticed.

This left-hand tunnel, like the right, curved quickly to one side and, she realized as she turned the last bend, had been similarly bricked up. Only this time, Aaron Moore stood there, his back against the concrete block wall, his gaze locked on Lucy's, brandishing a bread knife in his hand.

Chapter Fifty-five

Moore edged backwards, pressing himself against the wall, as if in so doing he might somehow be able to pass through it. His eyes were wide, his expression one of terror. Instinctively, he wielded the knife, swinging it in front of him to ward off Lucy's moving any closer.

'Mr Moore? My name's Lucy Black. I'm here to help you. Can you put down the knife?'

Moore stared at her, then flicked his gaze over her shoulder, towards the blackness of the tunnel behind her.

'It's just us, Mr Moore. Don't be afraid,' Lucy said, offering her two hands, palms up, to show she was unarmed. She guessed Frazer was behind her somewhere in the warren of tunnels. 'Your brother, Seamus, is up above. We've all been very worried about you. Will you give me the knife and come up with me?'

At the mention of the weapon, it seemed to come to life again, his grip on it strengthening, its erratic movement back and forth increasing.

'Please, Mr Moore. Come up to your brother.'

In the hush of the tunnel, she was sure she heard him snort derisively, but he did not speak. He moved forward a little, away from the wall, and shifted the knife to his other hand momentarily, before returning it to the right.

'I saw your pictures on the wall out there,' Lucy said. 'Is it a shrine?'

Moore glanced again behind her.

Lucy stood her ground, her hand still outstretched, though well clear of the arc of Moore's knife. 'There's only us. You don't have to be afraid. Is it a shrine?' she asked again, bringing his attention back to her. To her rear, she thought she could hear movement, probably Constable Frazer, though with the echo of the tunnels, it was impossible to say from how far back he was.

Moore nodded. 'Yes,' he managed, dryly, his lips smacking as he spoke.

'You must have loved looking after those horses,' Lucy said, moving a step now towards him, slowly.

Moore nodded, distracted both by her movement and by the sounds carrying along the tunnel from behind Lucy, growing clearer now. As she moved, Lucy became aware that her faint shadow was growing on the wall behind Moore. Constable Frazer was coming behind her with another torch.

The shadow darkened as both she and Moore simultaneously heard Frazer shout.

'Put the knife down or I'll shoot!'

Lucy turned to see him standing a few yards behind her now, just past the curve of the tunnel, his gun raised, his torch clamped against it, both trained on Moore.

'Don't shoot!' Lucy snapped, twisting again to Moore.

The man stood, one arm shielding his eyes, his knife still outstretched, its swinging increasing again,

307

wildly moving back and forth, blindly protecting himself.

'Mr Moore? Please put down the knife. No one wants to hurt you. We're here to help.'

'You said you were alone,' Moore said suddenly.

'If my colleague goes again, will you put down the knife?' Lucy asked, ignoring the comments of refusal from Frazer behind her.

'We'll go out together,' Lucy said. 'Put down the knife. My colleague will back down and you and I can go up together. You can tell me the names of the horses. Is Sefton one?'

The name was the only one Lucy could recall having heard in connection with the attack.

'Sefton lived. And Echo and Yeti,' Moore said, the knife lowering. 'They're dead now, too, though. They're all gone.'

'Show me their pictures,' Lucy said, moving closer to Moore, her hands out by her sides, both for his benefit and for Constable Frazer behind her.

Moore shifted back slightly, but did not raise the knife again. Lucy stretched out her hand. 'Just drop the knife, Mr Moore. My name's Lucy. I'm a friend,' she said, holding his gaze.

She heard the clatter as the knife fell to the ground, then Moore seemed to slump, almost as if in defeat.

'I'm sorry,' he said, the words bubbling on his lips.

Recalling Seamus Moore's comments about his brother's mental age when she first met him, Lucy reached out to him, put her arms around his neck and embraced him, shushing him as one might do a child.

'It's OK now,' she said. 'You're safe now.'

Sunday, 22 July

Sunday 22 July

Chapter Fifty-six

While Seamus Moore at least sat on the same sofa with his brother as Aaron was being interviewed in the PPU, there remained, throughout, a gap between them. For the first half hour of the interview the following morning, Seamus made apparent his displeasure at his brother's odour, a mixture of stale sweat and unwashed clothes that hung in the heat of the room.

In daylight, Lucy could now better see Aaron Moore. His features were weathered, his skin leathery, the crow's feet around his eyes deep, as if from constant squinting against the sun. His hair, straggled and unwashed, had once been brown but mousey grey now predominated. She noticed two of his teeth were missing towards the front of his mouth and his front tooth to the left had broken and was now little more than a shard of enamel. It was, however, the bruises that had caused most concern.

After they'd found Moore the previous night, they'd taken him to the hospital to have him checked over. In addition to recommending lotions for lice and flea bites, the doctor had called Lucy in to show her the extent of the injuries which Aaron Moore had suffered to his torso, none of it visible when he was clothed.

A series of bruises, at various stages of healing, criss-crossed his back and trunk. The most recent, about four inches wide and running almost the width of his back, ended just below the shoulder blade.

'Look at the end of the bruise,' the doctor, Kevin Lynch, had said, pointing to the outer edges of the injury with the end of his pen. Sure enough, as Lucy leaned closer to examine it, she saw that the bruise seemed squared off, its shape defined.

'What do you think?' she asked.

Lynch shook his head. 'It looks like he was hit with a lump of cut wood; like something used as a rail on a wooden fence.'

'How recent are the injuries?'

'Some are probably weeks old. The most recent, a week or so. Nothing fresher than that.'

Moore sat now, near his brother, staring around the room. When he'd first been brought in, to his brother's annoyance, he'd headed straight for the bucket of toys which they kept to help entertain children, the most frequent occupants of this particular interview room. Moore had sifted through the contents before producing a small toy horse, triumphantly. He brought it across to the sofa and tried standing it on the armrest next to him. The legs, bandy with overuse, kept buckling, causing the toy to fall to the ground. Now Moore sat with it cupped in his hand as he waited for Lucy to start.

'Mr Moore? Do you recognize this man?' Lucy began, handing Moore a picture of Kamil Krawiec.

Moore took the picture and looked at it for a moment, until Seamus Moore took it from him and examined it closely, as if the question had been directed at him.

'That's Crackers,' Aaron said. 'He's called Kamil, but everyone calls him Crackers,' he added with a smile, as if this was to be their secret.

'How did you know him?'

Moore glanced at his brother, looking for his permission to speak. Seamus Moore nodded lightly.

'We worked together.'

'Worked?'

Moore nodded. 'We were laying drives.'

'Whom were you working for?'

'The family,' Aaron Moore said simply, his hand closing tightly around the toy he held.

'What family?'

'The ones we worked for,' he said, as if explaining it to a child.

'Do you know their name?' Lucy asked, trying to maintain her patience. She was pretty sure it would be Nash, but she didn't want to be accused of leading Moore, especially if his brother decided against his being cooperative.

'The son was called Padraig. The father might have been called Roy.'

Lucy nodded, biting her lip to stop her correcting him to 'Rory'. 'You don't know for definite the names of the people you worked for?'

'We had to call them "sir",' Moore explained. Next to him, Seamus Moore shifted uncomfortably, lifting himself a little from the seat and pulling out the cushion from behind him, which he then set on the floor.

'How did you end up working with them?' Lucy asked. 'Take us back to where you first met.'

'I went to the soup kitchen on Great James Street,' Moore began, earning a tut of disapproval from his brother. Lucy shot a warning glance at Seamus, who nodded lightly in acknowledgement.

'You went to the soup kitchen ...' Lucy began, encouragingly.

'The father was there. Big man with red hair. He asked me if I'd ever done any building work. I told him I had, bits and pieces. He said he needed men for a job, if I wanted to earn some cash. He said I'd get £40 per day, and food and a bed.'

'And you went with him?'

'A couple of us did. Some of the other men got into the van so I thought it would be OK. I needed the money.'

Again, Lucy sensed Seamus Moore tensing where he sat, but admirably restraining himself from speaking. Lucy assumed his annoyance at his brother masked his embarrassment at the fact that his sibling had felt he had to eat in soup kitchens and take building work from strangers rather than ask his own family for help.

'So what happened?'

'They took us to a place, by the river. We slept in a stable.' His grip tightened again on the horse in his hand.

'A stable?' Lucy asked.

Moore nodded, simply, turning over the horse in his hand. 'There were maybe twenty of us in each room. We slept on the floor. There were bags of straw lying if you wanted to make yourself a bed.'

'You slept on the floor?'

Moore nodded.

'How far away was this place?'

Moore shrugged.

'How long did it take to get there from the soup kitchen? Do you remember?'

'Not long. Crackers lit a fag in the van when we got in and he was still smoking when we arrived. I remember because we were all glad to get out into the fresh air. Out of the smoke. I was in a room with Crackers and he smoked there, too.

'So what did they ask you to do?'

'We had to lay driveways.'

'Did they pay you?'

'I think so,' Moore said, dipping his head slightly, inclining it away from his brother.

'Did they give you money for your work, Aaron?' Lucy asked.

Moore shrugged. 'They said they would have to move our pay from their bank. They took my Post Office card to pay the money into it.'

'You gave them your card?' Seamus Moore asked. 'Where all your benefits are paid?'

Aaron Moore nodded, his head dipped, his shoulders rounded as if in the expectation of being struck. 'They said they couldn't pay me otherwise. I'd no choice. Some of the others said no and they … they beat them.'

'They hit them?' Lucy asked. 'With what?'

'Bit of wood,' Moore said, glancing at her. She was reminded of Dr Lynch's comments about the bruises on Moore's body.

'Did they hit you, Aaron?'

Moore nodded, silently.

'Did they feed you?'

Moore nodded again, more animatedly. 'Pot Noodles at night, bread and tea in the morning. They brought them on trays.'

'How could you have stayed there?' Seamus Moore asked, suddenly. 'Sleeping on straw? Like an animal?'

Aaron Moore opened his mouth, as if in preparation to answer, but made no sound.

'Why didn't you leave?' his brother said.

'That's enough—' Lucy said, but Aaron Moore raised his hand to stop her.

'We did try,' Moore replied plaintively. 'But they locked our rooms. This one night, though, the son brought food and, when he left, he didn't do it right. Some of the men were able to open the door. They said we should go. Run away from them. I didn't want to at first, because they had my Post Office card, but Crackers said it would be all right. We made it over the bridge, before the son caught us.'

'Which bridge? The Foyle or Craigavon?' Lucy asked. If they could deduce the nearest bridge, they could perhaps pinpoint where the men had been held.

'I don't know. It was only short. Right beside where we stayed. We made it onto the path on the other side when they caught us.'

'What happened?'

'They beat us. Crackers said they broke his ribs. But he wasn't the worst.'

Lucy shifted forward where she sat. 'Who was the worst?'

Moore shook his head. 'I'm not allowed to say.'

'It's OK, Aaron. No one is going to hurt you. I promise.'

Moore lowered his head, staring at the horse toy, turning it over in his hand. He closed his fist around it. 'The one who opened the door. The father came down. He was *so* angry. The man who opened the door, I don't know his name, but they held him down. They kept hitting him and hitting him.' He tried to speak but his breath seemed to catch. 'They made us help,' he managed, finally.

'How?'

'He was lying there, on the ground. They told us no one cared about us. No one had even noticed we were gone. We only had them to look after us, to feed us, to give us a bed.'

'Straw on the floor,' Seamus Moore muttered, earning a glance of disapproval from Lucy.

'Did you notice I'd gone?' Aaron Moore challenged him. 'Did you look for me?'

When his brother did not reply, Aaron continued. 'They said we had to prove we were grateful. Some of the men started first, like they wanted the father to like them more. Then we all took turns,' he said, lowering his gaze to the horse in his hands. Lucy could see the dimples in the skin of his palm from where he had been gripping the toy so tightly. 'We promised we'd never tell.'

'But you're telling now,' Lucy said. 'You're taking control of your own life again.'

Moore shook his head, his eyes glistening at the memory. 'It was the sound. Squelch and crunch. I can't ... Squelch and crunch, squelch and crunch.

317

On and on. Just like it was with the horses when they tried to move after … after the …'

Seamus Moore reached across and laid his hand on his brother's, the gesture enough to bring Aaron's attention back to his story. 'They took him over the green and dumped him in the river,' Aaron said.

A tear slipped down the side of his cheek and he rubbed at it with the back of his hand. Lucy wondered at 'the green'. Was it Moore's way of describing grass, or did it mean something more significant?

'What's the green?' she asked.

'Outside,' Moore said. 'The green. Outside.'

'That's OK, Aaron,' Seamus Moore said, laying a placatory hand on his brother's arm.

'So you went back?' Lucy said, moving on lest Seamus Moore called a halt to the interview in light of his brother's distress.

Moore nodded, his eyes wet. 'We'd no choice.'

'Did anyone else ever escape?'

Moore shook his head. 'Never.'

'You did,' Lucy said. 'Or did they let you go?'

Moore glanced at his brother. 'We were working on a house for a nice old woman. We were laying a drive and Crackers found a key for the house under a gnome in the garden that we'd had to move. He kept it. He said she had loads of jewellery in her house. If we went and got it and sold it, we'd not need to stay with the family no more. If we could get away.'

'How did you do it?'

Moore stopped for the first time in the interview and glanced again at his brother.

'You don't need to say anything,' Seamus Moore said. 'Not if it's going to get you into trouble.' He looked across at Lucy. 'I was very clear about this.'

Lucy nodded. 'I just need to work out a timeline of events for now,' she said. 'I'm only interested in what happened to Kamil Krawiec.'

'We were working on a house just up the road from the old woman's, a week after. Kamil had heard the old woman tell the father that she was going on holidays, so we knew the house would be empty. It was the son, Padraig, who was with us on the second job, keeping an eye. The owner brought him in for tea in the middle of the morning. Me and Kamil ran. We went in through the gardens, and out onto the fields that ran along the backs of them. We were able to find the old woman's house from the spare tar we'd dumped over the back of her fence, into the field, when we'd finished the job.'

Lucy nodded. 'So, you went inside the house?'

Moore blushed, lowering his head. When he spoke now, his words were soft, almost lost as they formed on his lips.

'We let ourselves in and took her stuff. We took some food too. We stayed there all day, until it was dark, until we knew that the rest of them would have left the other place. We found some money in one of her coats, a few pound just. There was a bus stop up the road. When it was dark, we went up and waited for the bus.'

'Where did you go?'

'Kamil stayed at mine for the night. The next day, he went and sold the things and came back so we could split the money. He left then. Said he had a friend he could stay with. I didn't see him after that.

I'd not have taken it, but they had my card, you see?' He stared pleadingly at Lucy.

'And you don't know what happened to Kamil?' she asked, refusing to offer him the forgiveness he sought for the theft.

Moore shook his head. 'No. Why? *Has* something happened to him?'

Chapter Fifty-seven

'How much can we believe?' ACC Wilson asked. They had gathered in the incident room in the Strand Road where Lucy and Fleming had shown the video of Moore's interview to Burns and his team.

'All of it, ma'am,' Fleming said. 'His account of what happened fits with the timeline.'

'Certainly it corresponds with what we know about the theft from Doreen Jeffries's home.'

'Where did Krawiec go after Moore went underground?'

'Terry Haynes's,' Fleming said. 'I'd guess he went to Terry for help.'

'Why?' Burns asked. 'Why not come to us?'

'And admit he'd possibly aided in the killing of another homeless man? And had just robbed an old woman's home?' Fleming asked, without looking at Burns directly. 'Terry would have understood. He'd have wanted to help. Especially if he knew other people were still being held. Maybe he wanted to check for himself first.'

'So you think he and Krawiec went to the soup kitchen and accepted work to see it first-hand?' Wilson asked.

Fleming nodded. 'Krawiec wouldn't know the city. Wouldn't know where the men were being held. Moore doesn't even know and he's *from* here. Maybe Terry reckoned he'd have a better chance of recognizing the place and being able to find it a second time if he did report it to us.'

'One way or the other,' Lucy said, 'the people running the gang found out about Haynes, though. And killed him for it.'

'And Krawiec, too,' Tara added. 'But why would he go back? After what he'd seen happen? And why would they take him back? Would they not have punished him for escaping?'

Lucy shrugged. 'Maybe he wanted to help his friends.'

'Perhaps they did punish him. Maybe he folded and sold out Terry Haynes to them?'

Lucy shook her head. 'Haynes was cremated hours before Krawiec was dumped. Perhaps once they knew Haynes was on to what they were doing, knew about their having killed one of the men, they probably guessed Krawiec was the one who'd told him, considering they were recruited together at the kitchen.'

'What about the man Moore claims they killed? Have we anything to substantiate that?'

'Bodies are pulled out of the river all the time, ma'am,' Fleming said. 'He might not even have surfaced yet. And if he was homeless, he might never have been reported missing. We can check back over records for the last few months.'

Wilson nodded, then moved across to the table at the head of the room and perched against it, her arms crossed. 'So why go to all that trouble with Haynes? Why hide his body in a coffin? And the cost of doing it, if they did pay off Duffy.'

'Krawiec being found in a bin wouldn't arouse suspicion. He was a street drinker, homeless. He fell asleep or passed out and didn't wake when the lorry came to empty the bins,' Lucy said. 'Even a street drinker being pulled from the river wouldn't raise any alarms.'

'But with Haynes though, you'd not have had that excuse. Haynes was known for working with the street drinkers and that. People would ask questions if his body was found,' Fleming said. 'Especially with an axe wound.'

'With Duffy, we just got lucky that the rain started and put out the car before the fire could take hold properly,' Lucy argued.

Wilson glanced towards Burns. 'What's your feeling, Mark?'

'It sounds reasonable,' Burns admitted. 'I do worry a little about the stables comment, mind you. We know Moore has a thing for horses. And there are no stables near the Craigavon Bridge, which is the shortest one over the river.'

'There's the Peace Bridge,' Mickey offered. 'Though no stables near that either.'

'There's more than one river near the city,' Wilson said. 'We've the Faughan, too.'

'Moore said the journey to wherever they kept them was short. A cigarette's length. That must be what? Ten minutes at best?'

'It depends,' Mickey offered. 'There's no way Moore could be certain that he started smoking as soon as the van started.'

'Still, he said it was short. Let's say twenty minutes. There's only so far they could have travelled in that time. Allowing for time to get out of the city,' Lucy argued. 'There can't be that many bridges within a ten- or fifteen-mile radius of the city.'

'We need to hurry on this, too,' Fleming offered suddenly. 'Sammy Smith is with this crowd and is diabetic. He had enough insulin to last him until last night at the most. If we don't find him soon and get him to a doctor, we'll have another death on our hands.'

Wilson raised her eyebrows slightly, then nodded in agreement. 'Take a look at the maps and see how many you can find. There's little uniform support available with the parades stuff still going on, so you might need to assign teams to check each location, Inspector,' she said. 'And do it quickly.'

'Yes, ma'am,' both Burns and Fleming said at the same time.

Chapter Fifty-eight

Burns deliberately told Fleming and Lucy that their help would not be required in arranging the division of labour for checking the bridges throughout the city and beyond. He would contact them, he said, in due course, to let them know where they would be searching, with members of the Major Incident Team.

As they reached the car, Lucy's mobile began to buzz in her pocket. She pulled it out and recognized the caller's number as Grace's.

'I need to take this,' she said to Fleming, gesturing that he should get in and wait for her.

'Grace?' she asked, answering the phone.

'Who is this?'

Lucy didn't recognize the voice. It was female, but the accent was Southern Irish.

'DS Lucy Black of the PSNI,' Lucy said. 'Who is this? Where's Grace?'

'DS Black, my name's Mary McGeady. I'm a nurse in Altnagelvin. Are you a relative of the girl who owns this phone? Did you say her name was Grace?'

Lucy felt the pavement tilt beneath her, had to put out her hand to steady herself against the thick wall of the compound.

'What's happened to her? Is she OK?'

'She's in A & E. You'd best come up.'

*

Fleming tried to insist on coming into the hospital with her, but she pleaded with him to stay in the car until she was done. Grace would barely trust her, never mind if she landed with her DI as well.

At the reception area, she was directed straight through to the cubicles at the rear of A & E, curtained partitions where patients were treated after triage. She found Grace in the fourth bed, with a nurse in attendance.

Grace was unconscious, her face so badly bruised and bleeding that Lucy was not entirely sure at first that it was her. A small oxygen tube was strapped below her nose and ran across the bruised cheek and looped over her ear. But she recognized her by the clothes she wore, the same ones she'd been wearing when Lucy had dropped her off in town.

'What's happened to her? Is she going to be OK?'

'She's being transferred upstairs,' the nurse said, extending her hand. 'DS Black?'

Lucy nodded, took the proffered hand, briefly, recognizing from the woman's name badge that she was the one who had called her.

'Mary McGeady. So, *are* you family?'

'She doesn't have family,' Lucy said. 'She's homeless.'

'I see. She was found by one of the street cleaners up on the Walls. Maybe she had a run-in with some of those young fellas that congregate up there drinking.'

Lucy nodded, unconvinced. 'Could have been,' she said. 'Have you called the police? Apart from me?'

'There was a uniformed officer came in about half an hour ago. But the girl – Grace – can't say anything. He said he'd come back when she woke up.'

'I'll handle it,' Lucy said.

'I thought you were family,' the woman explained. 'Your number was the only one that had rung the girl's phone.'

Suddenly, an alarm began to blare, its source seemingly a few beds further down the corridor.

'Excuse me,' Mary said, pulling back the curtain and disappearing out onto the corridor, leaving Lucy alone with Grace.

Lucy moved across to the bed and took the girl's hand in hers. Her hands were grubby, but not marked with blood. It meant that she'd not fought back, Lucy guessed, or that she hadn't much chance to defend herself from whoever attacked her. The bruising seemed to be restricted solely to her face. The unit fell suddenly quiet as the alarm ended.

'Grace? Can you hear me?' Lucy said softly, holding the girl's hand in hers, rubbing her thumb across the rough skin of the girl's knuckles. 'Grace? Who did this?'

There was no response from the figure on the bed, no sound save for her breathing and the hiss of the oxygen.

She heard the clatter of the curtain rings rattling against the rail as Mary re-entered the cubicle.

'She's out of it on painkillers,' Mary offered. 'We're admitting her, in case of concussion. We want to do a few more checks, too, that there's no serious swelling on the inside. You know?'

Lucy nodded. 'Call me when she wakes,' she said, handing Mary her card. 'Don't worry about the uniform. Come direct to me, OK?'

Mary nodded. 'As soon as she's fit to talk, I'll call.'

'Thanks,' Lucy muttered, turning again to Grace. 'I'll speak to you later, Grace? OK?' She patted her hand lightly, replaced it by the sleeping girl's side, left before Mary could see her face.

She stopped halfway between A & E and the car park and took Grace's phone from her pocket where she'd secreted it. She opened the call history but, as Mary had said, the only number on it was her own.

She flicked through instead to the Photo Album and opened it. She had to flick back a few shots to be sure that Grace had photographed it a second time. But she felt a queasy mixture of anger and guilt when she saw that the final picture Grace had taken had been a second shot of Bernadette Thompson's black Audi.

Chapter Fifty-nine

Fleming was leaning against the car when she reached it, his fingers drumming on the roof.

'I've been thinking. I—' He stopped, seemingly noticing Lucy's expression. 'Is everything OK?' he asked.

'Fine,' Lucy said.

'What's happened, Lucy?'

Lucy hesitated a moment. 'Grace – the girl with the red trainers who took us to where Krawiec was killed? She's been beaten up.'

'As a result of showing us the bank?' Fleming asked.

Lucy shook her head. 'I think it was one of her johns.'

'How do you know?'

Lucy started the engine and shifted into gear before she spoke again. 'The night of the heavy storm I called her and let her stay in my house. She was sleeping rough. She'd been hit by someone, a client.'

'Did she say who?'

Lucy shook her head.

Fleming said nothing for a moment, staring out the window. They reached the traffic lights outside the hospital before he spoke again. 'You called her to stay in your house?' he asked, finally.

'It was pouring down. I … I felt … I was worried.'

'Of course you were,' Fleming said, the admiration in his tone clear.

Lucy felt her mobile vibrating again in her pocket and, worried that perhaps the hospital had realized she'd lifted Grace's phone, she pulled it out quickly to check. It was her mother.

'Lucy? How did things pan out with that council worker, John Boyd, and his partner?'

The question was such an odd one, so unconnected to anything they had been discussing, that Lucy was automatically suspicious. 'What's happened to him?'

'Can you not answer a question with a question? How did it pan out?'

'She left him, I think.'

'You *think*? Did she or did she not?'

'She did. Then she found out I was a cop. I'd not told her. I'm hoping that doesn't drive her back to him again. Why?'

'Boyd has vanished. You need to come back in.'

Fleming accompanied her up to her mother's office. Her secretary was off, so they knocked at the main double doors and waited to be called through. When they went in, Lucy was surprised to see not just her mother, but also another couple – a young man whose face she recognized, and an older woman who she did not know.

'Tom, Lucy, come in,' her mother said, directing them across to the meeting table that sat to the left of the room. Six large leather chairs surrounded it. Fleming and Lucy took a seat. A tray with a flask of coffee and empty cups and saucers sat before them.

'Lorna's off, so I've no milk,' Wilson said. 'If you can take it black, go ahead.'

Lucy passed on the coffee, but did peel back the cling film from the small plate of biscuits and lifted the pink wafer, not least because she remembered they had been her mother's favourites when Lucy was young.

'This is Chief Superintendent Tracey Marshall,' Wilson said, introducing the woman who sat opposite Lucy. 'This is DI Tom Fleming and DS Lucy Black, as I explained.'

Marshall nodded at them both and smiled. 'This is Colm Elliot,' she added, nodding to the young man who had also moved across and sat next to her. 'Colm is—'

'An auditor,' Lucy said suddenly, not meaning to interrupt, then immediately apologized.

'That's right,' Marshall said. 'Can you tell that just by looking at him? I have that skill with accountants, personally,' she added, smiling.

'I saw you with John Boyd the other day. You were about to go out on a site visit.'

'That's right,' Elliot said.

'Tracey is with the Fraud Unit,' Wilson said. 'They've been investigating John Boyd for some time.'

Lucy was aware that Fleming glanced quickly at her, worried perhaps that, in getting involved with Fiona, she had somehow screwed up a fraud investigation.

'You've had dealings with him, DS Black?' Marshall asked, looking to Wilson to show from whom she had gained this knowledge.

'Tangentially,' Lucy said. 'My neighbour's sister is, or was, his partner. My neighbour was concerned that he was being abusive or controlling of her. I shared her concerns.'

'Why?'

'The description she offered of their relationship was of a controlling partner. He wouldn't let her handle her own money, her own bank accounts, discouraged her from maintaining any friendships she'd developed before she met him, discouraged her from visiting her family.'

'He's an unpleasant little shit all round,' Marshall said. 'Was he physically abusive?'

'On at least two occasions, I saw her with bruises or cuts which I suspected he'd caused.'

Marshall nodded. 'But you didn't arrest him? Or intimate that you planned to?'

'I was introduced to Fiona as a friend of her sister's. She didn't know I was an officer. Then, when I next met her, it didn't seem like a natural thing to drop into the conversation. Certainly, I encouraged her to seek help and to report him, but I'm not sure that she did.'

'Where is she now?'

Lucy shrugged. 'She had been with her sister. He called at the house last night and, in so doing, revealed to her that I was a DS.'

'Did she leave with him again?'

'That wasn't the sense I had from what she said,' Lucy admitted. 'But I can't know for sure. She was … unhappy that I hadn't been totally honest with her.'

'What is the Fraud Unit's interest in him?' Fleming asked, sparing Lucy further embarrassment.

'He's been under suspicion for some time,' Marshall said. 'Colm can better explain it.'

Elliot straightened himself in his seat and put down his coffee cup in preparation to speak. 'Boyd had limited purchasing powers on behalf of the council, to facilitate speedy remedial works that might be needed.'

'He was allowed to sign cheques to certain companies?' Fleming asked.

'Essentially, yes,' Elliot said. 'One company, actually.'

'Dynamo? Dynamic?' Lucy said. 'He told me the day I met him with Burns.' She glanced at her mother and Marshall. 'Chief Superintendent Burns,' she added.

'That's right,' Elliot said, a little deflated. 'Dynamic.'

'So what's happened?'

Elliot shifted in his seat again. 'He's been issuing more cheques than Dynamic have been receiving.'

'How?'

'We suspect he's created a bank account in the name of a second company, Dynamic Construction, and has been writing cheques to that company as well as the genuine one. They've been countersigned by his boss and passed through the council accounts because he has permission to write cheques to Dynamic Inc. Nobody picked up on the slight change in the name.'

'Not even the bank?'

'They did, eventually,' Marshall said. 'Which is where we got involved. But we think he's been doing it for some time.'

'What about the countersignatory? His boss. Is he involved?'

'She,' Marshall corrected. 'And no, we think not. We're fairly sure that it was carelessness rather than criminality in her case. Boyd wrote the cheques; she glanced at the name, saw Dynamic, and signed them off.'

'Can the bank check who set up the Dynamic Construction account? If it was Boyd, you'd have direct evidence to lift him.'

'That's the problem; it wasn't Boyd,' Elliot said. 'It is actually a real building company, set up three years ago by someone called Rory Nash, who does small-scale building works.'

Marshall offered Elliot a rebuking glance. 'That stays within these four walls for now.'

'We know Nash,' Fleming offered. 'In fact, we had him in for interview downstairs yesterday.'

'For what?'

'We believe he's been using vulnerable adults for forced labour.'

'Forced labour.' Marshall laughed, mirthlessly. 'Boyd wrote cheques of almost three-quarters of a million to Dynamic Con over the past three years. If the workers have been slaves, that money must still be somewhere.'

Lucy thought of Nash's house, of his comment about the work being there if you were prepared to chase it.

'Any idea where Boyd has gone?' Fleming asked.

Marshall shook her head. 'Colm's been trying to contact him all morning but there's nothing. We've been at his house and it seems deserted. We've got a warrant to search it, but it would be much quicker if someone who knew the place were able to tell us straight away if things were missing. Passports, bank books and that.'

'Fiona?' Lucy asked.

Marshall nodded her head. 'I was going to ask you to speak to her about helping us. Especially if she has reason to want to see Boyd locked up. But now that I've heard what's happened between you two, if she no longer trusts you, you might be the worst person to try.'

'Let me speak to her,' Lucy said. 'Please.'

Chapter Sixty

Fiona, Jenny and the children were in the kitchen, washing up after what appeared to have been an afternoon of baking. Two wire cooling racks sat on the table, both piled high with buns. One of the children, the youngest girl, stood at the sink with a plastic bowl encircled by her arms, running her small hand through the leftover icing, then sucking it noisily off her fingers, one by one. Two spots of icing dimpled her smile as she saw Lucy.

'Into the living room, kids,' Jenny said. 'Let's stick on a movie.' She smiled lightly at Lucy as she passed.

Fiona stood, leaning against the worktop, a mug of coffee in her hand. 'I said I didn't want to see you,' she said.

'I know. Fiona, I'm sorry I didn't mention I was a police officer. Growing up here, it's not the first thing you share about yourself with someone you meet.'

'I understand that,' Fiona said. 'But you actively lied. You said you were a fitness instructor.'

'I was.'

'But not now.'

'No,' Lucy admitted. 'When I met you, I did so as a neighbour. And a friend. Not as a police officer.'

'So which are you now?'

336

Lucy considered the question. 'All three, I guess. Look, Fiona, I have some news about John.'

Fiona snorted. 'Of course you do. What's he done now?'

'He's disappeared,' Lucy said. 'We've been looking for him, but we think he may have done a runner.'

'Because of me?' Fiona asked, then her expression quickly darkened as she considered all the alternative explanations for what may have happened to him. 'He hasn't … he hasn't … killed himself, has he?' Already the tears were welling in her eyes, her lip's quivering building.

'No,' Lucy said. 'John has been under investigation for a while, Fiona. Nothing to do with you. Or me. The audit at his work that he was talking about to you? He was being investigated for fraud.'

'Fraud?' Fiona repeated, incredulously. 'John?'

Lucy nodded. 'He'd been writing cheques to be lodged in a dummy company – £750,000 worth over the past few years.'

Fiona set the mug on the counter, its contents sloshing onto her hand as she did so, though she seemed not to notice.

'Why are you telling me this?'

'The Fraud Unit have a warrant to search his house. Your house. But it would speed things up *a lot* if someone who knew where he kept everything was able to check whether he was planning on leaving the country. You know, see if his passport, travel bags, bank books, that kind of thing, are missing or are still in the house. It means we'd know he was still alive. We haven't much time. You can help.'

Fiona shook her head. 'No. Not me. That's not fair.'

'It means *you'd* know he was still alive, Fiona,' Lucy said, moving across to her. 'Whatever happens to him as a result of this is on him alone. Not on you.'

'I'm not giving evidence against him,' Fiona said, staring at Lucy. 'I'm not doing that.'

'You're not being asked to,' Lucy said. 'All we need to know is that he's *chosen* to leave. Jenny can come with you, if you want.'

Fiona stared around her, as if seeing the kitchen for the first time. 'No,' she decided finally. 'I'll do it on my own.'

Lucy sat in the living room of the house Fiona and Boyd had shared while Fiona checked the bedroom. She'd been told by Marshall to make sure that she watched her as she searched, but, having already tested the limits of trust once with her failure to tell Fiona she was police, she thought standing watching her would suggest she didn't trust her at all.

The room was modern, the walls painted white, the suite cream-coloured cloth. Two pictures hung on the walls, in both of which red was the predominant colour. However, Lucy would have struggled to say what the pictures were of, carrying as they did the appearance of a Rorschach.

She wondered how much of the decor reflected each of the people who had lived there. To what extent had Fiona sacrificed her own personality to accommodate John Boyd's.

There was one bookcase to the left of the fireplace. Lucy moved across and scanned the spines, recognized a few of the authors. The books, she noticed, had been arranged on the shelves according to size, the larger volumes together, the smaller paperbacks on a shelf of their own. It was only when she turned to sit again that she saw, on the small alcove between the door and the back wall, half hidden by the open door into the hallway, a studio picture of Fiona.

Fiona herself appeared a moment later, a small overnight bag in her hands.

'Well?' Lucy attempted a smile.

'He's gone. The folder with both our passports and bank stuff is gone. So is his toothbrush and razors. He's taken a bag of clothes with him too. A couple of nice suits that he bought last year.'

'Anything else?'

Fiona shook her head. 'Whatever he's done, he's chosen to leave. And if he's taken all that with him, I assume he's not planning on topping himself.'

The visit to the house seemed to have helped her steel herself, her concern for his safety replaced now with anger.

'He has my passport, too,' she said. 'Everything.'

'Maybe he was in a rush,' Lucy offered.

'I'll need to get it replaced,' Fiona said. 'And get the rest of my stuff from here. I've brought a few things I meant to take last night, but I left so suddenly. My own toothbrush and that.'

She offered the bag for Lucy's inspection, its opening unzipped. Again, Lucy felt that to check the contents would further damage their already fragile friendship.

'You can search it,' Fiona said, as if sensing her discomfort. 'That's your job after all. That's why you're here.'

Lucy felt herself redden. 'That's a nice picture of you,' she said, gesturing to the alcove behind the door. 'Why did you put it in there? No one can see it.'

'John put it there,' Fiona said, simply. 'I hate the sight of it. He insisted I get it taken and insisted that it hang up there.'

Lucy phoned her mother after she had dropped Fiona back at Jenny's house in Prehen. 'It looks like a planned disappearance,' she said. 'His passport and bank stuff is all gone. And some of his clothes and toiletries.'

'We'll get an alert out to the ports and airports,' Wilson said. 'And hope he's not already out of the country,' she added. 'How's the girl?'

'OK,' Lucy said. 'He took her stuff, too. Passport and everything.'

'She wouldn't be planning on going with him, would she? Stringing you along, then vanishing herself and joining him somewhere?'

'I doubt it,' Lucy said, unconvincingly, unwilling to admit that she'd thought exactly the same thing the moment she'd seen Fiona holding the travel bag in her living room.

'We'll keep an eye on her movements, too,' Wilson said. 'Just in case she's planning on travelling anytime soon. You need to come back in; I believe the Chief Super is assigning search areas. You'll not want to miss that, now, will you, Lu?'

Her mother hung up before Lucy could register the warmth in the woman's use of the nickname that both her parents had called her when she was a child. Since their conversation about her father's deteriorating state, she'd sensed more than once that her mother was attempting, in some way, to rekindle their relationship, perhaps even going so far as to move Lucy back into CID as Burns had suggested, if Lucy so wished. It disconcerted her; at least they'd both known where they stood when she was simply Lucy's superior officer. Now, Lucy couldn't help but wonder for whose benefit was this attempted reconnection most intended: her own or her mother's.

Chapter Sixty-one

As it transpired, Lucy was too late for Burns's meeting. The team was filing out of the room when she arrived, loosely pairing up as they did so, presumably into the teams Burns had assigned.

Thankfully, she and Fleming had been put together. He was still sitting in the incident room when she arrived, flicking through the maps that they had been given.

'Sorry, sir,' Lucy offered to Burns as he passed. 'I was tied up with the ACC.'

Burns grunted an acknowledgement and moved on out of the room, not looking at Fleming.

'What's up with him?' Lucy asked.

'He's feeling the pressure,' Fleming said. 'He requested Police 44 to do a flyover the city, check out the various bridges, but both helicopters are being deployed in Belfast, trying to get pictures of protesters. He had to use Google Maps in the end.' He held up one of the sheets in evidence.

'So, where are we?'

'Drumahoe outwards,' Fleming said. 'We're with Tara and Mickey.'

'Does he not trust us to do it ourselves?'

'Clearly not,' Fleming said. 'I think I know where the men are being held, too. Here.'

He handed Lucy a map. She could see the curvature of the river, could see to one side what looked like a housing estate. A narrow line traversed the river.

'What is it?'

'Green Road,' Fleming said, 'in Ardmore. So called, because that collection of buildings you can see is in an area called Bleach Green.'

'*The Green*,' Lucy said. 'Moore said they'd carried the dead man "over the green". I thought he meant the grass.'

'It's an abandoned bleach works,' Fleming said. 'Thus the name. The river was used to power a flax mill nearby and the linen was taken to the bleach works to be bleached. They left it lying out on the grass area to dry in the sun: Bleach Green.'

'Why do you think that's where they are? Did they have stables?'

Fleming shook his head. 'No. But they did have a row of old terraced cottages where the workers lived. They've fallen into disrepair now. Maybe Moore was confused.'

'And that's a bridge, I take it,' Lucy asked, pointing to the thin line.

Fleming nodded. 'A very short metal bridge. Plus it's near where the Nash family live.'

'Sounds like a good place to start,' Lucy said.

'Burns didn't agree,' Fleming said. 'Not when I suggested that sending us out to every bridge in the city was a waste of time and we'd be better concentrating our efforts on this one. What with Sammy running out of time.'

'Thus the doubling up with Tara and Mickey.'

343

'As a sop; he knew I was right but didn't want to be seen to be backing down.'

Lucy gathered up the sheets. 'He must love you,' she said.

'He's only human. Any word on Boyd?'

'Fiona checked the house for us. He's taken his stuff with him: toiletries, passport and that.'

'At least it means he's still alive,' Fleming reasoned.

'For now,' Lucy said.

The door opened and Tara leaned in. 'We want to get started. Are you two ready to go?' she asked, then left again without waiting for them to answer.

Chapter Sixty-two

Bleach Green was much bigger than Lucy had expected. They'd driven past Ardmore graveyard, and the Beech Hill Hotel to their left, through into Ardmore itself, almost missing the turning to the left, down towards the river. After a few hundred yards, they spotted the first of the large grey buildings appear through the trees which lined the roadway and obscured much of the place from view.

They drove around the building itself, then pulled into an area of waste ground at the far end of the bleach works, next to the short iron pedestrian bridge which Fleming had mentioned. As they got out of the car, they could hear the rush of the river next to them. Lucy ventured across and, leaning over, looked down to where it had swollen almost to the limit of its banks. The river here was narrowed, meaning that the water travelling through the space did so with much greater pressure than at other spots along its length where men fished its meandering current.

'The rains must have flooded it,' Fleming offered.

They turned to the building itself. Nearest them squatted a long, low, red-brick building, the plaster crumbling from the sides, its low roof tiled but gaping with age and weathering. Next to it was a longer, wider building, its entrance closed off with sheets of corrugated metal that bore a NO TRESPASSING warning sign. High above this part of the works towered a red-brick chimney, its sides veined with tendrils of ivy, long since dead.

'So, how do we get in?' Mickey asked.

They approached the corrugated sheets; Fleming pulled on a pair of gloves and peeled back one of the sheets. It swung back fairly easily, grinding only slightly on the ground as it did so.

'Someone has been in here,' he commented.

The first room they stepped into was dark and, despite the heat of the recent days, the ground damp beneath their feet. The space itself was empty save for rubble lying scattered about. To the left, in the far corner, stood a ladder, which reached up to the ceiling above their heads. As they moved further into the room, they realized that the ceiling was actually the underside of a makeshift mezzanine level to which the ladder reached. From this angle, Lucy couldn't see what was above them. Following Fleming's example, she pulled on her gloves and, moving across, began climbing the ladder.

She'd climbed six rungs before her head was level with the floor above. The upper floor was unoccupied at present but, in addition to more rubble and three rusted iron girders, a stained and sodden mattress lay on the ground.

'Anything?' Tara called up.

'An old mattress,' Lucy said. 'It doesn't look like it's being used to be honest; it looks like a sponge it's so wet.' She glanced up to where the gap in the roof showed through to the afternoon sky, heavy-bodied clouds gathering above them.

'Come down and we'll check some of the other rooms,' Mickey said.

The next space they moved into was a wide, open corridor. The roof had completely gone here and the two side walls were bridged by a series of metal joists above their heads. The ground was concrete at one stage, but was thick with vegetation now. At various intervals, shafts of thick ferns curled upwards from the floor.

They moved along the length of the room. The walls were covered in graffiti, most proclaiming nicknames or political affiliations. As Lucy was reading one particularly lengthy proclamation, she felt the floor suddenly drop from under her as she fell off balance. Fleming, who had been alongside her, gripped her arm, quickly, with enough force to make her exclaim.

One foot dangled into the space below and she could feel coldness envelop her boot, could feel something leaking in around her feet, through the leather.

Mickey and Tara ran across and, grappling with her, managed to heave her back onto solid ground. Catching her breath, she looked down to realize that in front of her was a square hole in the floor, about two foot square, which dropped down to a lower level that, she could now see, was flooded with water.

'What the hell's that?' she managed.

'Are you all right?' Tara asked, her arm still around Lucy's shoulder. 'Are you hurt?'

'Embarrassed,' Lucy said. 'I should have been looking where I was going.'

'There are a series of them,' Fleming said, having moved further up the room. 'Every few feet, on either side of the floor. They must have been drains or something. It must feed down into the river.'

Lucy could see now, once Fleming pointed them out, that the holes were present, at intervals of about six feet, the entire way along the corridor. As they moved along, more carefully now, they glanced down into each. Two of them, towards the end of the corridor, showed metal barrels, some lying on their sides, leaking oily fluid out into the water around them.

'Fuel-laundering waste,' Mickey suggested, moving on.

'Are you OK?' Fleming asked, touching Lucy on the elbow.

'I feel stupid falling like that.'

'Easily done,' Fleming said. 'Forget about it.'

They moved on through the building, in places being able to step through the gaps in the walls where the brickwork had collapsed. Finally, they moved out into the evening sunlight again. Ahead of them, across a meadow, thick with grass and wild flowers, they could see a second building, lower than the first, stretching in behind the treeline.

'Those must be the workers' cottages, from when the bleach works was running. Families lived on-site,' Fleming explained.

It was then that they spotted a figure approaching the cottages from the river. It took Lucy only a second to recognize him as Padraig Nash.

Chapter Sixty-three

Nash spotted them at almost the same moment they saw him. He had been carrying a basin in his hands, which he dropped, then turned and sprinted away from them, hurdling his way through the thigh-high grass around them.

'Stop,' Mickey shouted, ineffectively, for Nash didn't even look back. Mickey set off in pursuit, Tara following behind, but already they could hear the crash of Nash breaking through the treeline into the wooded area that shaded the river upstream of where they stood.

'Looks like we're at the right place,' Fleming said, leading the way towards the row of cottages. 'Look for Sammy first.'

From outside, the cottages were clearly dilapidated. Like the main building, the roof showed gaps in the slate, the rough-stone walls crumbling in places. They reached the door of the first cottage and found it bolted and padlocked. Fleming shoved it a few times, testing it.

'Stand back,' he said. He shouldered against it, once, hard, the padlock rattling off the wood as he did so. He stepped back and shoved again, harder this time. The door strained against the dead bolt but still did not shift. He tried once more, charging the door this time, his shoulder lowered. They heard the crack of the wood around the lock and the door flung backwards, the now useless lock clattering to the ground.

A waft of heat enveloped them as they stepped inside. The air here was thick and heavy, trapped in it the smell of sweat and damp and, above all else, the stench of faeces.

Despite the gaping roof, the light inside seemed grey and still and it took them a moment both to acclimatize to it after the brightness of outdoors and to register that the object lying in the corner next to them was, in fact, moving.

Fleming pulled out his torch and directed the beam to the moving mass. It was a man, curled foetally under what looked to be coal sacking. Beneath him, serving as a bed, lay a scattering of straw. The man looked up at them, pathetically, from where he lay. His eyes were red, his face dirtied, his hair matted. He rubbed at the bristles of his beard with his right hand, as if stroking himself in comfort. His hands were thick and swollen with bruises. He raised his other hand, feebly, to shield his eyes from the light. In doing so, he dislodged the empty cider bottle that he had been hugging to him, which rolled onto the floor. He scrabbled to collect it up again, lest Lucy or Fleming tried to take it from him.

Lucy moved across to him. 'We're with the police? My name's Lucy Black. Are you OK?'

The man stared at her, his head swaying slightly with the exertion of raising it from the ground. This close to him, Lucy could see his beard matted with saliva from when he had slept.

'Is there anyone else here?' Lucy asked, as behind her she heard Fleming calling for an ambulance. 'We're looking for a man called Sammy.' The man held her gaze for a second, seemingly unsure if she was actually there, then lowered his eyes, directing her, she realized, to the next cottage down.

She followed his gaze and saw that, whether by accident or design, the internal walls, which would once have separated the houses, had fallen into disrepair, with the result that the entire terrace of houses was open from one to the next. As she looked, as if distilling themselves from the darkness of the rooms beyond, a series of figures began to emerge in the outer edges of her torchlight.

'Jesus,' she heard Fleming say. He had moved to the far corner and was directing his torch towards a bucket, the encrusted outer edges of which showed Lucy enough to know what it had been used for and helped explain the smell when they had come into the room. Fleming turned and saw now, too, the figures coming towards them from the rest of the building.

All were men, though ranging in age from one who appeared to be a teenager, to a man so old and weakened, he was leaning on two others, either side of him, to keep him upright.

'We're looking for Sammy Smith,' Fleming said, raising his torch towards the men who, almost in unison, retreated a step from the light.

'He's here,' someone from the rear of the group said.

Fleming moved towards them now, Lucy following. The men parted, allowing them through.

As she passed, Lucy tried to do a quick mental tally: including the man lying on the ground at the entrance, she reckoned there were fourteen occupants of the cottage, so far.

As she followed Fleming further down the line of cottages, however, she realized that there were a handful more, lying against the walls, in stupors of either sickness or alcohol, visible in the constantly shifting beam of Fleming's torch as he scanned from left to right, trying to identify Sammy.

'Here,' he said, suddenly, rushing across to where the old man lay. He knelt next to him and gripped his wrist in one ungloved hand, taking his pulse, even as he checked his airways and, laying his head close to the old man's mouth, searched for signs of breath.

'Sammy?' Lucy said. 'Can you hear us, Sammy?'

Fleming straightened, his face suddenly alert. 'He has a pulse. It's very weak but it's there.'

Fleming pulled out a pen and, tugging at the high-visibility vest which Sammy wore, exposed the soft skin of his belly and injected him. 'Niall Toner left over a few insulin shots at the station,' he explained. 'We need to get him to a hospital, though. Quickly.'

'I'll go out to the main road, see if the ambulance is coming,' Lucy said. When she turned again towards the entrance she realized that most of the men who had been in the cottage had already gone, leaving behind only those too drunk, or ill, to stand.

Chapter Sixty-four

Outside, she caught sight of a pair of stragglers from the cottage, making their way across the iron bridge that, she reckoned, would eventually bring them out onto the main Glenshane Road. Presumably the others from the cottage had already made it across. She took out her phone and called through for any available cars to be on the lookout for the men. They would at least need to be taken to the hospital to be checked over and, she suspected from the state of their living conditions, deloused.

To her left, Tara was moving back towards her, taking long strides to make her way through the thick grass. Mickey was trailing in her wake, visibly puffing for breath.

'He's vanished,' Tara said. 'Mickey went the whole way up to the road, but he's nowhere to be seen. Did you find anything?'

Lucy nodded. 'Take a look. There were over a dozen of them here, but most of them have scarpered. I've asked for support.'

'Are you going after them?'

'No. DI Fleming's called for an ambulance. I'm going out to meet it; we found Sammy in there.'

Lucy felt she should ask Tara to come along with her, as a sign of friendship, but she knew that

Fleming would need help inside too. In the end, it was irrelevant, for Tara moved on into the cottage as Mickey drew up behind.

'I can see how the little shit got away from you, too,' he said breathlessly.

Lucy retraced her steps towards the car, back through the main building. She was rounding the corner of the long central corridor, when she saw someone shifting suddenly to one side, through the gap in the wall leading to the adjoining room. Assuming it to be one of the homeless men, she stepped through, shining her torch onto the ground rather than at eye level so as not to startle them.

'Hello—' she began.

Padraig Nash exploded out of the corner where he had been trying to hide, knocking Lucy off balance. She stumbled over a scattering of rubble lying at her feet as she turned to try to follow, twisting her ankle as she did so, the pain shooting up her leg.

Nash rabbited his way through the gap in the wall, back out onto the main corridor, turning right in the hope, Lucy guessed, of making it to the bridge. Once across, he would have a range of directions he could run.

She pulled herself up quickly, using the wall for support, then wincing both as she put weight on her foot and at the thought of another chase with Nash, began the pursuit.

As she emerged through the gap, she shouted after him. He was halfway along the corridor now. Hearing her voice, he glanced around, for a second, clearly trying to ascertain how close she was to him.

Lucy knew what was about to happen the moment she saw him break through the line of ferns ahead of him. Almost instantly, he dropped, falling face forwards. From the sharp, wet crack of bone, she guessed he had struck his face on the concrete around the edge of the hole through which he had fallen as he disappeared from sight.

'Jesus!' Lucy shouted. 'Help!'

She struggled, as quickly as she could, across to where she had last seen Nash. The thickness of the vegetation growing around the holes made it impossible for her to see anything until she was almost upon it herself. Then she realized that the hole into which Nash had fallen was one of the ones that had contained the barrels of waste. And Nash was trying to claw his way back out of the hole, balanced precariously on the edge of the barrel beneath him, his head just below the level of the floor.

'Help me!' he spat at her, a bloody globule of saliva running down his chin. His nose had clearly been broken by the impact with the concrete, his lower face bearded now in his own blood. His hands clawed at the edge of the hole for purchase, but the damp had left the concrete slimy with moss and he couldn't get sufficient grip to pull himself up.

Lucy knelt at the edge carefully, her ankle still aching, stretching out her hand to grip Nash's.

'Pull me up,' he commanded.

Instead Lucy relaxed her grip. She knew how this would go. If she pulled him up, he'd run again and she was in no state to follow him. Even if he were caught, he would say nothing, feeling he had nothing to lose.

355

'What happened to Terry Haynes and Kamil Krawiec?' Lucy asked, sitting back.

'What? Help me out, you fucking bitch!' Nash shouted, struggling more wildly now to escape, then suddenly realizing that the more erratic his movements, the greater the chance of the barrel on which he stood toppling and his going under the water. Even he must have been aware that whatever was leaking from the barrel beneath him, it was probably not suitable for swimming in. Besides, he'd be trapped beneath the floor, in a flooded cellar.

'Terry Haynes. Someone killed him with a hatchet. Cremated him in another man's coffin. Why?'

'Fuck!' Nash screamed now, making one last effort to lift himself free. Finally, exhausted, realizing his efforts were in vain, he let go, almost as if to fall into the water below.

Lucy gripped his hands sharply, preventing him from falling. 'What happened to him?'

'Lift me out and I'll tell you,' Nash said, his eyes flickering past her towards the doorway that would lead out to the river beyond.

'Tell me and I'll lift you out.'

Lucy was kneeling low now, partially hidden from view by the ferns around the hole. She was using both hands to hold Nash, which meant she couldn't phone for help.

'You can't do this!' Nash protested.

'Do you see anyone to stop me?'

Nash lowered his head. The blood had begun to dry now, congealing around his lips.

'Why was Terry Haynes killed?'

'He wasn't who he said he was. We thought he was one of them. He wasn't. The Polish guy told him about the camp and brought him to the soup kitchen.'

'And?'

'He would have told someone. He knew things.'

'What things?'

Nash snorted.

'That you'd killed someone and dumped the body in the river here?'

She could tell from the flash of fear in the boy's eyes that Moore had told them the truth about the killing.

'So why hide Haynes's body? Why not dump it in a bin like Krawiec? Or in the river like the other man?'

'He knew people. Someone finds an alco sleeping in a bin, no one blinks. He wasn't an alco. It had to look like he done it all himself and then had done a runner. If he was never found then ...' He grunted, shifting his weight as he struggled to stand. 'Please let me up.'

'How did you do it? Swapping the bodies?'

'I knew Ciaran. I asked him to help. He brought the van with the body out here and we switched them round. He said the old guy in the coffin would sink so we dumped him in the water.'

'And you paid him for it?'

'Five grand.' Nash nodded, blinking furiously at the sweat stinging in his eyes.

'How did you know about Haynes? That he wasn't who he said he was? How did you find out?'

'Someone told me da,' Nash said, resignedly.

'Who told him?'

'Look, I don't know,' Nash said. 'Pull me out, my arms are cramping. I can't hold on.'

'Who killed Haynes? And Krawiec? And your friend, Ciaran Duffy?'

'It wasn't me,' Nash said. 'Please help me out.'

'Was it your father?'

Nash stared up at her pleadingly. 'It wasn't me,' he repeated.

Lucy leaned back on her good ankle and, flexing, began pulling Nash up through the hole. By this stage, she reckoned, his arms and legs would be cramping so much, he'd not be in much state for trying to run.

Sure enough, as he reached ground level, he lay face down, seemingly accepting that the chase, for him, was over. Lucy straightened up to get plastic ties from her belt to cuff him and, in so doing, realized that Tom Fleming was standing a little distance back, watching her.

'How long have you been standing there?' she asked, blushing.

'A while,' Fleming said.

Chapter Sixty-five

'Rory Nash and his wife were gone by the time a response unit made it to the house,' Burns explained an hour later. Padraig Nash had been brought to the station but had not requested he be allowed to contact his parents. Despite not doing so, half an hour after, just prior to Burns convening the team together, a solicitor had arrived and requested some time alone with the boy.

'We checked his phone,' Burns continued. 'He called his father minutes before DI Fleming called in his apprehension, which suggests that he tipped the parents off that we'd discovered the labour encampment. The parents have done a runner, presumably.'

'And left the boy high and dry,' Mickey said. 'Charming.'

'He knew what to expect,' Fleming commented. 'The fact he didn't call for them when he was brought in; he knew they'd send someone for him.'

'What do you think his strategy will be?' Tara asked.

'No comments all round,' Burns said.

'Where have the parents gone?' Mickey asked.

Burns shrugged. 'We've checkpoints on all the borders and we've contacted An Garda to check on their side.'

'Any luck with John Boyd?' Lucy asked.

Burns glanced to where ACC Wilson sat, at the back of the room, arms folded, watching proceedings.

'We believe he's made contact with the ex-partner, Fiona,' she said, standing.

'Are we watching her phone or his?' Lucy asked.

'His,' Wilson said. 'He made a call to her that lasted ten minutes. We were able to locate it to a bar in the city centre, but by the time we got someone there, he was gone. My own feeling is that everything has turned to shit on him at the same time. First the audit, now his partner leaving him and the Nash family being rumbled. I suspect he's running ragged at the moment, with no place to go.'

'Which makes him much more likely to implicate the Nash family than the boy is,' Fleming said. 'If we could find him, he'd spill his guts to try to salvage whatever he could.'

Wilson nodded. 'Of course, if the Nash family know him at all, they'll probably realize that. They know the son's not going to say anything, especially now that his lawyer is here. Boyd, on the other hand, is an entirely different creature. If they get to him first, he's dead.'

'Maybe the girl, Fiona, knows where he is?' Tara said. 'If he was on the phone for that length, maybe he was asking her to come with him.'

'Maybe she's planning on going with him,' Mickey added, nodding.

Wilson shook her head. 'We've been keeping an eye on her. She's not going anywhere by the looks of it. But I agree with DS Gallagher; I suspect Boyd was asking her to meet with him. Which means she may know where he is.'

'Do we bring her in?' Mickey asked. 'Put some pressure on her.'

'I think there might be a gentler way to get her to speak,' Wilson said, staring at Lucy.

Chapter Sixty-six

The bruising extended all the way down to Sammy's shoulder, though was partially obscured by the bandage that had been applied to his arm and shoulder which, the nurse said, had been dislocated. The drip standing next to his bed was an effort to rebalance his blood sugars.

As Lucy stared in at him, through the window of the hospital ward, she couldn't help but think of her father the night she had helped pull Stuart Carlisle from the River Foyle. She glanced across to where Fiona stood, arms wrapped around her, staring in at the man.

Fiona had initially refused to come with Lucy, especially as Lucy hadn't told her where they were going, just that she wanted her to see the consequence of John Boyd's fraud. In the end, she'd agreed. Lucy suspected she was now regretting that decision.

'There were almost twenty of them,' Lucy said. 'Most escaped, probably thinking *they* were in trouble. The ones that didn't escape were, to a man, too ill to do so. They were sleeping on the ground in an abandoned bleach works, being fed Pot Noodles. The people controlling them convinced them that they were the only ones who cared about them, then took their money, their bank cards, anything which might give them the sense of being in control of their own lives.'

'That's not fair,' Fiona said, blinking away the tears gathering in her eyes. Lucy knew that her complaint was more about her telling Fiona this, drawing attention to the parallels between them, rather than the act itself that she had described.

'Five of the men were malnourished,' Lucy said. 'We think they were there the longest. This man was sleeping in his own faeces as he'd grown too weak, presumably, to make it to the slop bucket they used as a toilet.'

'Why are you showing me this?' Fiona said, turning from the window into the room now, as she gathered her fist in front of her face.

'We know John contacted you,' Lucy said.

'You're watching my phone?' Fiona cried.

'No. We're watching his, to make sure he's still alive. We know he called your number and that the call lasted for over ten minutes.'

Fiona nodded. 'I told him I didn't want to speak to him.'

'I don't doubt that,' Lucy said. 'Did he ask you to go with him?'

Fiona nodded but did not speak.

'Did he say where he was going?'

She shook her head. 'He sounded wild, like he couldn't get his thoughts straight. He was jumbling everything up, speaking so quickly.'

'Did he tell you where he was?'

Fiona shook her head again, though this time her gaze dropped to the hand in front of her.

'Fiona. The man who kept these people in those conditions? We think he killed two other people, with a hatchet. That's the type of person John has got involved with. The man in question has abandoned his own son after we arrested the boy this morning. If he decides to go after John, to prevent John talking to us, he's not going to ask nicely. If you still feel anything for John, any small thing at all, you're doing him no favours protecting him. He'll be safer now if we can bring him in; if we can protect him from his own business partner.'

Fiona stared at her. Her jaw shifting as she chewed on her thumbnail now, her eyes flushed.

'Someone has to answer for what happened to the man in that bed,' Lucy said. 'Someone has to pay.'

Fiona shifted her gaze to the ward window once more, to where Sammy lay, but Lucy could tell that her eyes were not focused on him at all.

'He has a house he's having built out at Claudy, out near the park there, by the river. On the Donemana side.'

'Thank you,' Lucy said. 'We can take you back to Jenny's.'

Fiona shook her head. 'I'm OK. I'll go in a bit myself.'

Lucy stared at her quizzically. 'I can drop you back.'

Fiona held her gaze a moment. 'I'd rather get a taxi,' she said. 'Honestly? I curse the day I ever met you.'

Lucy watched her walk away, her face reddening as if she had just been struck.

Chapter Sixty-seven

'Where is she?' Fleming asked, when Lucy came back out to the car. He'd agreed to leave the two of them alone in the hospital, thinking that Lucy would have a better chance getting through to Fiona alone.

'She's finding her own way home.'

'Is everything OK? Did something happen?'

Lucy shook her head. 'I think I screwed up her life.'

Fleming tapped her on the leg. 'None of that. You helped her start living her life. Without you, she'd have ended up as a statistic on a domestic violence report some day.'

'Her, Robbie, Tara. Everyone I meet gets hurt.' She did not mention Grace, who had been left in hospital as a result of Lucy's involvement in her life, too.

'Everyone gets hurt,' Fleming said. 'Stop taking the blame for the world's problems. You can't change anyone but yourself.'

Lucy nodded, unconvinced.

'Do you know who told me that? Terry Haynes,' Fleming said. 'Now I'm passing it on to you. Do something with it.'

Lucy nodded. 'Thanks, Tom.'

'So, did she tell you *anything* useful or did she just insult you?'

'She says Boyd has a house in Claudy, near the river and the park?'

'I know where the park is,' Fleming said. 'I'll call it in while you drive.'

They reached Claudy within fifteen minutes, cutting down through the village, past the statue of the weeping child erected to commemorate the nine victims of the IRA car bombs, which exploded without warning one Monday morning in the village in July 1972.

They crossed the Faughan again over the stone bridge at the bottom of Church Road, which led out of the village itself. Fleming pointed to their right, to the road signposted for Donemana.

'The park is in there,' he said. 'Where's Boyd's house?'

Lucy turned right, driving more slowly now, scanning both sides of the road for a driveway, which might indicate where Boyd's house was. Sure enough, just over the brow of the incline on which they were driving, she saw an entranceway to the right. The road up from it was untarred, its surface pockmarked with potholes.

'Are you sure this is it?' Fleming asked, one hand held out to grip the dashboard in front of him.

'Fiona said the house was being built,' Lucy offered. 'It's worth checking.'

At first glance, the house looked deserted. The gloom of the thickening twilight was deepened by the ring of high, leafy trees that surrounded the perimeter of the grounds on which the house stood, meaning that Lucy had to turn on the car lights. In doing so, she spotted the reflective red strip on the rear bumper of a car, parked around the side of the house.

'Someone's here,' she said.

They pulled up outside the house.

'Should we wait for backup?' Lucy asked.

'If Boyd's there on his own, there's no need,' Fleming reasoned. 'If Nash is there with him, the longer we leave it, the less chance there is that Boyd is still alive.'

Lucy unclicked her seat belt. 'That's what I thought,' she said, opening her door.

As they approached the front of the house, they saw someone moving quickly inside, just behind the door. Although the figure appeared large-framed, Lucy didn't think it was Rory Nash.

Fleming thumped on the front door three times. 'Open up!'

The door clicked and opened ajar a fraction, just enough for them to see Nash's wife standing inside and enough time for her to recognize them, too. She tried, in vain, to shut the door again quickly, but Lucy was already wedging her foot in the gap, both she and Fleming pushing against her to swing the door back. Eventually it gave as she moved away from it. They had barely crossed the threshold, though, than she was on them, grappling at Lucy's face. Lucy felt the tear, as one of the woman's nails caught her just below the eye, felt the woman's hand grip her hair and pull.

The next minute, with a tug, the woman's grip released and Lucy turned to see that Tom Fleming had managed to subdue her, twisting one of her arms behind her back. Lucy grabbed at the free arm, flaying now at Tom, likewise twisting it backwards and pulling out a plastic tie with which to cuff her.

They heard the shuddering of the van engine outside coming to life all at the same time. While Fleming continued his hold on the woman, Lucy stood and moved to the door, in time to see Nash's blue van emerge from around the side of the house.

The woman realized that her husband was running without her, leaving her to the police in the same way they had abandoned their son hours earlier. She tried to raise herself from the ground, almost unbalancing Fleming in so doing, and bellowed, 'Rory! Rory!'

If Nash heard her, he had no intention of stopping, for they heard the revving of the engine and the grinding of gears as he tried to build speed. Lucy instinctively knew why; she had parked at the top of the driveway, essentially blocking the pathway for the van. Nash was planning on ramming her car.

She sprinted out through the doorway, the action accompanied by Fleming's call for her to come back and the woman's cries of anger and resentment aimed at her husband.

Nash was planning to hit the car at an angle, to push it to one side, but he misaimed and hit the bumper straight on. The car shifted forwards several feet, but the action did nothing to clear the path for his escape. She heard the gears grind as he tried to reverse and attempt the manoeuvre again.

She was almost on him when the van smashed into her car for a second time. This time it did shift across a foot or two, but Nash hadn't built sufficient speed to move it enough to get past it. He was struggling to shift the van into reverse again when Lucy pulled the door open.

The van jolted as he took his foot off the clutch, the action knocking Lucy unexpectedly. Her grip on him released, Nash tore off his seat belt and came at her, bringing his full weight to bear as he threw himself from the cab of the van.

Lucy fell backwards, the back of her head striking the rough stonework of the driveway. As she looked up, Nash loomed above her. She saw him tug at something on his tool belt, saw his thick hand clamped around a small hatchet as he pulled it free and raised it above him, ready to strike.

Absurdly, Lucy raised her hand to protect herself, just as she heard the first loud pop. She felt the skin of that hand suddenly slicken. She looked up at Nash now as a gash of blood unfurled itself on his chest. A second pop and Nash dropped sideways to the ground next to her.

She twisted to see Fleming walk towards where she lay, his gun raised. He approached, as Lucy kicked the weight of Nash from her legs, scrambling to get away from him. Fleming stood above her, his gun bucking in his grip as the air filled with the sound of the gun firing for the third time and, behind them, the wailing of the dead man's wife.

Thursday, 26 July

Chapter Sixty-eight

Fleming was suspended while the Ombudsman investigated the shooting of Rory Nash. Nash's wife claimed that she heard gaps between the shots being fired and that she believed Fleming had used unnecessary force on her husband. In her interview, Lucy simply said that her life had been at risk and that, in shooting Rory Nash, Fleming had saved her.

Despite her complaints regarding the shooting, both Nash's wife and son began to talk when they were interviewed again after Rory Nash's death. Padraig had clearly been given the same advice as his mother by the family lawyer, for both laid full responsibility for all that happened at Rory Nash's feet, including the killing of Terry Haynes, Kamil Krawiec and Ciaran Duffy, who had gone to Nash to tell him that the police had started investigating the identity of the body in the coffin. It had been Rory Nash's idea too, they claimed, to use Terry Haynes's car both to dump Kamil's body and in which to burn Duffy's as a way of implicating Haynes in their murders. John Boyd had arrived out to inspect one of the work sites and he had recognized Haynes somehow. Haynes had challenged Boyd over the treatment of the men and the killing of the man Moore said they had dumped in the river. Having begun to piece together Boyd's involvement in the scam, Haynes threatened to report him to the police so Nash attacked him. Padraig claimed to be terrified of his father, having suffered beatings at his hands since he was a child. Upon medical examination, there was no doubt he bore the scars of historical injuries. His mother likewise claimed to have been controlled by Nash, afraid to leave him in case he harmed their son.

Her mother relayed all of this to Lucy as they sat in her office with Chief Superintendent Marshall.

'What about Boyd now?' Lucy asked. 'Any sign of him?'

'Actually,' Marshall said, 'he tried accessing one of his accounts in Lincoln on Monday morning. We'd managed to get every account he set up frozen over the weekend; he left empty handed before the local police arrived.'

'How much did you recover?' Lucy asked.

'Over £300,000,' Marshall said. 'We know the Nashs took some as well, though they're not admitting to it. There's still quite a chunk missing. But Boyd won't have it as easy as he thought he might. We'll get him at some stage.'

Wilson asked Lucy to remain behind as she walked Marshall out to the car park. She helped herself to tea and a biscuit while she waited, deciding, as she did so, to pour out a second cup for her mother. She set the remaining pink wafer on the saucer next to the cup.

Wilson came back into the office, glanced at the cup on her desk. 'Is there sugar in that?' she asked.

'One,' Lucy said.

Wilson nodded her thanks and lifted the wafer. She snapped it in half, offering a piece to Lucy, who took it with a brief smile.

'I had an interesting phone call from a woman called Bernadette Thompson earlier,' her mother said. 'She knew my name, but seemed surprised to learn that I was ACC.'

Lucy struggled to swallow the crumb of wafer that seemed stuck in her throat.

'She claimed I had called her the other day about her husband.'

She stared at Lucy, willing her to react.

'And?'

'She wanted to report him. She said she'd asked him about the claims I had made in *my* call to her and he'd denied it. But he went out that night. She found blood on his clothes yesterday. She challenged him about it and, eventually, he admitted that he had been using the girl. He said he lost it after his wife questioned him the first time. He thought the prostitute had made the call to her. He went to ask the girl and, when she denied reporting him, he became enraged and gave her a beating. Is that true?'

Lucy nodded her head. 'She had to be hospitalized,' she said. 'She's being discharged today.'

'Will she make a statement?' Wilson asked.

'She might not want to,' Lucy said.

Her mother nodded. 'She might not have to. He confessed to his wife to save their marriage. If he talked that easily with her, I suspect it'll not be too difficult to get the truth out of him. I'll leave that in your capable hands, shall I?'

Lucy nodded, briefly. 'I'm sorry about using your name. It was the first one that came to mind,' she added.

'Well, there's some comfort in that, Lu,' her mother said.

Lucy couldn't help herself but smile. 'Thank you,' she said, then added, 'Mum.'

Later that morning, Lucy went with Tom Fleming to a second funeral in so many days. Having attended Ciaran Duffy's the day before, they now sat at the memorial service for Terry Haynes. The congregation who had gathered in front of the small plastic urn of his ashes, to pay their respects to the man, was one of the most varied Lucy had ever seen, ranging from those clearly affluent to some of the street drinkers she'd seen at the Railway Museum platform.

At the end of the service, Lily Hamilton, Haynes's neighbour, approached Fleming with a small photograph album. 'I thought you might want something,' she said. She handed him a photograph of himself and Terry Haynes standing side by side, smiling.

'The leaving picture,' Fleming said, smiling sadly. 'Terry took a picture with each of the people he helped on the day they left him, just for himself. It was part of *his* recovery.'

'He kept it as a reminder of all the lives he'd touched and those who'd touched his as a result of his staying sober,' Lily explained. 'Anytime he felt like drinking, he could look at the pictures and see how far he'd come. How much he'd done for others. That's mine.'

Lucy looked at the first page of the album at the picture of a much younger Lily, standing next to Haynes.

'I was his first,' the woman explained, her eyes brimming despite her smile. 'I'm trying to give them out to anyone here who was with him,' she explained. 'I thought people would like to have them back, to remember Terry. There's still a few faces I don't recognize. Do you know any of them?'

She handed the book to Fleming alone and Lucy understood that, having not been one of the Haynes's guests, the album was not for her viewing.

Fleming flicked through the pages, then stopped. 'Lucy,' he said, nudging her. She looked at the proffered page, and saw a picture of Terry Haynes standing smiling next to a younger-looking John Boyd.

'John Boyd was helped by Haynes?' Lucy asked.

'Must have been a few years back,' judging by the position of the picture in the album,' Fleming said, sadly. 'That's how Boyd recognized Terry. Terry would have known Boyd's position in the council, would have guessed that he was using slave labour for public contracts.' He took the picture from the album and handed the book back to Lily.

'This one doesn't deserve to be in there,' he said, tearing the picture in two.

Lucy was leaving her house just before 4 p.m. when she recognized a figure appearing from across the street and coming over to her.

'I wanted to catch you before you left,' Fiona said. 'I wanted to say sorry. About what I said in the hospital.'

Lucy waved the comment away. 'No need,' she said.

'I shouldn't have blamed you. What I said, it wasn't true. I'm sorry.'

Lucy nodded. 'Thank you.'

Fiona stood a moment, as if she had something further to say.

'Do you want to come in?' Lucy asked. 'I was just going out, but—'

'No, I need to … I'm staying over with Jenny and Dermot until things …' The sentence trailed off. She straightened suddenly. 'I went to the bank first thing on Monday to change the details on my account, before John was able to do it,' she said, her words spilling now as she finally said what she had wanted to all along. 'They sorted it for me. They told me there was £20,000 in it. John must have put it in there a few months back to hide it.'

Lucy stared at her, Fiona pale and fearful. 'The Fraud Unit have frozen all the accounts John Boyd set up,' Lucy said. 'I take it *you* set up your own account initially.'

Fiona nodded. 'Years ago, when I was a student. He had nothing to do with it until we started dating. The account wasn't connected to him at all. He just took my bank card. What do I do about it?'

Lucy considered the question a moment. 'You should keep it,' she said, finally.

'But, that money, it's not mine.'

'Well, it is now,' Lucy said. 'Use it to get yourself back on your feet.'

On her way to the hospital, Lucy stopped at Robbie's. He was working in the garden, trying to clear weeds from the flower bed close to the road. The soil was baked hard with the heat, his trowel making little impact on its surface.

'Hey, stranger,' he said, standing as she approached, his hands fitting instinctively into the back pockets of his jeans.

'It's looking good.'

They both glanced at the bed, thick with dandelions and dock leaves.

'So, how have you been?'

Lucy nodded. 'OK. Busy.'

'I thought you were,' Robbie said. 'Ever since I asked you to move in. Or I hoped you were. That you weren't just ignoring me. Not calling.'

'You didn't call me,' Lucy protested.

'I was giving you space,' he said. 'I didn't want to be pressurizing you.'

Lucy knew her comment had been an unfair one. Even had he called, she wasn't sure she'd have answered. Not until she'd made her mind up.

'I've had the house redecorated,' she said. 'My dad's house.'

'Really?' Robbie's face brightened. 'To sell it?'

Lucy shook her head. 'No. I just felt it was time. He's not coming back.'

'You're staying where you are then?'

'I'm sorry,' Lucy said. 'It's not that I don't want to be with you. I just … I'm just not ready to move in. I like things the way they are at the moment.'

'I don't,' Robbie said simply. 'I want you here, with me, every day.'

Lucy smiled sadly. 'I appreciate that, Robbie. But I'm not ready for it just yet.'

'What are you afraid of? What do you think might happen?'

'Nothing.'

'You think we'll fight?'

'No.'

'You don't want to be with me?'

'Of course I do.'

'Then why not move in with me?'

'I can't be responsible for you, Robbie!' she said finally.

'You're not responsible for me,' he said, moving towards her.

'I feel like shit every time I see your leg, every time I see you limp. I feel constantly guilty. And do you know why? Because I *am* guilty. I'm sorry for what happened to you. I wish it had been me. But I don't want to confuse guilt with love. And when I move in with you, Robbie, it will be because I know for certain that it's because I love you, not because I feel sorry for you.'

'Sorry for me? I don't want your pity, Lucy,' Robbie snapped.

'That's not what I meant,' Lucy protested, moving towards him.

Robbie stepped back from her, his hands raised. 'Don't! You know what, I think you're right. Moving in would be a terrible idea. I don't think I could stand the looks of sympathy every day,' he snapped.

'I'm sorry, Robbie,' Lucy said.

'That's all I hear from you, Lucy. How sorry you are. Maybe it's time you changed the tune. Started living.'

He turned from her and went inside the house, closing the door behind him. Lucy stood in the garden, feeling suddenly alone.

*

Grace was already coming through the foyer by the time Lucy made it to the hospital. She looked younger than her age, her frame narrow, her hair tied back from her face which still bore the marks of the beating Thompson had given her.

She smiled lightly when she saw Lucy. 'Are you in visiting someone?' she asked.

'I'm here to see you,' Lucy explained, causing the girl to blush. 'I thought you'd want a leaving party for getting out.'

'Are you my armed protection?'

'You don't need one,' Lucy said. 'The guy who did this? His wife reported him. He's been arrested.'

She could see the girl's shoulders slump slightly in relief, though she said nothing.

'So? What do you fancy for your party?' Lucy asked.

'I'd murder a burger,' Grace admitted.

'I think we can manage that,' Lucy said, taking her bag from her.

'Are you all right?' Grace asked. 'You look like you've been crying.'

Lucy shook her head. 'I'm OK,' she lied.

Grace stayed where she stood a moment, even after Lucy had started moving towards the main doors.

'And what then?' Grace asked, as if afraid to step out through the doors, into the sunlight beyond. 'After we eat?'

'Then?' Lucy repeated, moving back and linking arms with her. 'Then we're going home.'

Acknowledgements

I'm indebted to a number of people for their help with various aspects of this book. My sincere thanks to Tara Vance, Dr Ciaran Mullan, Mark Quigley, Bob McKimm and Michael McAleer. I also owe belated thanks to Father Paddy O'Kane for his assistance in a previous work.

My thanks to all the team in Constable & Robinson, most especially my editor, James Gurbutt, and to the team at Witness Impulse: Dan, Margaux, and my US editor Emily Krump.

Particular thanks to Jenny Hewson in RCW and Emily Hickman in The Agency for their invaluable support and guidance over the past number of years.

Thanks to the McGilloways, Dohertys, O'Neills and Kerlins for their help and support, especially Carmel, Joe and Dermot, and my parents, Laurence and Katrina, for all that they have done and continue to do.

Finally, my love and thanks to my wife Tanya, to whom this book is dedicated, and to our children, Ben, Tom, David and Lucy.